WANTED: ROWING COACH

WANTED: ROWING COACH

BRAD ALAN LEWIS

shark
press

1995, 2007

ALSO BY BRAD ALAN LEWIS:

ASSAULT ON LAKE CASITAS

WALKING TOWARDS THUNDER

A FINE BALANCE - DOCUMENTARY ON DVD

BOOKS AND DVD AVAILABLE THROUGH JL RACING:
1-800-831-3305 / WWW.JLRACING.COM

FRONT COVER: *THE GATHERING* BY KIT RAYMOND
BACK COVER: AUTHOR AND NIECE UNDER THE RAINBOW AT BURNING MAN,
2007 - PHOTO BY TRACY LEWIS

AUTHOR'S NOTE: THIS IS A WORK OF FICTION. NAMES, CHARACTERS, AND INCI-
DENTS IN THE NOVEL ARE EITHER THE PRODUCT OF THE AUTHOR'S IMAGINATION
OR, IF REAL, USED FICTITIOUSLY WITHOUT ANY INTENT TO DESCRIBE THEIR ACTU-
AL CONDUCT. REFERENCES TO THE UNIVERSITY OF CALIFORNIA SANTA BARABARA
ARE NOT INTENDED TO DESCRIBE THE ACTUAL CONDUCT OF THIS ORGANIZATION,
ITS EMPLOYEES OR STUDENTS.

WANTED: ROWING COACH
COPYRIGHT © 1995, 2007 BY BRAD ALAN LEWIS
ISBN: 1-888478-02-0

CONTACT INFORMATION CAN BE FOUND THROUGH MY WEBSITE:
www.bradalanlewis.com
DROP ME AN EMAIL ABOUT THIS BOOK - ABOUT ANYTHING - I'D LIKE TO
HEAR FROM YOU

WANTED: ROWING COACH

Caution: Omen Crossing

Coach is a powerful word. I've fought rowing coaches on many fields of battle. Once or twice I had even fought for them. Certainly, I knew enough to make me think twice, no, twenty times, about trying to be a coach myself. But the life of a rower-turned-writer is fraught with challenges, especially those of a financial nature, so I figured I might be able to parlay my twenty-odd years of experience in the world of rowing into something that could pay the bills - a college coaching job. It might be refreshing, even fun, to work with some college rowers, to teach them what rowing is all about.

Word got out that I was in the mood to coach and within a short time an offer came my way. Far from being an offer I couldn't refuse, I considered refusing it many times. VISA won out and before I knew it I was on my way to an interview at the University of California, Santa Barbara.

I've never been a particularly superstitious person, but perhaps I should have paid more attention to that first cautionary omen. I was driving toward the coast on Highway 46, a desolate stretch of road from Interstate 5 to Highway 101, having a long, involved self-discussion on the merits of square-blade rowing. Not a soul in sight, emptiness all around. Suddenly, a blue sedan appeared in front of me, poking along at 45 miles an hour. When the road was clear I signaled to pass, and moved out and around. As I returned to my lane, I saw the CHP, California Highway Patrol. Our eyes met and without even knowing why, I knew I was sunk. Sure enough, he soon pulled me over and proceeded to give me a ticket for having completed my pass outside the legal passing zone. My first moving violation in many years.

"Where you headed?" he asked, as he copied the information off my driver's license.

"Santa Barbara," I said. "I've got a job interview this afternoon at UCSB. I might be coaching their rowing team." In a long shot attempt at dodging the inevitable, I asked him, "Did you ever row?"

The result of this query was an odd look and a gruff, "No."

One more such question, I sensed, would be enough to bring forth his breathalyzer kit. I held my tongue, signed the bottom line, and continued on my way. So much for ignored omens.

Within an hour I was sitting across from Ms. Elizabeth Pearson, Director of Club Sports at UCSB, learning the details of my coaching duties. They seemed straightforward: coach the varsity heavyweights and varsity lightweights, keep the launches in running order, repair broken equipment, make sure the boathouse stays clean and neat, raise a lot of money and put out a newsletter at regular intervals. How hard could it be?

I stood up, shook hands with my new boss and thus began a magnificent adventure filled with life lessons, mice and crabs, wins and losses, and wonderful, awful, endless days.

Our big recruiting meeting was held this evening at the Isla Vista Theater. Flyers had been hastily posted all over campus. Word-of-mouth running high - an Olympic gold medalist coaching a humble school like UCSB? Let's check it out! I dreamed, as has every coach, of an overflow, turn-away crowd. As I walked toward the theater entrance, I heard Jimi Hendrix blasting from a nearby stereo, All Along the Watchtower for the ten millionth time. Hendrix, like rowing, is timeless. Given half a chance Jimi Hendrix could have been a decent rower. Left handed. Tall, wiry guy. Good sense of rhythm. He was a dedicated free thinker, probably better suited for sculling than sweep.

The Isla Vista Theater seated about two thousand people, and for the weekly showing of The Rocky Horror Picture Show or the occasional surfing movie it was inevitably jam-packed. I looked around as I walked through the entrance. This evening empty seats outnumbered the full, twenty to one. As I surveyed the meager crowd, a young man walked up and asked if this was Chemistry 101. "Yes," I said, "take a seat. It's just about to start."

The house lights dimmed and Terri Larson, the new women's head coach, strode to the microphone. Terri had rowed at UCSB for four years and had previously coached the novice women. Like myself, today marked the beginning of her tenure as varsity coach. Sincere as ever, she promised everyone in attendance that salvation could be found through rowing.

Men's varsity lightweight captain, Clement Nash, took the stage after Terri. Clement spoke eloquently of the beauty of the lake and the wonderful friendships to be earned from the sport. Then he made the mistake of saying, "Yes, the early mornings are brutal, the drive to Cachuma is long and tiring and the workouts are hellish, but you'll love it." I doubt if that last part, although honest, helped convince anyone to join the team. Clement handed the microphone to heavyweight rower, Gordon "Gordo" Rollins, who, for his testimonial, said succinctly, "Because of rowing, I lost twenty-nine pounds." Gordo looked as though he could stand to lose a few more.

My turn had arrived and as I stumbled to the podium, the cavernous hall seemed to grow even larger, as though an outer space black hole had squatted on the theater. My heart rate zoomed toward maximum. Every seat magically filled with a potential gold medalist. The tie encircling my neck tightened of its own accord. The notes I clutched in my sweaty left hand - important points I wanted to make - began to disintegrate like some ancient parchment. My voice, suddenly hollow, thin and reedy, seemed not to carry beyond the edge of the stage. I was nervous.

Keep in mind, I've given dozens of talks. I know exactly how to do it. I understand well the first rule of Toastmasters: nervousness breeds incoherence. But somewhere between my cushioned seat and the podium, I lost my brain. Talking to old men at the Kiwanis Club is one thing. It's quite another to have all these kids staring at you with unabashed curiosity. And while a little case of nerves can sometimes be a good thing, when on stage it is pure hell, enough to make you sick to your stomach.

I began, saying, "Thanks for having me. It's really great to be at UCSB. Some of you may know that during the 1984 Olympics the rowing teams stayed right here on campus. I was in Anacapa dorm. Yeah, I have a lot of nausea about this place."

Suddenly the hall filled with laughter. Immediately I retraced my verbal steps. Damn, did I say nausea?

"I mean nostalgia," I said, feeling the color of my face turn beet red. "I have a lot of nostalgia about this place." For some reason this provoked even more laughter. I stepped back from the podium and took a deep breath.

"Geez, talk about catching a crab right off the start," I said, trying to regroup. "Take two. Rowing is a fantastic sport. In fact, I'm reluctant to call it a sport. I think of rowing as a discipline. Baseball is a sport. Tennis is a sport. Rowing is an incredible, powerful discipline."

In the back of my mind I was thinking - or maybe it is a sport? Or does it even matter? A moment later someone called out, "Tell us more about the nausea."

"You must have your priorities straight," I continued, ignoring the heckler. "Your first priority is to yourself. Keep yourself healthy - mentally, physically, spiritually. Your second priority is to your family and close friends. If someone needs your assistance, go to them immediately. Your third priority is to school and academics."

Beyond the 250 watt footlights, I could see some of the veteran rowers shaking their heads in disagreement.

"The final priority is what I call the wild card. This wild card can be surfing, part-time job, reading to old people in a nursing home - any of ten thousand things. The wild card can determine your future. My wild card was rowing. Maybe it should be yours."

Okay, I was back on track. Now, if I could just hurry up and finish, I might make it out in time for Seinfeld.

"Rowing can offer many things. You gain awesome physical and spiritual strength. You learn the secrets of focus and discipline, which are critical for success in any arena. You make friends that will last a lifetime. All good reasons. All worthy reasons. I'll end with a quote by one of my favorite authors, William Gass. 'If you were a fully realized person - whatever the heck that is - you wouldn't fool around writing books.' Nor would you fool around rowing. To spend copious amounts of time going backward on a self-propelled craft at 6:00 A.M. is not for everyone. We row to fill in some missing piece of ourselves. If you stay with it long enough, take enough hard strokes, win and lose enough races, you will find what you're looking for."

I limped off the stage as tired as if I'd run a marathon. Number of recruits recruited? Hard to tell. I wouldn't be surprised to learn that my speech had convinced a few prospects to take up surfing or reading to old people in a nursing home.

Afterward, as my heart rate returned to double digits, I met with my rowers-to-be, the varsity heavyweights and lightweights. One man, Jeff Beldon, told me that his life's dream was to make the first lightweight boat. A quick head count led me to conclude that should he merely stay alive, he was virtually guaranteed the realization of his dream. Not too many rowers were vying for a place on the varsity squad, one boat of heavies, one boat of lites and a few men left over.

"Listen up," I said. "Since agreeing to take this job, I've thought about my own college rowing experience. I asked myself, what did I learn that was useful later on? In a nutshell, I learned to do everything-rowing. That includes rigging the boats, lifting weights, rowing properly, training hard, racing well. I've decided that I want you to learn the same things - about the whole damn world of rowing." The men stared at me with unblinking eyes. Did they already know everything about rowing? I might have been a little presumptuous to assume they didn't. Well, those details would be sorted out soon enough.

"For starters, I want everyone to keep a journal. Make some sort of entry every single day. Describe the work we did, how you felt about it, how your blisters are healing, how things are going in general. Otherwise you'll never remember how much fun we had along the way." The journal - the dreaded journal. Despite repeated entreaties, the only member of the team to keep any sort of journal was me.

"Next, from now until the last stroke of the last race, we'll have some sort of competition practically every time we meet. It's more important to be an expert at competing than to have perfect technique or awesome endurance. The only way to become such an expert is to practice, practice, practice. Here's today's competition, a test of your rowing knowledge: who is the most famous rower in the world?"

After a brief pause, someone offered, "You?"

"No," I said, "definitely not. Dr. Benjamin Spock, in my opinion, is the most famous. His Baby Book sold more copies than any book except the Bible. Dr. Spock won a gold medal in the '28 Olympics, in the eight." Trick question.

"Lastly, I'll read you various pieces over the course of the year. I believe that you must look far and wide for your knowledge - movies, books, magazines, search high and low. So much good information is available, just waiting to be plucked like fruit from a tree. All you have to do is keep your eyes open." I paused for a second and looked at everyone in turn.

"While all that knowledge is great, the driving force must come from right here," I said, thumping my chest. "Find your inspiration in the mirror!"

The General Rule in Hoplology
Wednesday, September 29

I stepped out of my car, straightened my parka and looked around me. Pitch black. Couldn't see a thing. Black like the outside of a dream on a cold winter's night. As I walked toward the coaching launches - or at least where I thought the launches were located - I stumbled over naked tree roots and kicked unseen rocks. Finally, I found the storage box containing the gas tanks.

A piercing pain shocked my fingertip as I felt around the lid for the padlock. What the hell? Something was biting off the tip of my finger. A leech. Yes, a carnivorous leech must had sunk its spiny fangs into my flesh. I quickly pulled my hand away, cursing under my breath. Leeches. I'd never encountered a leech before but instinctively I knew this had to be a big one, a quarter-pounder, six or seven inches long, razor sharp teeth like a movie monster. I grabbed a heavy rock and slammed it against the padlock-and-leech combination. That should do it.

A few yards behind me, barely enveloped in the pitch darkness, were a full-grown mountain lion, several black bears, and a trio of thick rattlesnakes. Yes, the deep mountain dark-before-dawn was doing wonderful things to my imagination.

A few days ago a friend of mine had said, "UC Santa Barbara? I didn't know they had a rowing team." Yes, we have a team. We practice at Lake Cachuma, in the middle of the Los Padres National Forest. Wild animals not only live here, they are encouraged to roam free as though they own the place, which in fact they do.

I returned to my VW and looked for my flashlight and air pistol. After a night of car-sleeping, my life's contents had been thrown into a jumble. Finally I found the flashlight - no pistol - and returned to the gas box. Using the flashlight, I looked for the monster leech. Unfortunately, he had left. In his place, a rusty fishing hook was cleverly wrapped around the padlock with a length of nylon line. I stripped away the hook and opened the box, all the while cursing the shots that I'd no doubt need to counter any assorted rusty fishing hook diseases.

Faint scurrying noises kept just ahead of my beam of light as I lifted out a gas tank. Then I untangled a hose from the knotted mess, a sight not unlike a dense ball of milk snakes in mating fervor. With gas tank and hose in hand I walked a dozen feet or more to the dock, where our fleet of coaching launches bobbed quietly.

After depositing the gear in the stern of my launch, I went back to the gas box and grabbed a cushion and megaphone. When I lifted out the cushion, I saw my first Cachuma mouse - little critter, healthy coat, comically big ears, slightly annoyed look on its face. Apparently I had interfered with his nightly routine. I dropped the lid and let him return to whatever I'd interrupted. I soon had the outboard engine purring, my gear stowed and all other pre-practice preliminaries out of the way. The gray-pink light of dawn was beginning to filter over the lake - calm and inviting. My watch read 6:20. I was eager to get going. Damn it, where were my rowers? Certainly they would be arriving any moment.

A new challenge always seems particularly inviting and as my launch slowly rocked on the water, I found myself wondering, who should I be? Which coaching persona would get the best results? I could be stoic-stern Harry Parker, the legendary Harvard coach. Say ten words all season and have them crush their opponents by lengths. Or maybe Ted Nash, with a drill for every day of the year and a race plan that describes every solitary stroke. Coach Nash had the distinction of being one of the few rowers who was both an Olympic gold medalist and a world-class coach. Maybe I should be Kris Korzenowski, the king of negative coaching, who could find serious fault with anyone - anytime, anywhere. Maybe I should simply be me. Yes, that would certainly be easiest but would it be enough?

I shut off my launch and walked to the boathouse, expecting any moment to hear cars pulling into the dirt parking area.

Before I arrived last night, I had not been to Lake Cachuma since the spring of 1982, over a decade ago. I clearly recall the occasion for my previous visit, the West Coast regional rowing championships. I remember the hurricane force winds that caused my opponents to abandon the competition in mid-race. In the raucous cross-wind, I won the open single only by staying afloat and continuing to move, however slowly, in the direction of the finish line.

Still no rowers had arrived, although daylight had appeared right on schedule. At the boathouse I unlocked the side door and then unlatched and slid open the bay doors. Nothing much had changed since my last visit, at least nothing I could see. The boathouse was the same industrial strength rectangular building, single boat-bay, single story, corrugated-metal. No amenities such as showers, toilets, running water, phone or electricity had been added.

Hanging over the entrance was a long blue and gold sign, "UCSB Rowing." On the concrete floor was painted a large letter "G" for Gaucho, the school mascot. Skylights built into the roof illuminated a banner against the rear wall that commemorated a victory in the 1987 Pacific Coast Rowing Championships Men's Novice Lightweight Eight. Did such an event actually exist?

As I lowered my gaze, I took in the general state of the boathouse. Scrap wood dumped against the walls, stray riggers piled in the corners, a rack for holding seats, falling to pieces. Covering everything, walls, floor, rowing shells, was a half-inch of dirt. The place was a frigging mess.

I stepped inside and walked to the rear of the boathouse, but after a few steps, I turned around and headed back out. More overpowering than the sight of this shabby boathouse was the rancid smell, like a hamster cage that hadn't been cleaned in a decade. A closer inspection could wait until later. I'd been in countless boathouses. None had ever sunk so low. Coach Parker would have bolted. Somebody had some serious work ahead of them - most likely, me. I couldn't help but laugh out loud. My boss, Ms. Pearson, had said that I was to keep the place clean and neat.

I had assumed by her statement that it was already clean and neat. Ms. Pearson, I suspected, had not visited in quite some time.

Outside, on either side of the boathouse, fenced-off areas stored the less valuable novice boats. This Gaucho program didn't lack for equipment. Offhand I counted fifteen eight-oared shells, a half-dozen four-withs and innumerable small boats.

Like an elephant's graveyard, several derelict hulks were scattered outside the fence, boats that no one was going to row again. Neither would T.G.I. Friday's want them for a salad bar either. I bent down next to one boat and ran my hand across the hull. Someone had built a fire in the stern, and the black mottled wood was a repulsive sight. Rowing shells aren't supposed to meet such a disgraceful end.

I walked around the parking area for a few minutes, picking up trash, waiting.

Last night I had driven up Highway 154, the endless road from Santa Barbara. Soon after cresting the San Marcos Pass I stopped at a view point with a dozen other spectators. A red glow could clearly be seen to the east. The mountains were on fire.

I'd heard on the radio that a fire was raging due east of town. By late afternoon billowing smoke-clouds had blotted out the sun. With this evil eclipse came the distinct smell of forest being burned along with a fine, gray ash that covered everything. This disaster, running out of control, burning thousands of acres, had been caused by a solitary lit cigarette tossed by a careless deer hunter. As daylight eased into darkness, the flames took on an independent spirit of their own, as though they hung suspended from the heavens. The fire was ten miles away - not close enough to be threatening but not so far that it wasn't unsettling, the flames and ash somehow setting off a primal smoke detector within my subconscious. Still, it was phenomenally beautiful, hot energy given form and substance.

When I eventually arrived at my camping spot next to the boathouse, my home until I found an apartment, I parked facing the fire. All through the night I woke and watched for a few seconds and then fell back asleep, dreaming fiery dreams.

Now - 7:00 A.M., my first day of coaching - I returned to my launch and sat on the bench seat. The water was smooth, my launch was ready to go, an antique stroke watch hung around my neck, a huge conical megaphone stood poised at my feet.

For a few minutes, I looked over an article that I had planned to read to the men, part of my Lewis life lesson series. Who better to inflict it on than a captive audience of college rowers? Today's article came from Handguns magazine, May '93:

> The general rule in hoplology [the study of weapons] is that the more primitive the weapon, the greater must be the skill of the user. A pistol is a complicated weapon. Hundreds of parts must fit together in well-oiled symmetry in order for it to function. The skill necessary to successfully engage in a gun fight is minimal. A pound of pressure on the trigger delivers a bullet toward any target at 2300 feet/second. A knife, however, is simplicity incarnate. No moving parts. But the skill needed to survive a knife fight is prodigious.

When I sailed in the America's Cup, I witnessed first-hand the sporting equivalent of a gun fight. The 12 meter yachts were expensive, complicated and varied. The outcome of a Cup race was defined to a large extent by the inherent speed of the boats rather than the skill of the sailors. Rowing, however, is like a knife fight. The equipment is simple and fairly equitable. The skill of the rower reigns supreme.

I returned my gas tank to the storage box, locked up the launch and boathouse, stalled for a few more minutes in the parking lot and then finally went to my VW. I learned later that the men had been told by lightweight captain Clement Nash that the first practice would take place at the ergometer room and not the boathouse. Signals crossed. Tomorrow would be better.

I stood in front of my men for a few seconds, not saying a word, just looking. At the recruiting meeting a few days ago I hadn't been sure who were the real rowers as opposed to the Lookie Lou's hanging around to inspect the new coach.

Now I had my first chance to see, up close and personal, who would actually be rowing. All through history, coaches have stood in front of their charges much like this, trying to sort it all out, trying to imagine the long adventure that lies ahead. I had saved up a million things for this moment, life lessons for each day of the week, drills that would have them rowing like Tom Bohrer, workouts they'd be telling their grandchildren about.

I took a few more seconds to see if any of the men had that special spark. Who had something upstairs besides unruly long hair and an earring. Who, among all these rowers, would eventually win an Olympic gold medal? No one jumped out at me as a gold-medalist-to-be. In fact, they all looked a little sleepy and indifferent. Had I come face to face with the infamous Slacker Generation? No, I don't think so. They looked pretty much the way I must have appeared two decades earlier.

In keeping with the traditional Gaucho fall schedule, we were meeting this morning on campus, at the ergometer room. Monday, Wednesday, Friday and Saturday at Lake Cachuma for rowing. Tuesday and Thursday on campus for ergs and running. Weights on Tuesday and Friday afternoons. Since we had only seven ergometers and twenty rowers, I decided to take the easy way out.

"Okay," I said, "tighten up your laces 'cause we're going running."

The words were fresh out of my mouth when I was confounded with the beginning of an on-going challenge given human form: Gordo Rollins.

"I can't run," Gordo told me. "Knee trouble. What should I do?"

Hmm. My immediate impulse was to say that I had no idea. In all my years of training, I'd never had to consider such a limitation.

Over the next nine months I'd have to consider this limitation and many similar ones. Gordo was a big guy, 6'4" at least, which in rowing is a good thing. But he was also a Mr. Softee, carting a Goodyear tire around his waist. That's a bad thing, which also leads to such unpleasant nicknames as anchor, manatee, sluggo. Gordo, no matter what he was called, did not waver. He was a damn good guy, never late for practice, never complaining, always paying attention and paying his dues. None of these characteristics worked to make him a rowing success, but maybe that would come later. I do believe Gordo was the only rower who learned how to properly strap a boat onto the trailer.

"Take a spin on the ergs: sixty minutes, steady state." That should keep him out of mischief.

"What rating?"

"Let me think. Twenty-four strokes a minute."

"What sort of pace?"

Now I was stumped. I'd never used ergs to train, so I had no idea of the proper pace.

"Heart rate at seventy percent of max."

"I don't know my max."

"Then use the hour to figure it out."

Before Gordo could ask another question, I yelled to the crew, "Let's go."

We ran through campus to the beach and then along the shore for about a mile, heading north. A hard right turn across the soft sand took us up a flight of concrete stairs to the town of Isla Vista.

I-V, as Isla Vista is called, was still sound asleep. Supposedly these few square miles contain the most concentrated population of students in the United States. The architecture is like a proving ground for HoJo's, Days Inn and Econo Lodge. Dilapidated two and three story apartment buildings stand shoulder to shoulder, block after block, nearly all of it devoted to student housing. The names of these sad, unwieldy masses of stucco and pink paint come straight out of psycho-Las Vegas, The Tropicana, The Matador, The Flamingo. Street names, too, are in line with a dream far beyond eventual reality, Picasso, Cervantes, El Greco.

It's quite a sight, this beach front property being used in such a rough and tumble way.

As we ran, I remembered when this little town had its fifteen minutes of fame. In 1971, during a mad season of student rage and rioting over the Vietnam War, the Bank of America building was burned to the ground. A small park, now lush with trees and grass, is located where the bank once stood. Kevin P. Moran, a student at UCSB, was killed during the riot, supposedly by a policeman's ricocheting bullet, although no one knows the actual circumstances. He happened to have been a member of the UCSB rowing team.

This morning, in the soft gray light of dawn, we chugged through the streets, occasionally passing a surfer heading toward the ocean, his board tucked securely under his arm.

I yelled to the rower closest to me, "You know what an Indian run is?" He nodded yes. "Okay, listen up," I yelled. "Let's try an Indian run with lightweights in one line, heavies in the other."

After the expected stomping on heels and pushing aside of the slow pokes, the group formed two undulating columns. We held this formation for a few blocks until the pace evened out. Then, on my command, the men at the rear of the line sprinted to the front.

My job through all of this was to keep from collapsing from exhaustion. I was wearing a blue nylon jacket and snug gray sweat pants, and as we passed the five-mile mark I began to notice that I was leaking perspiration at a prodigious rate. With my head spinning from the lack of oxygen, I cursed myself for having gotten so fat and out of shape. I found myself digging deep into my training history for the poise needed to make the few words I spoke sound moderately intelligible.

"Next pair," I yelled. "Ready, go!"

At the northern edge of campus, as I approached melt-down, I called for an end to Indian running. We shifted into an easy cruise for a half-mile or so, finally arriving at Storke Field, the well-known softball, Frisbee, volleyball, hackey sack, hang out playground. Near the edge of the field we stopped at the pull-up bars.

"It's time for our first competition of the year," I said, "a drill I practiced when I was training called Hang Time."

I gave a quick demonstration, grabbing hold of the highest pull-up bar and hanging by my fingers for a few seconds.

"No re-gripping allowed," I said. "Simply jump up and hold on, for as long as you can."

I learned this drill years ago from a legendary rock climber named John Bachar, who happened to give me a ride when I was hitchhiking out of the High Sierra. Bachar specialized in free-climbing, a particularly dangerous style that renounces ropes, carabiners and any other gear. In free climbing, hanging by your fingers is not merely a drill but a life-or-death matter. Bachar told me he could hang for five minutes. Besides strengthening forearms, hang time is a great way to thoroughly explore the subject of pain.

"Go ahead and take a crack at hanging as long as you can," I said. "Once everyone has had a chance, the best four hangers will compete in a head-to-head final."

As I watched, the rowers began pushing each other aside, eager to get at the bar. No doubt the rowers were anxious to impress their new coach and to take a long, satisfying drink from the golden cup of wisdom they must have assumed I carried with me at all times. Certainly to this point, we'd done nothing even remotely extraordinary, a beach jog and an Indian run. You don't need a gold medalist coach for those drills.

As I thought might happen, only a short time was needed before the rowers were pushing aside the cup of wisdom and grasping their forearms and moaning. Yes, it hurts. Makes your eyes bug out. The competition went much too quickly, with most of the rowers hanging so briefly that I barely had time to start my watch before they let go.

In anticipation of the finals, the four rowers who had hung the longest stood beneath each of the pull-up bars. On my command they jumped up and began hanging. One man dropped off at thirty seconds, another stayed on for a minute and a third slipped free at ninety-four seconds. A tightly muscled lightweight named Robert Churchill endured the longest.

Every student of physics knows the axiom "nature abhors a vacuum." A little known corollary is that "rowing coaches detest sending their crews in early." Coaches will always find something to fill the end-of-practice vacuum. This morning, as the rowers relaxed on the grassy field next to the pull-up bars, I used my few minutes to offer up a Lewis life lesson.

"In its most basic form," I said, "we've just explored the whole world of competition. Lots of challengers. Some tough combat. One eventual champion. And to the victor go the spoils." I unzipped my jacket, withdrew a sweat-softened Crunch candy bar and handed it to Robert Churchill, who seemed quite surprised at receiving his unexpected reward.

"Last night," I continued, "I was trying to decide what would be the best way to go about teaching everything-rowing. Some points are obvious: we'll lift weights to get strong, we'll run and row to get fit, we'll practice lots of drills and row lots of miles to become good technical oarsmen. We also need to train from the shoulders up. I have a whole list of mental drills that we'll do throughout the year. After the mental and physical, only one thing is left."

"Yeah," someone yelled. "Breakfast!"

"Give me one more minute," I said, somewhat surprised by the interruption. The old men at the Kiwanis Club never interrupt.

"Besides the physical and mental," I continued, "I want us to become X Factor experts. The toughest part of the whole damn sport is the X Factor. To me, the X Factor is your soul. It's your courage. It's your unique driving force. Suppose for a moment that Churchill and I were doing the hang drill. Suppose that in every possible way - physical and mental - we were identical. Which one of us would emerge as the champion?"

The rowers were leaning back, their elbows resting on the deep green grass. About half of them were listening to me. The others, I could tell, were looking at the eucalyptus leaves rustling overhead or contemplating whether to have Sugar Smacks or Count Chocula for breakfast. Nonetheless, I kept on.

"You'll all agree that at a certain point during this hanging drill a million screaming voices within your body were telling you, 'Let go!'

I call this point the critical crossroads. What happens if you obey all those screaming voices? If it's an important race - the Olympics, for example - and you let go, you're in for an extended visit to a deep, miserable hell."

As soon as I said the O-word, the cereal eaters pulled their attention back to me. From now to the end of the season, I'd have to work the word Olympic into every other sentence.

"Don't worry, I'm well aware this was a dinky competition, the first of the year. But by starting now - acknowledging our X Factor, learning about the critical crossroads, and working to strengthen our response - we'll eventually be ready for a major test. Today is the beginning of our X Factor training. Your homework is to think back on you're races and come up with one or two where, for better or worse, your X Factor came into play. See you tomorrow at the lake, 6:30 A.M.."

The team jogged back to the erg room to reclaim their warm-up gear. I walked to my car, sore and tired.

Robert Churchill, the lightweight who had won Hang Time, came up as I was walking and asked, "How long can you hang, Coach Lewis?"

"I don't go by time," I said. "I just go by how I do in competitions."

"Well, how do you do?" he wanted to know.

"I've never been beaten."

Was that true? Certainly I hadn't been beaten in this decade. True or not, I would have said the same thing. I didn't want to sabotage my coaching image so early in the game.

SWEET SPOT
Friday, October 1

I spent the night in my favorite camping spot overlooking the lake, sleeping fitfully, listening to the uneven wind course through the branches of the oak trees, smelling the remnants of the forest fire. Mysterious mountain mammals danced the mambo, paw-in-paw, around my car, although whenever I raised my head to take a look, they ducked out of sight.

Not surprisingly, I was excited about our first on-the-water workout, coming right on the heels of yesterday's run. But before rushing out of the car, I took a little extra time to clean myself up so that I didn't look as though I'd spent the night sleeping in a VW Golf. I wanted the team to respect me and appearances weren't a bad place to start. A clean T-shirt, a comb through the hair, and I stepped outside, ready to go.

As I locked the door I saw the first faint sign of dawn, a lavender glow in the far eastern sky, so light and elegant that I had to stop for a moment to acknowledge the fresh beginnings of a new day.

My path was blocked at the boat bay doors by a dozen prostrate women who were stretching out on the ice cold concrete. I watched them for a moment trying to pick the best line through the mob. At the same time, they stopped and looked at me. By Gaucho tradition, the women owned the front half of the boathouse, with the men taking the rear. I walked back and stood in front of my men, trying to do my best imitation of Harvard coaching legend Harry Parker, whose success as a coach was matched only by his minimal use of words. I soon discovered that my Parker-parody, dead serious, quasi-angry, wholly intent, was somewhat akin to holding my breath underwater. It had an effect, nonetheless. The men stretching out on the bare concrete floor stopped moving and stared up at me.

"First off," I said. "Don't sit or lie on the concrete. If you must stretch out, do it at home. The only part of your body that should touch the floor are your feet." None of them moved. Perhaps they had a hearing impairment. Too much Nirvana through the Walkman? English a second language? With a little more force, I said sharply, "Get off the floor."

This time the rowers heard me, and reluctantly they rose to their feet. Some of these men had been stretching out like this for three years. Changing their routine was not going to be easy.

"Why shouldn't we stretch out?" one of the men asked.

"The concrete is too cold," I said. "And I have a feeling that all these little pellets scattered around are rat shit. Not too healthy." As I was talking, I noticed that some of the men were looking at the ceiling. I glanced up and saw the source of these droppings, a healthy adult rat, bigger than a kitten but smaller than a cat, walking calmly along a rafter. Another one followed. Rats. But no boathouse cat. Apparently the rats had eaten the cat. Given half a chance the rats would probably eat me.

Since I knew only a few of the men, I called upon veteran coxswain Adam Weinstein to suggest a line-up. Besides Adam, we were lucky to have two other coxswains, both women, Elaine and Eileen. Due to a cruel trick of fate, these two women, at least to my untrained eye, were identical: five-feet tall, 120 odd-pounds, shoulder length brown hair, pleasant smile, shrill voice, similar names.

In a few moments Adam had scratched out a lightweight eight, a heavyweight eight and a four-with coxswain. Two rowers were left over, chunky Gordo and his shorter equal Herb Griffith. They stood patiently in the middle of the bustling men awaiting their marching orders. "Do you guys know how to scull?" I asked them.

"Yeah," Gordo said. "I did a little sculling last year."

"Great," I replied. "Why don't you and Herb take out the Maas Aeros. Stay close to shore for this first outing. Help each other out." I figured they'd be fairly safe on their own. Not even a quivering blob like Marlon Brando could tip over a Maas Aero.

On Adam's command the heavies lifted their boat off the rack. You can tell a lot about a crew by the way they handle their equipment. My rowers, it seemed, managed the task somewhat clumsily, although they did avoid scraping the oarlocks of the boat above. I stood off to the side and watched as they eased the eight onto their shoulders and walked toward the dock.

When plastics were invented, I don't think anyone had in mind a plastic dock. Nonetheless, that's exactly what we had, a series of floating plastic pontoons, two foot-square pods in a checkerboard puzzle. The pods were cleverly linked together into a rectangular strip, twenty feet across and a hundred feet long. One of the rowers told me that this very dock had been used at the '84 Olympics. Along the perimeter, fishermen had cut holes into the hard plastic to anchor their poles, and at various places the squares had cracked open, creating hidden death pods. One false step could punch right through and easily break an ankle or dislocate a knee. Somewhat miraculously, my rowers managed to sidestep the death pods. I could only assume that they had walked across the dock enough times to know exactly where not to step. In my head I added onto my growing list of boathouse chores, fix dock.

After the usual commotion, finding the right oar, locating a missing inhaler, running back to the boathouse to retrieve a water bottle, both crews pushed off the dock and prepared to row onto the lake.

"Stop, stop, stop," I said. "Where you going? You haven't tuned up yet. Before you can play your guitar, you've got to tune up. Same with rowing."

The rowers looked at me blankly.

"What's wrong?" I asked. "No budding guitar players in the group? Pretend this is your first day of rowing. I want you to sit tall, so that you're sitting on your buttocks and not your lower back. The taller you sit, the bigger lever you can wield." Everyone stretched up a bit, breaking free of the slouched-in-front-of-the-TV posture.

"Excellent. Now we're off to the races. While still sitting tall, come to the finish and bury your blade so that the top edge is one centimeter underwater." I held my thumb and forefinger half an inch apart.

"With the blade buried, find the exact place where the handle strikes your ribs. This is called the sweet spot. No matter the conditions, no matter how tired you are - on every stroke you must find the same exact sweet spot. Feel how steady the boat is? Okay, sit easy." The rowers shook the stiffness from their shoulders and arms.

"I want you to perform the same ritual every workout: establish the right posture and then identify the sweet spot."

"I don't see the point of doing it every time," one of the men said.

"What if some little gremlin messes with your rigging?" I said. "If that gremlin changes the rigger height, the sweet spot will also change."

"Like that master's team," Churchill shouted out. "Last year they borrowed our boat at the Crew Classic and screwed up the rigging. We never got it right again." At least one man was listening.

"Okay, you get the picture. One last thing: never begin rowing from the finish. Always come up to three-quarters slide and then go. The reason is simple - you'll never start a race from the finish position. By commencing each piece at three-quarters slide, we'll have ten thousand practice starts in our bag of tricks by the time race season rolls around." I had to remind my rowers countless times before this change took hold, and even then it was an iffy proposition.

"Coxswains, sit tight a minute while I get my launch." Within a few minutes I was motoring alongside the eights and four-with on our first lake tour. Gordo and Herb in their Aeros followed in our wake like kid brothers trying to keep up.

I positioned my launch away from the crews, fifty yards to the side, trying to take in the whole angry picture. The crews, to put it bluntly, looked raw. Timing was haphazard. Even worse, the rhythm-thing was nonexistent. Good rowing has a very specific look to it. At any pressure, light paddle to race-force, a good crew manages to spend more time on the recovery than on the drive. My rowers had the dreaded inverse ratio, less time on the recovery than on the drive.

Rather than dwell on their technique so early in the practice, I turned my attention to the lake. We soon passed the opening of Cachuma harbor, where fishermen launched their bass boats every day of the fishing season, a schedule that omitted only Christmas. A mile farther along the shore we came to Bradbury Dam. Lake Cachuma is wholly man-made. During the recent severe drought, when the water level dropped dozens of feet, old roadways became exposed along with foundations of long forgotten houses.

The crews turned around at the dam and rowed in the other direction, toward the rising sun. After a mile-and-a-half we passed a floating outhouse, installed to keep fishermen from polluting the lake. Further east we came to a huge conical tower that looked like an elevator shaft coming straight out of the water. This intake tower was connected to a massive pipe that provided drinking water to the town of Santa Barbara. A string of buoys kept all boats well away from the powerful vacuum suction of the intake. A mile past the tower was Arrowhead Island. In the weeks ahead, I often had the men row one steady piece from the floating outhouse, around Arrowhead Island and then back to the outhouse, a little over two miles altogether. This morning we kept going until the lake finally narrowed into a skinny channel that ended 1000 meters later at a heavy log boom.

Over the next ten months, I would get to know this body of water exceptionally well, the hidden inlets, the deer that fed along the shore, the eagles and osprey, the bass and bass fishermen, the contrary winds and bedeviling fogs, the frigid temperatures and gloriously warm sunshine.

At this quiet time of day, the crews gliding along, the wind nonexistent - it was a religious experience. The lake was exquisite beyond words. No Citgo sign, no houses crowding the shore, no factory smokestacks, no roads alongside the lake, no bridge abutments to smash into, no other crews on the water except for the women who were off in some private side channel. I tried to focus on my rowers but I found myself distracted by the overwhelming natural beauty.

When we reached the log boom, I had them turn around and row one long piece to the dam, low rating, half-power, about three miles. I was being paid to coach, so I forced myself to watch. By my own admission, my eye for technique is untrained. When I row, I rely on the tactile sensations conveyed through the seat, foot boards and oar handles to determine how efficiently the boat is moving through the water. The caliber of my technical eye, however, didn't matter this morning. In fact, a blind man could have critiqued the crews simply by using the discordant sound of their catches. Without looking too closely, I saw that the rowers had no slide control, their balance was shaky, their finishes were as soft as fresh-fallen snow. Average rowing. C-plus.

A half-hour later, at the dam, I had the crews turn toward the boathouse. Once in a straight line, I shut off my engine and offered my coaching wisdom for the day.

"For the next week," I said, "we're going to work on only one aspect of technique. We might as well start with the finish. Don't worry about the catch, the drive, the recovery - just think finish!"

The rowers shifted uncomfortably on their seats.

"Pretend you have a tennis ball hovering just in front of your stomach. Draw the oar handle to the sweet spot, then press down-and-away in one smooth motion, so that the handle follows the contour of the imaginary tennis ball. Easy day."

Easy for me to say. The limiting factor is the rower's arm-and-lat strength. Before I could add anything more, I found that I had drifted a good distance from the crews. I re-started my launch and came alongside.

"Into the sweet spot - around the tennis ball - out towards the catch," I yelled through my megaphone.

I saw two rowers in the lightweight boat talking to each other and then laughing. My engine was too loud for me to hear what they were saying. How much would an electric launch cost? I shut off my engine and asked, "Any questions? Okay, let's go rowing."

Results were mixed. The rowers who now pulled into the sweet spot were overpowering the rowers who pulled in low, thus ruining any semblance of balance they might have previously enjoyed. Tomorrow would be better. The good news: Gordo and Herb made it back in one piece.

I had not been inside a weight room more than three times since I stopped training a decade before. Too noisy. They smelled bad. Weight rooms attract weirdo's as sure as Dunkin' Donuts attract cops.

Promptly at 2:00 this afternoon, I unlocked the door to the UCSB weight room, a boxy, free-standing structure near the basketball gym. By any measure, the weight room was a modest affair, the size and feel of a weathered mobile home, complete with wall to wall artificial grass carpeting that had worn down to the black lining in places. In one corner stood a file cabinet that contained stacks of workout sheets dating back to the mid-1970s. Huge doors at either end of the room, when opened, allowed a steady ocean breeze to flow through. If nothing else this kept the collected fragrance from years' worth of arduous human effort somewhat tolerable.

The saving grace of weight lifting equipment is its indestructibility. No matter how you abuse it, a 45-pound plate is pretty hard to ruin. Through attrition, the UCSB equipment had been reduced over the years to only the basic, hardy tools of the lifting trade. Two Universal all-in-one machines, both vintage models, dominated the middle of room like the World Trade Towers. Three well-worn bench presses stood near the Universals, the padding now gone, leaving the plywood bench exposed. Along the wall, two squat racks were bolted into place. A plentiful supply of 45-pound bars and iron plates of every denomination completed the inventory. Being a strong proponent of power-lifting, I figured we had all the tools we'd ever need.

Before we commenced our workout, I implemented my first and, as it turned out, my best organizational effort of the season. I took a photograph of each rower, a mug shot, and I had them fill out a sheet with their name, address, phone, port or starboard, year in school, sculling experience, other interests, parents' address. The photographs and information found their way into a thick three-ring notebook, my prime ally in the coaching war. Besides the rower's resumes, I kept all my receipts inside, along with important phone numbers, maps of the campus, the lake, the world, any piece of paper that I thought had relevance. Whenever I was stumped for an answer I simply opened the book and pretended to read from some random page. Quite handy to have.

As the crew plowed through the paperwork, one of the rowers asked if we could talk outside. On the landing, in a hushed, conspiratorial tone, he asked, "Can you do me a big favor and not get in touch with my parents?"

"Why not?" I asked.

"They think I should be studying and not messing around in boats." I assured him that I'd keep his parents off the mailing list.

With the paperwork out of the way, we got down to business.

"First off, you guys know those MTV Unplugged specials?" I asked. Without waiting for a reply I yanked the electrical plug out of the wall socket, cutting the power to the noisy little radio that had been buzzing away for the last ten minutes. "Same drill here. Unplugged. No music. The only sound I want to hear is your rhythmic exhalations as you squat twice your body weight. Lifting is not a game - it's serious business. Ninety percent of rowing injuries have their origin in the weight room. I don't want any unnecessary distractions - not when the stakes are so high."

The rowers accepted my little quirk without obvious complaint. I doubt if they'd even been aware the radio was playing. The music had been distorted and unappealing, as if it were coming from an underwater speaker. More likely, the music had been serving as background noise, masking the silence that often makes people uncomfortable.

"Too often rowers simply play at lifting weights," I said. "They run through meaningless circuits or bogus high-repetition drills. In my opinion that's all wasted effort. The only lifting that has any real effect is low repetition, heavy and hard, and for that you need a few basic lifting tools, no radio, and a partner. So find a partner, preferably someone about your size and strength."

The men, without delay, began bouncing around the room, trying to hook up with their friends. As the rowers paired-up, I posted the workout sheet and they finally began lifting.

Ah, the sweet taste of power, ordering people around, giving commands, watching them being carried out. You could learn to enjoy the sensation, a feeling perhaps similar to what Donald Trump relishes as he bosses his minions around the Taj Mahal. I was in charge, on a roll, cracking the whip. I was The Man. My education as The Man was just beginning. I would need many hours of study, years more likely, before I'd have it mastered. Having been on the job only a few days, I could already see why coxswains so often become coaches. Coxswains love to give orders, to scream and shout, to pretend they're General Patton and Ross Perot at the same time. It's a natural evolution to put those same talents to work in the coaching arena. Scullers are the exact opposite, going about their business in a quiet, furtive manner, wasting neither words nor energy. Being an ex-sculler, I had my work cut out for me.

Since this week's technical focus was on the finish, I had several pull-in exercises on my sheet: one-armed bench rows with dumbbells, two-handed sitting pull-ins on the Universal machine. The scarcity of equipment necessitated a new drill: corner rows. I put one end of a 45-pound bar into an empty corner. On the bar's free end I loaded two 25-pound plates. With one knee resting on a flat bench, I had the rowers draw the heavy end of the bar up to their arm pits.

The rowers did well. Unlike our workout on Lake Cachuma, I could give hands-on advice to improve their lifting technique. Even Gordo managed to keep the pace. Now, if he could just lose the blubber.

Forty minutes later, I yelled, "Time for abdominals."

The crew quickly racked the weights and we walked as a group to the adjacent grassy field. Once on the grass I said to the squad, "Bob Ernst, my old college coach, taught me that having strong abdominal muscles is essential for healthy rowing. He likened it to a beer can that could easily be crushed should a flaw exist in the perimeter wall. The beer can represents your lower abdomen-back-and-flanks. To endure the rigors of hard rowing, you must have a strong cylinder. With that in mind, the last fifteen minutes of each weight workout will always be reserved for abdominal exercises, performed as a team, preferably outside, away from the weight room."

Besides the much needed conditioning of abdominal muscles, these few minutes were perfect for airing any grievances, sharing something important, telling a particularly good joke or simply expressing your wholehearted pleasure at being alive. When I look back on my own college rowing, these sessions were the best of times.

After my stomach refused to perform any more crunch sit-ups, I stood up and talked to the rowers. "No more Birkenstocks or Tevas in the weight room," I said. "Wear your running shoes." The Birk and Teva wearers moaned their disappointment.

"Listen up," I said. "This is more important. Lifting weights is an ongoing process. In a similar way, building a bullet-proof X Factor is also ongoing. A few days ago, we established a language to discuss it: in every close race you will reach a critical crossroads. The way you respond at this crossroads is determined by your X Factor, your courage, your soul. The challenge is essentially the same at every level of competition, whether it's the San Diego Crew Classic, the Christmas Regatta, the Olympic Trials or one of our inter-squad workouts. At some point you will need a powerful, invincible X Factor. You'll need courage beyond anything you've ever dreamed possible."

I looked around, trying to see if they were listening. Or was I boring the hell out of them? Tough crowd to read.

"When you don't respond the way you want at the crossroads, that's called failure. But to ignore when you have failed is a cop out. On rare occasions, we can fail at the crossroads and still win the race. You may rejoice at your victory but deep down you don't feel so good. Suffice to say, only through failure do we learn the importance of answering the challenge in a positive way. Don't think for a moment that failure is somehow unique to you. Everyone has their share of failures. Failure at the critical crossroads teaches us that our X Factor needs work."

I took a deep breath and prepared to wind up this little speech, which turned out to be one of my longest of the season.

"For me, the changes took place over years. Gradually I began making commitments and promises to myself that simply could not be broken. My promises didn't necessarily have anything to do with the coach or my teammates or even the race I was gearing up for. What mattered is the way I felt inside. I wanted to know that when I reached a critical crossroads, I would answer the challenge in the affirmative, with unbending resolve, with the strongest strokes I was capable of making. I want you guys, throughout the year, to continually examine your X Factor. If you don't like what you're seeing, then experiment, change it, make it work for you. Okay, see you tomorrow."

As the rowers headed to the locker room Robert Churchill came up to me. "I know what you mean about winning but not feeling good," he said.

"Really?" I said, somewhat surprised.

"Yeah," Churchill continued, "last year we raced Cal and won, but it was close and in the tough part of the race I backed off. I never said anything about it, but I felt really lousy afterward."

I thought for a moment and then said, "A lot of times we don't realize how much significance we put on our performance until something like that happens. Suddenly the truth cuts through like a knife. So we won't leave it to chance. We won't wait until race day to think about it. We'll work to make our X Factor respond the way we want. That's how champions do it." As he walked away I found myself thinking, maybe this coaching gig would turn out okay.

Freebirds
Tuesday, October 5, continued

Later in the evening I walked through downtown Isla Vista, looking for a place to eat dinner. I passed a VW repair shop, three pizza parlors, five beer bars, two expresso shops, and a Rasta man selling incense from a sidewalk table, ten sticks for a dollar. Finally I arrived at a funky burrito cafe where the line for ordering snaked out the door. Without much effort I had found the culinary hub of I-V, Freebirds.

For under five dollars you could eat like a king at Freebirds. Pretty healthy, too, so long as you watched the cooks when they prepared your meal. The twenty second rule was always in effect. Any food item that hit the floor was still considered edible if it was retrieved before twenty seconds had expired. My men often patronized Freebirds, especially when another rower, past or present, was working behind the counter. This guaranteed an unwieldy large portion at an all-time low price.

As I ate my veggie burrito, I looked through the information sheets my rowers had filled out. I already recognized some of the men, such as Robert Churchill, the curious lightweight who had won our first two inter-squad competitions. He wasn't the best athlete on the team, but for some reason I often found myself handing him the winner's Crunch bar after a competition. Besides being curious and a skilled competitor, Churchill served as the team's comedian, poet and rapper-provocateur. As a poet he was all too predictable, starting nearly ditty with, "There once was a girl from Pawtucket." I can only imagine the relief his parents felt when he went away to college. Churchill, at his best, could do a wicked imitation of Ed McMahon, Snoop Doggy Dog, and eventually me, (the lowest form of flattery), although he never quite perfected my walk.

Churchill once asked me about drinking alcohol - whether I thought it had an effect on a rower's ability. I told him, yes, studies had shown that alcohol hurts your performance. I also told him that most rowers, from Olympians on down, drank on occasion, some more than others. The less you drink, I told him, the better off you are. Some months later I found out that both his parents had severe drinking problems.

With his prominent pecs and bulging quads, I could not have overlooked Matthew "Moose" Morse, the captain of the heavyweight squad and a dead ringer for Fabio, poster boy of romance novels. Moose added to his budding bodybuilder physique each afternoon in the weight room. Yet, at the same time, I had noticed that in running practices he was quite slow. A dozen times I told him, "Moose, your training should concentrate on your weakest link. You'd be a national team contender if your engine could match your strength. Run some hills in the afternoon instead of lifting."

He'd inevitably say, "Yeah, but I like to lift."

Clement Nash, the lightweight captain, was from Manhattan Beach. He surfed, he played ultimate Frisbee, he looked like a young movie star. Throughout the season I had ample opportunity to marvel at his utter boldness when it came to meeting people. At every regatta he'd inevitably march up to an attractive young woman, usually the girlfriend of an opposing lightweight captain, and engage her in conversation.

"How the hell do you do it?" I asked him once.

"It's easy," he said, the faintest hint of pride in his voice. "Just walk up, stick out your hand and say, 'Hi, my name is Clement.'" His greatest triumph was having once slept with "an older woman," who had appeared on Robert Palmer's Victim of Love music video. "You'd know her if you saw her," he assured me. "She was the one standing next to the girl who was actually next to Robert Palmer on his right. Or was it on his left?" I assured him it didn't matter.

Clement was a great runner and as tough as they come. Unfortunately, his rowing technique was dismal. At the catch, after his seat had rammed into the front stops, he insisted on reaching forward about fifteen more inches. Whenever we practiced in singles, he inevitably had his ass handed to him, and for no other reason than all his toughness and endurance stayed bottled up, held captive by lousy technique. He had learned to row on ergometers and in eight-oared shells, neither of which is particularly technique-sensitive. I tried everything short of hitting him on the head with a spiked club to improve his catch, but with limited success. I have a sneaking suspicion that after ten days of rowing, your technique is set for life.

Another lightweight, Andrew Moore, was the only guy I knew who could make a JL uni-suit look baggy. Sure he's skinny now - give it a decade or two. He'll long for the lean old days. He was also the prince of sweat, often looking as though a garden sprinkler was attached to his head. On the ergs the other men refused to row next to him. Andrew Moore, the "More Man," always wanting to row more miles, more days of the week, more ergs. Andrew, wound tighter than a spindle.

Soon enough I'd learn all their names: Rick Trout, "Short Stack" Smith, Johnny Bender, Glen Mung, Jeff Beldon, Michael Kolbe, Björn, Antonio, Elaine-Eileen, Philip Shapiro, Rupert Foster, Herb Griffith. Taken together, a motley crew, and one that I'd get to know well.

SCULLING 101
Wednesday, October 6

Sculling is my passion, hardly a surprise given my background, and I was keen to have my men learn the symmetrical side of the sport. Over the past week, once or twice, I'd contemplated switching over the whole Gaucho program from sweep to sculling. In short order, we could become the finest sculling college in the country. Of course we would also be the only sculling college in the country. Another excellent idea to be filed away.

We were lucky to have a modest array of training singles at our disposal and plenty of oars. All we needed was a quiet place to practice. I thought that perhaps the Black Lagoon, located right on campus, would do. The lagoon's only limiting factor was its length, about 300 meters. Graceful white limbs of eucalyptus trees stretched over the lagoon waters, serving as house and home to cormorants, pelicans, seagulls, terns. Each morning the heavy, ungainly cormorants perched on the lowest branches, wings uplifted, drying their feathers in the first warmth of the day.

The most curious aspect of the lagoon was the texture of the water, dark and foreboding as in a children's fable. A rare combination of stale runoff, infused with fresh salt water, with a generous seasoning of guano had created a spunky little colony of micro-organisms that could not be found anywhere else on the planet. The Gaucho rowers were terrified of falling in. You'd become deathly ill, they claimed, by swallowing even a single mouthful. All the more reason not to tip over.

At the lagoon this afternoon I met my first sculling student, a heavyweight named Philip Shapiro. He was not much over six-feet tall, stocky, thick chest. He'd come to Santa Barbara intending to play football, only to find out that the football program had been dropped. Inevitably Shapiro won our bench press contests, once maxing out at 335 pounds, fifty pounds more than I could have ever done on my best day. He wore his black hair quite long, a pony tail at times, until a day in December when he cut it off. "Gonna see Dad soon, and I need to borrow some money" was his brief explanation for the new doo.

I'd heard that Shapiro's father was a successful lawyer in Los Angeles, and certainly he carried himself with the entitled demeanor of someone who was comfortable with the privileged life. Shapiro didn't live in the crew commune on Trigo Street, which served as ground zero for the social side of Gaucho rowing, the parties, gossip, binge drinking, projectile cookie tossing and endless failed seductions of novice women. No, Shapiro stayed somewhat aloof. A born sculler if I'd ever met one.

Before we launched, I gave Shapiro a photocopy of "Notes on the Sculling Stroke as Performed by Professional Scullers on the Thames River, England," by George Pocock. I'd been given a copy twenty-odd years ago when I had first taken up the sculls. "Put it in your training log," I told Shapiro. "It's good stuff to have."

> The art of sculling is like any other art. It is perfected only with constant practice so that each movement is graceful and is done correctly without thinking about it. It takes a lot of thinking about before this can be accomplished however. Note that all of sculling movements are smooth, flowing, rhythmic. They must blend. Remember you are dealing with natural elements: water, waves and wind. They have a rhythm and so must the sculler. He must have his mind on this rhythm to get in tune with his art.

We launched our singles sculls and set off across the lagoon. The only spectators were hundreds of birds, curious to see who was invading their private domain. As always, the water was as smooth as a kitchen table top. Our boats left behind clean tracks of streaming bubbles. The remnants from each stroke made minuscule waves that slowly eased towards shore.

As I watched Shapiro I contemplated taking the wheels off his seat, which would force him to row flat slide and hopefully perfect the finish motion. In terms of technique, great crews have only a few common points: positive ratio; the oars enter the water with lightning speed; and not a sliver of blade breaks the surface until the finish. This final point - the buried-blade finish - is especially key for single sculling, since all balance and stability hinge on the finish.

"I bet you're left handed," I said to him as we paddled.

"Yeah, I am," he said. "How'd you know?"

"Your starboard blade stays buried. Takes a lot of strength to draw the handle through like you're doing. Your port side isn't quite so strong. See how the top of the blade pokes through the water near the finish?"

"How should I fix it?" he asked.

"Exaggerate drawing the port blade in high. That'll make the blade go too deep. Once you can do it consistently, back off slightly, until both blades stay buried. You'll get it."

As the session progressed, the lagoon seemed to shrink in size, so that by the end I felt as though we were mainly practicing turning around. The final frontier was just beyond the bluff, the wide open Pacific Ocean, a straight stretch of a couple thousand miles. Tempting. Very tempting. Maybe tomorrow.

Home Sweet Motel 6
Friday, October 8

Since arriving in Santa Barbara a little over a week ago, I've been diligently searching for an apartment. My timing was less than ideal - school was in session, sabbaticals in place. What could I find in October?

First I scoured the town of Isla Vista. Tens of thousands of students had long before snapped up the more habitable places, leaving only the dregs. As my search slowed down, I actually considered taking one of these hovels. The only reason I didn't was the late-night noise factor in I-V, a taste of future hell for those of us who needed to get up early. The actual city of Santa Barbara, where the regular folk live, offered only slim pickings. I didn't bother with Montecito, the ritzy enclave to the south, home to countless celebrities including Don, Melanie, Sly and Jack.

I spent most of my time searching the community of Goleta, which lies between Santa Barbara and campus. Local farm workers had claimed the majority of places, bringing with them the accoutrements of their culture as surely as the students had done in Isla Vista. Goleta pulsed to the rhythm of mariachi music and low rider Chevy Impalas. The inviting smell of warm bread from the numerous Mexican bakeries along Main Street was enough to make you renounce bagels and cream cheese.

A few stray apartments were still advertised in the classified section of the Santa Barbara News-Press, and after inspecting assorted trailer parks, rooming houses and dilapidated hotels, I finally found something decent. My new home was more of an unfurnished Motel 6 than a real apartment, a generic, overpriced one bedroom, a solitary cell set among several hundred identical cells in a sprawling two-story honeycomb. As long as I could find my own door, I'd be okay. My apartment was close to campus, only three miles by bike path, and close to the freeway, the back wall of my bedroom serving as the retaining wall for the southbound 101. The sound of cars and trucks zipping along the freeway was the last thing I heard going to sleep and the first thing I heard in the morning, a soothing hum not unlike waves crashing on the beach.

On those mornings when we rowed on Cachuma, I rose extra-early to drive the 25.4 miles from my apartment to the boathouse. Does a program exist that requires its rowers to traverse a greater distance? I seriously hope not. Nor were these easy freeway miles. Highway 154, the long and winding route to Cachuma, was rated as the second most dangerous stretch of road in the state of California, based on the number of accidents-per-mile.

The trek from campus to Cachuma starts in Isla Vista, rolls along the 217 Freeway, then eases onto the 101 Freeway for a few miles to the State Street exit. Follow State Street to Highway 154. Eight miles up 154 brings you to the top-of-the-world, the San Marcos Pass. To the west, the Channel Islands rise out of the Pacific ocean like ancient volcanoes. To the east, fire-blackened mountains stretch into eternity. Tucked behind one of these mountains is Michael Jackson's famed Neverland Ranch, complete with Ferris wheel, exotic zoo and massage parlor. Shift into neutral for a screaming downhill stretch, which finally bottoms out on a rolling, two-lane road for a dozen miles, all the way to the entrance of Lake Cachuma State Park. Along the way you pass a well-stocked ostrich ranch and also the hidden mansions of assorted famous people, Eddie Murphy, Ronald Reagan, Fidel Castro, Elvis.

Highway 154 lacks only one thing, a passing lane. Most of the accidents occur when a speed demon tries to pass a slow poke. Ninety-nine percent of the time, the demon pulls it off. That errant 1% is what makes the drive so exceptionally grim. Through the course of the year, I jammed on the brakes a dozen times to keep from being crushed by an on-coming car.

According to Gaucho rowing tradition, the crew endures numerous speeding tickets each year along with at least one or two accidents. A few years ago, a rower on his way home from practice crossed the center divider and rolled his car, killing himself and severely injuring the other occupants. The police surmised he fell asleep at the wheel. Early on I instructed my rowers to wear seat belts and drive safely.

"I'd rather you got here fifteen minutes late," I told them, "instead of driving like a maniac to be on time." On this occasion they must have been listening because my rowers consistently arrived fifteen minutes late.

Exactly three weeks into the season, Adam the coxswain asked if we could get together and talk for a few minutes. "How about after weights tomorrow afternoon?" he said.

"No problem," I said.

Hearing his request, I was struck by an odd sensation, best described as a sinking feeling. It reminded me of the feeling you get when the national team coach asks if you can talk and within five minutes you're studying the Greyhound bus schedule for a ride out of Dodge.

Over the next thirty hours I found myself wondering what the hell Adam could want. Things were going along nicely. Or were they? The sculling indoctrinations were nearly complete, although on occasion my students had showed little or no interest in the two-handed stroke. More than once I found the Pocock missive that I gave each rower neatly deposited in a nearby trash can. But overall, I felt good about our progress. At least no one had quit. Then why did this underage contender for a Clearasil commercial have me worried?

Adam and I sat on a bench near the weight room, watching students roll past, most of them utilizing the three prime achievements of the wheel: bicycle, skateboard and rollerblade. After exchanging a few of the usual rower-coach pleasantries, I took the lead by saying how much I appreciated his help with the line-ups and all. "You're like my assistant coach," I told him, which was true.

"Wow," he said. "Does that mean I get paid?"

"No. So, what's on your mind?"

"One or two things," he said. "First off, your speech at the recruiting meeting got a few of the guys a little upset."

Was it that bad? I wondered.

"Rowing is the first priority for us," he continued, "the only priority. Forget the rest of the stuff - school, family, anything. All that matters is defeating the Cal Berkeley lightweights."

The whole time, as he spoke, Adam kept opening and closing his notebook, working off nervous energy. By nature, Adam was a tad high-strung. When he got a quick injection of adrenaline, watch out. He was tall for a coxswain and scrawny, of course. Had he treated himself to a few decent meals at Freebirds he would have ballooned to rower-weight. As is, he looked as though a moderate crosswind might knock him off his feet. Adam had the most important coxswain characteristic, a good set of lungs, altogether sufficient to snap a drowsy, hungover rower to attention.

"Sure, rowing can be your first priority," I said. "That's fine with me. But before it can be your first priority, you've got to satisfy those other things. What else is on your list?"

"The Pacific Coast Rowing Championships, PCRCs, is the big race we're all shooting for," he said. "I know it's a long way off, but if we keep the goal in mind, it'll happen for us."

"Right," I said. "PCRCs, here we come." As he spoke I began to wonder why the hell I was sitting here? I was in charge. I was The Man. The longer we sat, the more this idea protruded into my thoughts.

"I want to tell you a little of the history of Gaucho rowing," Adam continued. "Here at Santa Barbara the lightweights pretty much rule the roost. We've won the lightweight event at the PCRCs for the last six years. Hopefully we'll win it again this year."

"What about the heavies?" I asked. "What's their history?"

"The heavies," he said, doing his best to stifle a smile. "They do the best they can."

"What's their problem?" I asked.

"They don't like to work as hard as the lites," he said, responding quickly, as though he'd often discussed the matter with the other light-weights. "Basically, they're lazy. But the lites love to work hard. In fact, if they don't pound themselves at least once a day, they feel cheated. That's the next thing on my list: some of the rowers think you're going too soft. They want more pain."

"Don't worry," I said, "you'll get it."

Finally Adam said, "Our slogans at UCSB are 'Go Gauchos,' and 'Gauchos Never Die.' Shout them to us, to get us fired-up."

"I'll do my best," I said. For some reason I could never say Gaucho without smiling. Wasn't a Gaucho a Girl Scout cookie? At our regattas I came to curse the word. Whenever a Santa Barbara crew went past, the supporters would break the word into two, long sing-song syllables. Gow-Choz! Gow-Choz! Gow-Choz!

As he was getting up to leave, Adam remembered one last thing: "I'd appreciate any help with my coxing technique."

Was he joking? Adam must not have known that coxswains had inspired me to take up sculling. "Here's my only advice," I said. "Steer straight and say little."

Cleaning Up the Old Pad
Wednesday, October 13

Before we launched, I invested a minute to address a point I'd been mulling over since my talk yesterday with Adam.

"Just to clear up any confusion," I said, "this is a competitive crew, as opposed to recreational rowing. We are training in order to win our races."

"You are right, sir," Churchill said, using his Ed McMahon voice, a pretty good imitation and always good for a laugh, although eventually I told him that if he ever did it again I'd cut out his tongue.

I continued: "Way back at our first orientation meeting I described the order of importance. First, keep yourself healthy and centered. Second, your family and close friends. Third, school. Lastly, wild card, in our case rowing. Several of you have mentioned that I'm wrong, that rowing comes first - specifically, beating the Cal lightweights at the PCRCs."

I glanced at Adam. His head was going up and down like a hyper dunkit bird.

"Here's the deal. College rowing operates under the umbrella of real life. After college, when you're training for the Olympics, you can justify pulling out the stops and going hog wild. For those few months or years rowing can be everything in your life. Many rungs of the rowing ladder must be climbed before you've earned the right to make this final commitment."

I noticed that Adam's head had stopped moving.

"To summarize: we train to win. We'll do it under the umbrella of real life. Besides, it's more fun this way. Juggling one ball at time is as dull as oatmeal. When you have to juggle a lot of balls - classes, girlfriends, Green Day concert, rowing - that's more fun and a lot healthier, too."

The response was mixed. No one came up to me and said, hey, right on. No one took exception to my statement. If nothing else, I felt as thought I was doing my job. We launched straight away and proceeded to have one of our better workouts, all of it with eyes closed, feet out of foot stretchers, off-blade-side-hand only and on the square. Good for the concentration.

During a break I said to the rowers, "I thought of another point, relating to our earlier discussion. Make sure you're getting some manner of satisfaction from your rowing endeavor. Right here, today, right now. A well-rowed piece this morning should be as satisfying as a well-rowed Olympic final."

As the crews worked through their lone hard piece of the morning, I thought of a story I'd heard, about a college athletic director who wanted to initiate a rowing program. The director telephoned the legendary boat builder George Pocock to get an idea about how to proceed. "Do you want to have a winning team?" old George asked the director. "Yes, absolutely, more than anything," the director said. "Too bad," George Pocock replied, "because the substance and beauty of rowing have nothing to do with winning races." Pocock was right. Certainly you must train to win in order to keep focused and motivated. But if winning is the only determinant of success, then your program is doomed. Winning and losing, treat both these impostors the same way.

After the boats were put away and the rowers departed, I looked around the boathouse, contemplating the clutter and confusion. Enough was enough. I wasn't going to take it any longer. A stray sheet of plywood caught my eye and became my first victim. I carried it outside and dumped it behind the boathouse. As I threw it to the ground, I noticed a map of Lake Casitas painted on one side, showing the warm-up pattern to be used on the Olympic race course.

Lake Casitas, fifty miles from Lake Cachuma, was the site of rowing, kayaking and canoeing for the 1984 Los Angeles Olympic Games. This plywood map had been part of UCSB's inheritance from the '84 Games, along with the pontoon dock, miles of galvanized steel cable, several dozen half-inflated buoys, and innumerable scissors-style slings. Except for the dock and a few slings, none of it had been used. Instead, it was strewn in and around the boathouse, until today.

I brought out another identical sign and stacked it on the first. So much for the '84 Games. Don't get me wrong, I am a big fan of Olympic memorabilia and scrap lumber. I simply didn't want it in my boathouse.

In addition to the historical debris, the Gaucho boathouse had an unbelievable collection of ordinary junk. Scattered over the concrete floor were riggers from boats long forgotten, discarded seats, cracked foot boards, tattered shoes. Even less useful bits of rowing detritus were strewn around - leaky water bottles, smelly socks. A heavy layer of dirt, dust and cobwebs colored everything with the same drab gray-brown hue. I remember saying earlier that the place was a frigging mess. The last few weeks had only made it worse.

Like candy sprinkles on a birthday cake, topping it off were mouse and rat droppings, literally by the millions. Of mice and men, only a few common traits exist - one of these traits is a penchant for mating. Judging by the sheer numbers of mice, I quickly concluded that in non-rowing hours a veritable mouse orgy was taking place inside the boathouse. The stench of their many mouse nests evoked a deep revulsion, a smell that worked into the weave of your clothes and wouldn't go away without a good laundering. Had the Pied Piper of Cachuma come along at that moment, I would have paid handsomely for his services.

I'm not a clean-house freak. I have the requisite dirty dishes in the sink and last month's newspapers piling up by the front door. But a boathouse is different - it's special. It should be treated with care and respect. All the best boathouses, from Ratzeburg to Harvard, are kept clean, well-organized and well-maintained.

Besides a desire to keep up with the Rowing Jones's, I had a health reason for wanting a clean boathouse: Hanta virus, also called Four Corners disease. This ultra-deadly disease is spread by contaminated mouse droppings that dry out, become airborne and are then inhaled. Granted, we were in the middle of a forest so some rodents would be inevitable, but because of Hanta virus I had a real concern about controlling the level of droppings. Once I'd removed the bulk of the droppings, I set to work to clean up this boathouse/mouse cage.

I had plenty of company as I worked - not the other coaches who fled after each practice as though a radiation leak had been discovered - but the innumerable common crows, Corvus brachyrhynchos, or simply black winged-hunger. At exactly 10:10 each morning, they perched in the oak trees around the boathouse and commenced a riotous racket. After an hour or two, the noise was enough to make even the most ardent animal lover reach for a shotgun.

As I listened to their arguments, I couldn't help concluding that the crows had a vocabulary that rivaled some of my rowers. I actually struck up a modest friendship with one crow. At lunch time I'd set my beach chair on the end of the dock and eat a peanut butter and strawberry jam sandwich. Mr. Crow would stand near me, clicking his claws on the plastic pontoons, cocking his head back and forth, staring at me with his marble-black eyes in hope that his magnetic personality would convince me to share my lunch. Of course I did.

For the most part, I enjoyed the two-week long cleaning marathon. The lake was quiet and beautiful. The boathouse acoustics were suited for both music and books-on-tape. Once, buried in all the junk, I actually found something useful, the team's lone heart rate monitor, its stopwatch racing along madly. Gradually a new boathouse emerged, one of which perhaps Coach Harry would have been proud.

I had an exceptionally low threshold for boredom when I rowed. Now, as a coach, I've been trying to keep the same monotony-monster at bay. This task was proving to be tougher than I had first imagined. Varied and challenging workouts don't grow on trees. Barely a week into the season I abandoned one of my original goals, to never repeat a workout. Hell yes, we'd repeat certain workouts - all the time.

Today I introduced a drill that none of the rowers would soon forget, touch monkey. The origins of touch monkey are unclear. I suspect that it was invented eons ago by some young man who could find relief no other way. Certainly these days everyone knows how to touch monkey, but can they do it in public, with their friends watching, when they're tired, when the pressure is on?

Two days earlier, in preparation for TM, I tested each rower's vertical jumping ability - for one leap only - and carefully recorded the numbers in my notebook. As with most rowers, each Gaucho crewman had a vertical jumping ability somewhat less than their respective shoe size.

On this TM day I woke extra-early, drove to the erg room and posted a sign on the door directing the rowers to run as a group to Goleta Pier, about a mile away. I drove to the beach and parked near a stand of palm trees. Between the palms, I strung assorted lines, each line at a different height, corresponding to the jumping ability of the different rowers. To these lines, I duct-taped a monkey playing card. The scene was set.

When the rowers arrived, I assigned each man to the particular monkey-card station that matched his jumping ability. On my command the rowers jumped up continuously for one minute and tried to touch their monkey card. After resting, they jumped again for three minutes and then rested. Next was five minutes of continuous jumping.

The coxswains, Adam, Elaine and Eileen, kept careful account of the exact number of successful jumps made by each rower. This gave a special significance to the workout, as though I would later submit the numbers to an obscure FISA world-ranking committee. When people are watching and numbers are being recorded - in pen, no less - an athlete tends to try a little harder.

Rather an insidious workout, touch monkey, obviously devised by someone with far too much time on his hands. You needed leg strength and good endurance and a relentless attacking willpower to keep touching the card. If you lacked one of these talents, you would suffer. Of course, you were going to suffer regardless, but if you could keep touching that monkey, your teammates and coach would be duly impressed.

The champion monkey toucher was Andrew Moore. He was able to touch his card the same number of times, per minute, regardless of the duration of the piece. Tough guy. I gave him a Crunch bar.

UCSB, The High School After
Friday, October 15

"Time on the slide is time wasted" might have worked for the great single sculler Tiff Wood, but we mere mortals must use some measure of control as our seat rumbles down the tracks towards the front stops.

Since Monday, when we began Slide Control and Rhythm Week, I've been trying to teach my rowers to use poise as they approach the catch. Exercise control. Be patient. Yet regardless of the cleverness of my drills or the comeliness of my words, they still consider the last six inches of slide to be a bottomless chasm that must be crossed as quickly as possible. Maybe I should extend slide control and rhythm week for a month or the rest of the year.

As usual, I played the Oly card: "At the Olympics," I told them, "all the best rowers control their slide on the recovery. Every single one. Feel the pressure on your hamstrings as you make your way up the slide. Pretend an egg is lodged under your foot - don't crack the egg on the recovery. By controlling the recovery you can get a sense of the right-rhythm, a three count cadence: one count on the drive, two counts on the recovery, ONE, two, three, ONE, two, three."

Perhaps I could teach slide control and rhythm in the weight room, specifically through squat lifts. This afternoon I had three different flavors on tap, regular bar-behind-head squats, front squats and my new favorite, overhead squats. No sooner had I posted the workout sheet when lightweights Jeff Beldon and Andrew Moore walked up to me.

"We're not doing squats," Jeff said.

"Why not?" I asked, somewhat surprised by this mild mutiny.

"They're too dangerous."

Certainly if you have a problem with your knees or back, then yes, stay away from squats. For that matter, stay away from rowing altogether. But with good instruction and a watchful spotter, squats are fantastic for developing leg strength, balance, rhythm, slide control. I told the non-squatters to use the Universal leg press station and invited my first candidates, Glen Mung and his lifting partner, Michael Kolbe, into the squat cage.

Mung stood towards the front of the squat rack with Kolbe right behind him. I took my place off to the side and directed the action like a movie maker.

Mung and Kolbe, until I learned their names I thought they might be brothers. No, not even close. While Kolbe was singing in the men's chorus, Mung was trying to seduce the whole women's choir. Mung was a proud young man, proud of his skateboarding scars and the sexually transmitted diseases he'd endured and the barbed-wire tattoos on his upper arms, which he called a permanent record of his momentary lapses of intelligence. If fearlessness equaled success, he would be unstoppable. When he filled out the information sheet, he included as other interests, "Hunting Beemers." When I asked his what hunting Beemers meant, he said, "I like to roam around I-V after midnight and shoot BMW's with my paint gun." Made me glad I drove a VW.

"Press the 45-pound bar over your head," I told Mung. He easily lifted the bar off the supports and overhead. "Okay, now rock back and forth on your heals a few times, to find the balance point."

As he rocked, the bar swayed overhead. Gradually he brought the balance into focus.

"With your knees wide apart, descend until your quads are parallel with the floor. Be extra slow at the bottom end of the squat. Use your hamstrings like a brake to slow your descent. That's exactly the motion you want to duplicate in the boat. Super-control in the last six inches of compression."

As Mung lowered himself, his partner mimicked his movements in tight harmony. At the bottom end, Mung pressed back up to the standing position. Through the whole lift, the 45-pound bar continued to sway slightly over his head. The balance factor is so tricky with overhead squats that little weight, if any, is needed to make for a good drill.

"One squat down," I said. "Only 99,999 more and you'll be an Olympic contender."

Mung repeated the motion nine times and then racked the bar. The two men switched so that now Kolbe was lifting and Mung spotting. The beauty of two-man lifting teams is that the rest period between sets is just about right.

After Kolbe lifted, I added two 25-pound plates, making the whole contraption weigh ninety-five pounds. Again Mung worked through ten repetitions.

With the added weight came a marked increase in his concentration. White Hot Concentration is the unappreciated fruit of hard lifting, especially squats. When you're in the squat rack, with a serious amount of weight overhead, your life literally depends on maintaining concentration. You learn to block out the swirling images in the mirror, the obnoxious chatter of the people next to you, the fat drop of sweat running down your nose. Once you've mastered this concentration in the weight room, duplicating it on the race course is relatively easy. Champions have only a few things in common. One weapon they all possess is White Hot Concentration.

Later in the afternoon I met a prospective UCSB student, a tall, enthusiastic, high school senior from Long Beach named Walter O'Connor.

"I can't wait to get into the rowing here," he said. "I think I can go somewhere in the sport. Hard to say for sure, but maybe."

As he talked on and on about rowing, the whole time ignoring the young coeds who nearly ran us over on their mountain bikes, I told him, "Walter, if you're serious about rowing, I'd recommend you go to a serious rowing school. If you want to rollerblade around campus hand-in-hand with a future super model, then UCSB is your best choice."

He looked at me for a moment, perhaps stunned by my statement.

"My sister once gave me a book called The Write Stuff," I told him, "The author said that the most important thing in writing is putting yourself into an environment where good writing can take place. The same is true for rowing. If I'd gone to school here, I'd never have gotten to the Christmas Regatta, much less the Olympics. Surfing, yes. Rowing, no."

Walter shook my hand, said he appreciated my honesty and walked to his car. Yes, recruiting comes easy to me.

I once saw this message on a T-shirt: "UCSB - The High School After High School." The accompanying drawing showed Calvin and Hobbes engaging in an illegal, impish performance.

UCSB students lived in a fantasy world. Everything they had wanted to do in high school - but were prevented from doing by their parents - was now at their fingertips. Perhaps this is true of college students all over the country. I don't know. I do know that three basic pastimes comprised the average Gaucho's life - drinking Bud, watching MTV, having sex. Having grown up in a ridiculously ordinary time and place, I couldn't help but envy the students. No doubt some of them were serious about their studies and would eventually become doctors, lawyers, Indian chiefs. These students, I never met. It made me want to turn back the clock, slip an earring into my ear and another through my nostril and watch marathon showings of Ren and Stimpy.

I had to admire my rowers for at least attempting to do something as difficult and counter-cultural as crew. It would have been so much easier, so much more pleasant, to simply sleep in. God knows, they had to get up at 4:45 to be on time for practice.

Don't get me wrong - they rarely missed a party. In truth, they couldn't have missed a party. The noise factor in I-V was incredible, a nightly battle of the mega-stereos. As the year progressed, this hard style of living took its toll, with the rowers often sick with a cold or the flu or some other ailment. The wild life is not an easy life.

CLEMENT IS DEAD
Saturday, October 16

Parents love to clip articles out of the newspaper and send them to their offspring, an act somehow akin to a mother bird regurgitating worms for its chicks. A few days ago, my father sent me an article that caused me to lose a few minutes' sleep.

UC IRVINE AND COACH NAMED IN WRONGFUL DEATH SUIT
Parents of a soccer player who died while training allege the university and coach were negligent and careless. Freshman Terrie Cate collapsed with about a mile remaining in a six-mile run on the first day of practice. Cate was taken by ambulance to Irvine Medical Center, where she was in critical condition until she died three days later.

This article was on my mind as I drove to the local supermarket where I bought a case of bottled drinking water, ten pounds of oranges and several small boxes of chalk. The UC Irvine soccer player had died in part because of a lack of water during the run.

Without a doubt, this morning's workout was intended to be a killer: five times five minutes, running up a steep hill. At the end of each five-minute piece we would slowly jog back to the same starting point. This, in my opinion is the toughest workout known to man. With running, technique is not a factor. By the time you're three years old, you possess all the technique you'll ever need. Equipment is not a factor nor is the ability of your teammates. Nothing short of an earthquake can interfere with your physical expression. That's why it's so tough. That's why I like it.

The last great unknown, in terms of physiological training, is the optimum length of a piece. Is three minutes enough? Is ten minutes too much? No one knows. Perhaps someday the question will be answered - we'll find out that thirteen minutes is the perfect length for a training piece when preparing for a 2000 meter race. Until then, coaches will continue exploring the whole scale, up and down, from thirty seconds to sixty minutes and more, in hopes of capturing the optimum time. My personal favorite is five minutes, not too long, not too short. Just about right.

From the market I drove to the base of Old San Marcos Pass Road, on the western side of the mountains. My rowers were waiting when I arrived, along with some additional competition. For the first time this season we were blessed with the company of the men's novice team. I was glad the novices had decided to participate - more competition and good for team bonding.

The novice coach, Fred Checks was also taking part. I'd met Checks briefly at the recruiting meeting but had seen little of him since. His squad had used the Black Lagoon for their initiation rows and were only now venturing to Lake Cachuma. Checks was a true novice in terms of his coaching experience. In fact, he was still in college, trying to earn the final credits for an undergraduate degree. He wasn't coaching for the money, that's for sure. The salary he was paid wouldn't cover his gasoline to the boathouse. To supplement his income Checks worked at a shoe store in Goleta. Like everyone involved in rowing, he was coaching because he loved it.

We jogged as a group up the hill a few hundred yards to a straight stretch. When the road was clear, I drew a line across the pavement with a piece of white chalk - this would serve as our starting line. Then I instructed the coxswains to hand out a piece of chalk to each rower.

"Listen up," I said. "Here's the drill: we'll run uphill, full-tilt-boogie, for five minutes. Then we'll jog back to this same place. Once we're all gathered we'll start the next piece. This should give us lots of rest between pieces - ten minutes or so. We'll run five pieces altogether." As I was talking, the rowers began drawing obscene pictures on the pavement. "At the end of each piece, use the chalk to write your initials on the pavement. This way you'll have a definite goal - try to match or better the results on each subsequent piece."

"Car!" someone yelled. Everyone scooted to the side of the road. I hoped we wouldn't encounter too many cars over the next hour.

"We're damn lucky today. We have a steep stretch of road. We have plenty of competition. You'll be running against each other, against the novices, against the coaches. And we'll have accountability, in the form of your initials on the pavement. Usually one or the other is adequate, either competition or accountability. Once in a while it's good to have both."

With the drop of my hand, we started running. The novice rowers blasted ahead as though the piece were only a hundred yards long. My varsity rowers stayed close on their heels. I brought up the rear, chugged onward, cursing the lousy shape I was in. Fuck it. Show me a skinny writer and I'll show you a coke addict. By the end of the first five minute piece I had caught a few of the rowers. We scrawled our initials on the pavement and then jogged down to the starting line. Between pieces I had the coxswains hand out drinking water, although it wasn't much needed, the gray overcast sky keeping everyone relatively cool.

On the last few pieces my X Factor was severely tested, thanks to Fred Checks. I suspect that at any school the competition between coaches is as acute as that between rowers, perhaps more. In regards to Checks and myself, so many ingredients came into play: the fact that I was exactly twice as old as Checks and would do anything to keep from showing it; the fact that he was a nobody in the world of rowing while I was relatively well-known - I had my reputation to uphold; the fact that I was trying to establish my place at UC Santa Barbara while he was a veteran Gaucho. As long as Checks and I restricted our combat to the running course, I could see no harm in doing battle.

Checks stayed alongside for about three minutes, forcing me to endure the intense discomfort that such competition creates, hustling along well above my body's ability to re-supply oxygen to the major muscles, legs, arms, heart. A trained athlete, or an overweight ex-athlete, can insist that his body ignore the brain's sensible entreaties to stop the madness. Eventually lactic acid will shut down your body the way a strike by workers will shut down an assembly line. But until that happens, your heart pounds against the walls of your chest like a kettle drum and your head spins. The big ouch.

I didn't want to lose to this guy, Fred Checks, whom I inevitably wanted to call Fed Ex. Bull elephants bang their tusks to establish dominance. Checks and I ran against each other. When the light tapping of his shoes against the pavement softened and then faded into the void, I concluded that nothing is finer.

After the last piece I took my time coming down. Damn tired, exhausted. My eyes stayed focused on the uneven pavement as though it held some fascinating secrets. Halfway down, as I came around a sharp bend in the road, I saw Clement Nash, captain of the lightweight team, stretched out flat on the pavement, face up, lifeless. Dead.

Seeing Clement dead was the most frightening experience of my life - certainly of my coaching life. Two rowers, Churchill and another man, were bending over Clement, trying to revive him. My heart nearly exploded I was so scared. I ran to the lifeless figure and leaned over him. What the hell should I do? Then I noticed that the two rowers did not seem to be concerned with their captain. What the hell? Instead of jumping on his chest or blowing into his mouth, or whatever you were supposed to do, they were drawing his outline with their chalk. A joke. It was all a big joke. Seeing my concern, they quickly finished their drawing, helped Clement to his feet and jogged down the hill.

I was so glad to see that Clement was alive - that he was mobile and upright and not dead - that I was speechless. To this day the memory of him lying on the pavement dredges up a full-sensory recollection of fear in motion.

This little incident, probably long forgotten by the three rowers, made a deep dent in my consciousness. I took a CPR/Adult Lifesaving class and later enrolled in an emergency medical technician course, eventually becoming a certified EMT. I never again wanted to feel unsure about what to do.

X Factory
Tuesday, October 26

The UCSB campus is an intoxicating place. At one time it had been a sprawling military complex, specializing in the study of agricultural science. After World War II the site was decommissioned and donated to the University of California. A few of the drab military buildings still remain, filled through and through with asbestos.

This morning I stood next to the erg room, smelling the pungent odor of eucalyptus trees that enveloped the whole campus like a dreamy mist. From a distance I saw Clement Nash, hands in his pockets, not a care in the world, riding his skateboard toward me. At UCSB, the skateboard ranked second only to the bicycle as a means of inner-campus locomotion. The proper posture for skateboarding is a modified slouch, utterly relaxed, almost asleep. The rear leg should be slightly bent and the feet splayed to cover as much of the board's surface area as possible. Clement had it just about right, cruising nonchalantly as though the board were nothing more than an extension of his feet. That changed abruptly when the wheels of his skateboard met one of the thousands of seed pods dropped by the many eucalyptus trees. His board stopped. Clement kept going, airborne, a half-dozen feet and then boom. Luckily he landed on his head. He stood up, brushed himself off and walked the rest of the way to the erg room.

I had a hard running drill in mind for today's workout. We jogged to the school's quarter-mile tartan track and then ran two laps as a warm-up. This track is like the jewel in the heart of the campus. Surrounding it are coastal redwood trees and more eucalyptus. The grassy infield is as finely manicured as a putting green.

As the team stripped off their sweatshirts, I described what I had in mind. "We're going to run as a group," I said, "lots and lots of quarters. I want you to find a manageable pace - in the neighborhood of two minutes per quarter-mile. Once you find the right pace, try to relax and lower your heart rate. We'll check our heart rate every mile or so, to gauge our progress. The purpose of this workout is to learn to stay cool under duress."

We started off, rolling along, around and around, until I eventually lost count. Actually, I lost count soon after the third lap. I pedaled my bike alongside the pack, shouting instructions: "Arms relaxed. Face relaxed. Save every little crumb of energy."

After fifty minutes I told the crew: "Two laps to go - time to sprint." The best runners, lightweights Clement Nash and Rupert Foster, sprinted ahead as though freed from captivity. Within a few seconds they'd opened up a huge lead. At the same time, several runners, Moose, Bender and Björn, fell back and lumbered behind the group. Clement and Rupert soon crossed the finish line. These two men, best of friends, could be counted on to push each other to the absolute edge of consciousness. Afterward, as the team rested on the bleachers next to the track, I elaborated on what I'd said during the workout.

"In a close race, something has to fuel your X Factor," I said. "The fuel comes from having been stingy with your energy in the early going. The goal is to stay in contention while burning a little less fuel than your opponent. Then, when the time is right, throw out the kitchen sink, the microwave, it's X Factor time."

"What's the difference between X Factor and sprinting?" Robert Churchill wanted to know.

I scratched my head for a moment. "They're definitely related," I said. "To me, sprinting is a race strategy that comes from your head. The X Factor is a response comes from your heart."

I looked at my men. Three or four were listening carefully, which was enough to keep me talking.

"The window of X Factor opportunity opens up in the closing seconds of a race - you might be sprinting at the time or just hanging one, trying to get across the finish line. With a supreme act of will, you can prolong your effort, essentially fighting off the inevitable lactic acid shutdown. You'll have little time for contemplating the options: either wholeheartedly go for it, or back off. You must train your X Factor to unequivocally respond the way you want - go for it. Once the window is closed, it's closed forever."

THE CATCH
Wednesday, October 27

I left my apartment at exactly 5:03 this morning and walked down the stairs to my car. When I slipped the key into the ignition, I noticed the dashboard clock read 5:17. Somehow time had zoomed ahead by nearly fifteen minutes. How could that have happened? I have been wondering about the missing minutes all day. I wouldn't bother mentioning it at all except that the same exact thing occurred throughout the year, dozens of times. I want those minutes back, right now!

The technique we're emphasizing during this week's training-cycle is the toughest part of the stroke, the catch.

Our training-cycles are also work related: we begin with an easy workout, build to a crescendo at the halfway point and then drop back down, consummating the cycle with a semiformal race on Saturday. Many sports use a cycle method of training. It's too damn hard, mentally and physically, to always be flogging yourself. By adding a rhythm to the work, an athlete's life becomes livable. I would have preferred a continuous two-week cycle such as I used when I was training - twelve days on, two days off - but that wouldn't work with my rowers. Nothing could budge them from their Sunday-long slumber.

As the crews paddled toward the dam, I spoke to them about the catch: "The recovery is calm, serene, Buddha-like, in perfect balance with earth, sun and water. The drive is a violent explosion, Sly, Seagal and Van Damme rolled into one. The transition between these two temperaments takes place at the catch. The mechanics are simple. As your hands pass over your foot boards, extend and lift. Your head, shoulders - everything else - must stay fixed and steady. The lower edge of the blade should kiss the water as the wheels of your seat touch the front stops. Press with your legs and hang on for dear life. Speed is all important. The blade must enter the water at a speed greater than the speed of the boat."

I told the rowers to imagine that they had just finished writing a letter to some distant girlfriend. The all-important letter was taped to the end of the blade. The envelope for this letter - already addressed and stamped - was bobbing upright in the water at precisely the point of full reach. Without hesitation, drop the letter into the envelope. Verve. Exactitude. With utmost confidence. Not too deep. Speedy into the water, the same way a rattlesnake strikes a mouse.

Swimmers use kick boards and pull buoys to strengthen particular segments of their stroke. In a similar way, so must rowers. I gave each man a short wooden dowel and instructed them to bring their seat forward and place the dowel at the end of the slide. As expected, Clement the stroke tried to poke Adam the coxswain in the eye with the dowel. Two of the heavyweights fought each other as in a duel.

At last, with dowels in place, they rowed with the front five inches of slide only. Results were mixed. For some reason the slowest blade entering the water seemed to dictate the blade speed of the whole crew. The men soon complained of sore backs from having to stay in the forward position without respite. Finally I had them put the dowels aside and we began the meat of the workout, five times ten minutes, with two minutes rest between pieces, all at low rating.

After practice, one of the lightweights came up to me and said, "From now on, I only want to row port."

"Are you sure?" I said.

"Yeah, I just don't dig that starboard-thing. Makes the fillings in my teeth hurt."

"Okay," I said. "We don't want to mess with your teeth."

As he walked away I looked up his name in my maxi-notebook. Antonio Zancos, from Pomona, California. In regards to the side he rowed, I crossed out "either" and wrote "port."

Antonio was unique among the UCSB rowers for the simple reason that he wasn't one-hundred percent Anglo-continental-white. People have considered this dilemma for years, for decades, but as far as I know, no one has found a way to create a more ethnically diversified bunch of rowers. Energetic, zealous people - of any color - can thrive in rowing. Why the sport doesn't better reflect the mosaic of America, I honestly don't know.

Johnny Bender came up to me after Antonio and said, "The three seat in the Carrie On feels sort of funny."

"What do you mean?" I asked. "Was the pitch off? Rigged too high? Tracks loose?"

"I don't know," he said. "It just feels funny."

Johnny Bender is a funny guy. Sophomore. Heavyweight. Long blond hair. Several randomly placed earrings. Big kid, 6'3", 195 pounds, strong in the weight room, iffy endurance. Johnny rowed in high school, which should have served to his advantage now that he was in college. Yet he had a slight tendency to whine, a characteristic that will eventually frustrate even the most patient coach. Once or twice I took him aside and told him, "Big guys like you and me aren't allowed to whine. That's one of the down sides of being big."

CHAOS THEORY
Thursday, October 28

This morning, as we ran through the deserted pre-dawn streets of Isla Vista, I had each rower shout his name, one by one, at the top of his lungs. "My name is Johnny Bender and I'm a rower. Johnny I am!"

Part of being a champion is learning to eliminate all inhibitions. You must not be afraid to try new things, to risk being embarrassed. Break down all the barriers. Scream it out. Besides, this sort of thing is completely harmless since the denizens of I-V sleep like the dead.

Once on the beach, we continued running, a herd of giant sand fleas, heading north until we had the whole sandy world to ourselves. No surfers ventured this far from the point. A mile offshore the usual fog bank drifted over the water. Snow white pelicans took turns circling and diving in the shore break, searching for their morning meal. The distinctive salt water and seaweed smell floated heavily in the air. When you grow up with that smell, it gets into your head and never leaves. Finally we stopped, three miles up the beach, at a telephone pole planted in the soft sand. While the rowers rested, I talked the coach's talk:

"Listen up," I said. "Not long ago I read a story about an elementary school principal who had his pupils practice fire drill evacuations for months on end until the whole school, every solitary student, could be out in six minutes - a world's record. They had a big party to congratulate themselves. Then the recess bell rang and in less than two minutes the whole damn school was empty."

Every rower, myself included, could relate to recess, the best time of the school day.

"That's the direction I'm going this year, chaos theory. Orderly, predictable patterns of behavior are not as efficient as mildly chaotic systems that are more flexible. Nor are they as much fun. I prefer the mad, scrambling chaos of a recess bell to the orderly directions of a fire drill. This morning's workout is in line with chaos theory. I want you to break into three-man teams. As soon as I cut you loose, each team must decide the best and fastest way back to the erg room. Any of a half-dozen options are open, you can head inland and run through the hills or stay on the beach. Talk among your teammates as you run to solve the problem."

"How the hell does this relate to rowing?" Andrew Moore asked.

"The eight-oared shell makes you lazy," I said. "You assume the coxswain and stroke have all the answers. Close your eyes and pull. Wrong. Every man is stroke, coxswain, bowman, rigger, coach. Each man must be capable of solving every challenge. If you're in the finals of the PCRCs - two seats down with twenty strokes to go, and the coxswain's megaphone short circuits - you'd better be able to think on the fly and act under duress. Go ahead and pick your teams."

Instantly five men tried to convince Clement to join their team. At last, when everyone had a team to call his own, I drew a line in the sand and told them to get ready. One team was clearly stocked with lumbering hippos. I started this team first and then everyone else a minute later.

After they began running I loped back to the erg room, lost in my own thoughts, occasionally wishing I had my bicycle so that I could make some decent time. When I eventually arrived at the erg room only one team was still standing nearby - the winning trio of Johnny Bender, Philip Shapiro and Andrew Moore - waiting patiently for their Crunch bars.

Antonio Gone
Friday, October 29

We rowed a series of pieces, one minute regular rowing at 24 spm full effort, then a minute of front-half-of-the-slide only, then back to regular rowing, full-power for a minute. Seemed to work pretty well, although they mostly wanted to row the full-power part.

After practice, as I was putting away my launch, Antonio came up to me and said with great solemnity, "I quit."

"Good luck in all your future endeavors," I said. He looked shocked, as though he had been expecting me to talk him out of it. No thanks. Rowing is so darn relentless that if you doubt whether you should continue, then most likely you should not.

At weights this afternoon I brought along the handle portion of a broken oar and a rolling seat. Throughout the workout I spent a few minutes with each man, trying to teach him the correct catch-technique. This required that I act as a human rigger, holding the oar in place while they rolled forward on the seat, handle in hand.

"Extend and lift your forearms," I told Moose, "while keeping your head and shoulders fixed like a block of stone." Most of the rowers, Moose included, held their arm as stiff as broomsticks on the recovery. Thus the only way they could make a catch was by lifting their whole upper body. By the time the blade was firmly set in the water, much of the slide had been wasted.

During our abdominals session on the grassy field, I borrowed Adam's bicycle and turned it upside down, so that it rested on the handlebars and seat.

"Listen up," I said. "I'm going to show you the essence of the catch. Suppose for a moment that the race was only one stroke long. You'd have Swartzenagger-type rowers reefing on the oar." I spun the front tire with all my might and then watched it hum along for several seconds.

"That's the equivalent of a one-stroke race. But as you know, the race is a series of strokes, approximately one every two seconds, 240 altogether."

I spun the tire, but this time I grabbed it and brought it to a halt. Once fully stopped, I spun it again. I repeated this several times, spin, grab, stop, spin, grab, stop, spin.

"What I'm showing you here is Swartzenagger rowing a 2000 meter race. This is also the way we were rowing today. Lots of muscle. Not efficient. I want you to learn to row like this." I spun the tire, and then commenced tapping it lightly so that the revolutions did not decrease.

"Each time my hand strikes the tire - that's the equivalent of the catch. I can keep the tire spinning far more easily by simply tapping it along rather than muscling it. The catch must be quick and decisive and subtle, otherwise you'll lose your momentum mojo."

ANTONIO BACK
Saturday, October 30

As soon as I stepped into the boathouse, Antonio came up to me and said, "I don't want to quit after all. I was upset yesterday because it seemed just like last year when the coach put me in the four seat and blah, blah, blah."

I let him drone on for a few seconds, until I sensed that he was repeating himself. Then I said, "Every person is important to this team - you, me, everyone. But if you're not enjoying the process, then quit. If you are enjoying it, stick around. As far as boatings go, I pull everything out of a hat."

As Antonio walked away I started counting heads, to see who had made it to practice. Heavyweight Michael Kolbe was missing, but that didn't surprise me.

Kolbe is one of those rare rowers who makes you think, if I had seven more like him we could take on Harvard. Religious young man. Lean, blond-hair, wiry, like an oversized lightweight. In fact, he was as fast a runner as the lightest lightweight. When I learned his last name - Kolbe - my heart skipped a beat. Could he be related to the German sculling genius? Kolbe told me his name was as common in Germany as Smith in America. Deep down, I still think he's a close cousin to the champion single sculler Peter-Michael Kolbe.

At the beginning of the season Kolbe told me that his father had died the previous summer and now he must go home on weekends to help his mom. Yes, I said, by all means. Family obligations take precedence over rowing. It's the only way.

Lately I've been having the team watch a short video before we launch, so that an identical image of good rowing would be implanted into their collective gray matter. I select the video depending on whatever point I'm trying to emphasize. Since we're starting Lightning Leg Drive Week, I chose a video of an exemplary team, the New Zealand eight, which won the '82 World Championships. With the rowers gathered in the back of the boathouse, I hit the play button.

"Check out the New Zealand crew," I said. "Phenomenally fast leg drive. When it comes to moving the boat over the water all that matters is how quickly the blade gets from the catch to the finish. In theory you could use any sequence of motions. You could pull the arms first, swing the back and then press with the legs. But what seems to work best is a quick leg drive, followed by a strong back swing and lastly the arms squeezing toward the sweet spot."

As the raced played on, I looked around the group. Two of my men, Andrew Moore and Antonio, were talking to each other and not watching this incredible race unfold. I shut off the machine and confronted Andrew: "What's the problem?"

"It's a waste of time," Andrew said. "We should be rowing, not watching TV."

"No," I said, "it's good stuff." I grabbed my maxi-notebook and found an article I'd been planning to read to the crew at the right time. That time had arrived.

"This article comes from Sport Climbing magazine, an interview with a champion rock climber named Tony Yaniro." I read:

> When I used to Nordic ski race, I attended a couple of National
> Nordic ski seminars and the Norwegian coach put on a two-
> hour video of a top racer and the team just sat there, absorbing
> the skier's technique. I swear, if you watch one and a half-hours

of skiing, then go out and step into your skis, you will ski better. Same with climbing.

"Same with rowing," I said. "Before we can make the proper motions, you must have a precise mental picture of these motions. And it's essential that everyone in the boat use the same model." We watched the last ten strokes of the race, and then I said, "Okay, now let's go wake up some fish."

One of the unique aspects of rowing is that novices strive to perfect the same motions as Olympic contenders. Few other sports can make this claim. In figure skating, for instance, the novice practices only simple moves. After years of training, the skater then proceeds to the jumps and spins that make up an elite skater's program. But the novice rower, from day one, strives to duplicate a motion that he'll still be doing on the day of the Olympic finals.

Without further delay we launched two eights and headed out for three long steady state pieces. Long, for my crew, is about fifteen minutes. Anything more lengthy and their concentration drops below an acceptable level. It might be interesting to connect electrodes to a rower's head to see exactly how long he can concentrate. I suspect it might be far less than fifteen minutes - more likely ninety seconds. At some point, the annoying sound of the outboard engine, the graceful soaring of a turkey vulture overhead, the foul smell emanating from the man behind him can crack a rower's concentration.

The only way to stave off loss of concentration is by close-quartered racing, which I tried to introduce every workout. On the first piece this morning, I started the boats even, to see which crew had better speed. On the second piece, I handicapped the crews, giving the slow boat a lead. On the last piece I made the necessary corrections to the previous handicap.

On all three pieces I yelled to the crews, "Pretend you're in that New Zealand eight. The instant the blade enters the water, drive your legs as fast as you can." My yelling seemed to have only the slightest effect, so I tried an old coaching trick - I moved my launch a good distance from the boats. It worked. The farther away I was, the better they looked.

After practice I spent the morning re-rigging both the lightweight and heavyweight eights. Both squads use Dirigo shells, neon-yellow, 99.8% wood-free, simple rigging mechanism. They seemed wholly adequate for our needs.

I checked the big three, height, spread and pitch. I also inspected the heel-ties, replacing where needed. Finally, I measured the oars for overall length and inboard. Our Concept II oars had been cut down and retrofitted with big-blades. By my measurements, several of the oars were too long by an inch or more. With Skilsaw in hand, I quickly trimmed them down.

I was hating life until the boathouse warmed up, going from ice cold to quite warm in a matter of minutes. As the temperature increased, the whole rigging process became far more pleasurable. Rigging is like Zen meditation. You must bend over the boat until your back is breaking, until your brain is filled with numbers and fractions of numbers, until you can accurately measure an oarlock's pitch without bothering to use the pitch meter. Only then will you see the way of eternal rigging happiness.

Do Not Take
Tuesday, November 2

Way back in 1989 I found myself in deepest South Africa, working as a journalist, covering a team of renegade American track and field athletes as they made a sweeping tour of that tumultuous country. At one stop in the township of Soweto, the Americans gave a track and field clinic to several hundred young athletes who lived nearby. I stood off to the side as John Powell, a great discus thrower and Olympic medalist, addressed his charges: "It took me forty-five years to learn what I know," he said. "I'm going to teach it to you in two hours. You can build on my experience. That's the way society advances."

As with John Powell, I had achieved a certain level of enlightenment while weaving my way through life's wins and losses. According to Zen practice, I was now obligated to teach what I'd learned. The toughest part, I've found, is deciding the proper time for teaching.

This morning we ran as a group from the erg room toward the Goleta Pier. Not far from the beach, we came across a bicycle that had been lost-stolen-abandoned or simply left for a moment by the owner. Jeff Beldon climbed on the bike and began riding it downhill. When he reached the cliff, he jumped off and let the bike cascade over. A second later it smashed to the sand, thirty feet below.

Once on the beach, we continued our run, heading south for half a mile, still warming-up. At the Goleta Pier we turned around and headed back to the cliff, the starting point for our morning races. In a general sense we were previewing the course, something I considered essential regardless of the competition's degree of importance. To race without having previewed the course is to swim in a sea of ignorance.

After taking off our warm-up jackets and separating into fleshy snails, reluctant possums and jacko rabbits, we ran the first of seven full-speed, full-power pieces down the beach, around the pier and then back to the starting point, about a mile. As always I had the men stay in the soft sand, as opposed to the hard packed sand nearest the water. Soft sand running makes for an unsurpassed quad-burning effort.

"Listen up," I said, during the rest between the first and second piece. "Something important: Do not take anything that does not belong to you. Got it? Leave it alone. The bicycle that we encountered this morning - the one that Beldon rode over the cliff - did not belong to us. Perhaps the owner was watching the sunrise. Perhaps he'd be back in a minute looking for it. The circumstances aren't important. What matters is that you have no business messing with something that does not belong to you."

My men were listening, but were they hearing me? Most of them looked down at the sand, a little embarrassed.

"We've left our warm-up clothes on the sand," I continued. "I think we would be pretty angry if someone took our clothes while we were running. The same holds at regattas. Do not take banners, signs, posters. Nothing. If you want a souvenir, buy a T-shirt."

After running another pier-piece, I added a corollary to my do-not-take lesson: "Don't destroy something for no reason. Riding a bike off a cliff accomplishes nothing. Leave it alone."

Once we had finished I made Beldon return the bike to the place where he'd found it. He hated doing it, cursing under his breath every step of the way. After everyone had left and we were standing by the bike, I told him, "People have a tendency to dismiss things without taking the time to study the situation. Makes for problems. So chill out." The look on his face told me he'd rather be eating a broken-glass omelet than listening to me.

PRESSMAN RETURNS
Wednesday, November 3

When I entered the boathouse this morning I saw someone standing off to the side. Without hesitation he came up to me and said, "Coach Lewis, if it's okay with you, I'd like to start rowing."

The man in front of me was Lawrence Pressman, last year's team captain. I'd met Pressman only once, at the recruiting meeting, when he'd told me that he wasn't going to row this year.

"What changed your mind?" I asked him.

"Well, I miss rowing," he said. "I miss my friends. And from what I hear, you guys are having a lot of fun."

"Welcome back," I said, shaking his hand. He could have told me he'd returned in order to meet underage novice women and I'd have been just as happy. We needed someone like Pressman. He was a natural leader, a good athlete, easy going, pleasant to be around and a fierce competitor. If Pressman continues rowing after college, I predict he will make a national team. Of course, it might take a year or two or ten, but he'll make it.

To properly celebrate his return, the whole team jumped him, gang style, pummeling him with hard punches and kicks until he cried out in pain. That's how they do it in Compton. Works just as well at Cachuma.

We boated two eights and a four-with. By now everyone knew the boatings, lites in one eight stroked by Clement, heavies in the other stroked by Moose. With Pressman back, I bumped one of the less promising heavies, Rick Trout, into the "goofy guys" four-with coxswain, along with Herb, Short Stack Smith and Björn. Gordo brought up the rear in the Maas Aero.

Last week Björn told me that he doesn't appreciate being called a goofy guy. I can see his point, but it's a tough habit to break. I'm a little worried about Björn. He's from Norway and yet he has never heard of the famous double scull team of Frank and Alf Hansen. This immediately made Björn suspect, as though you could find a kid in this country who'd never heard of Michael Jordan or Shaquille O'Neal. I thought these Nordic-types were fierce, lean fighting machines? Björn must have got off the bus a little early.

We rowed a series of five minute pieces, all at super-low rating, ten to twelve strokes-per-minute. Even at the low ratings, the lites were faster than the heavies. A tad worrisome. Aren't the heavies supposed to be faster at low ratings? Better check my coaching manual.

We had one bit of excitement this morning, the sort of event that makes coaches go crazy: a novice rower nearly drowned. Fred Checks, the novice coach, had sent a man onto the lake by himself, in a tippy single scull - not one of the Maas Aeros. The novice had never sculled before and, to make matters worse, the water was quite bouncy. Not surprisingly, the novice flipped over. He told me later that he was probably a few   seconds away from succumbing to hypothermia. Good-bye, novice. Good-bye, UCSB rowing program. Hello a lifetime of nightmares. Through sheer luck, a fisherman came along and dragged him out of the water. We lost the seat from the single scull. We nearly lost a novice. Singles sculls are great teaching tools but they should not be used by beginners unless the coach is nearby.

The problem was not with the novice rower but with the novice coach, Fred Checks. He seems a bit lacking in that most un-teachable area known as common sense. Here at Cachuma, where the dangers are altogether real and the stakes exceedingly high, common sense counts for a lot. I also think that good a teacher should be a good role model. Yet several times Checks has passed me on the way to the boathouse, driving his Jeep Cherokee about ninety miles an hour. I wouldn't mind so much except that he inevitable has a few of his novices with him. I'd gladly give a month's salary to get rid of Fred Checks before he kills someone, which is saying a lot considering the state of my bank account.

From my experience, I've concluded that a college rowing coach has two basic goals: first, to provide a safe setting for rowing to take place; second, to instill in the participants an appreciation, a respect, an affection, perhaps even a love for rowing. Only after these goals have been realized can anything else be considered. Fred, it seems, has other goals in mind. Safety be damned. To hell with love-of-the-sport. His existence has only one purpose, to defeat the Stanford novices. Having seen the Gaucho novice, I considered this to be a risky proposition. When watching them row this morning I was reminded that "Nova" was showing a special on centipedes.

As I began another day of sorting through the remaining junk in the boathouse, I thought about how, at the collegiate level, one can become a rowing coach with only the slightest qualification. This is especially baffling when you consider what a litigious society we've become. Perhaps we should have some sort of examination to determine if the candidate has the knowledge or the experience or, heaven forbid, the formal training to competently perform the job. I'd vote for a two-year program taught at some junior college, an Associate Degree in Crew Coaching. The students could learn the basics of physiology, the fundamentals of technique, dieting for lightweights and coaches, rigging, trailer driving, boat repair, CPR/First Aid.

I'm no exception. I, too, would benefit from such a course. When being interviewed for this job I wasn't asked about my college coaching experience. Obviously I knew what I was doing for myself way back in

1984 - elite double sculling - but as far as college-level sweep rowing, I had little or no experience. My only training was on-the-job, trial by fire.

RACE EVE
Friday, November 5

The rowers were talking during a break about some movie they'd all watched on television the night before. In fact, all practice long they were talking and joking and performing marvelous imitations of Beavis. Heh, heh. I could imagine an eight made up of Ren, Stimpy, Beavis, Butt-head, Bart, Homer, Bullwinkle and Rocket J. Squirrel as stroke. But who would cox? Duck Man.

Once or twice I told them, "Your chatter isn't going to get you down the race course any faster."

They'd quiet down for a few strokes and then start up again. I was trying to think of a way to get a semblance of control when Michael Kolbe, the only rower to have seen the inside of a church, took it out of my hands by shouting, "Shut the fuck up!" Yes, that seemed to do the trick.

I seconded Kolbe's statement with one of my own. "Any of you guys tea drinkers?" I asked. "The Japanese have a wonderful custom called the tea ceremony. During the tea ceremony nothing can be discussed except the actual events transpiring at that moment - the wonderful taste of the tea, the elegance of the setting. Strictly forbidden from the tea ceremony is any mention of the sordid facts of our everyday existence."

"Did you say tea smokers?" Churchill asked.

I ignored the comment and continued: "Rowing should be an aquatic version of the tea ceremony. In the big picture I want you to leave the real world behind when we push off the dock and not let it return until practice is completed."

Back at the boathouse Kolbe came up to me and said, "The tea ceremony stuff was great, but they need more."

"What do you suggest?" I asked him.

"Tell them that to win the PCRCs," he said, "they must concern themselves with today, this very moment, to strive to be the best at this instant. If they can conquer this moment then by the time the PCRCs roll around, everything will be in order."

"Yeah, that's good stuff," I told him. "I'll do my best."

For a moment I wondered if perhaps Kolbe should be coaching the team. He was absolutely right. If you aren't self-disciplined, rowing soon turns into a perverse waste of time. When I first arrived at Santa Barbara, I had thought that everyone would be self-disciplined by this stage of their rowing lives. Wrong. Big time wrong. Clearly I had much to learn about coaching.

On my way home, I stopped at a hardware store in downtown Santa Barbara and had an extra set of keys made for the gas box, erg room and team van - all the important keys except the one for the boathouse, stamped "Do Not Duplicate."

After five weeks at UC Santa Barbara, I'd learned something of the politico-administrative side of club sports. Granted, it wasn't very exciting and I avoided it whenever possible. We club sporters dealt in pennies, while the varsity people concerned themselves with big fat dollars. I learned that while my boss, Ms. Pearson, could be counted on to give sweeping gestures of leadership, the details of club sports life were handled by a different person, administrative assistant "Queen" Wendy Collins. The details, I quickly realized, were far more important than the grand gestures. Queen Wendy had sovereignty over the two things that really mattered, the checkbook and the keys.

When I was first hired, Queen Wendy handed me a fat key ring, loaded with forty keys altogether. But she had refused to give me the boathouse key until I handed over $20 in cash, as a deposit. "After you leave us and give me back the key," she said, "I'll return your money." At the time she said these words, no more than twelve minutes into my tenure as coach, I couldn't help but think, am I going somewhere?

I returned to Lake Cachuma in the late afternoon to meet the rowing team from my alma mater, University of California, Irvine. Yes, tomorrow is our first race: the Anteaters of UC Irvine versus the Gauchos of UC Santa Barbara. I was excited at the prospect of racing. Obviously we weren't up to race speed, but I assumed that Irvine wouldn't be either. Mostly I was hoping for a chance to see what my rowers needed to improve the most.

RACE DAY
SATURDAY, NOVEMBER 6

Actually, it wasn't supposed to be a race, only a scrimmage: UCI versus UCSB, three times ten minutes with ten minutes rest between pieces. Since Irvine was using our boats, two sets of races were scheduled. First up, UCSB lightweights against UCI-A boat.

The lightweights, once they had their boat on the water and the oars in place, huddled together by the coxswain's seat. I stood to the side and listened as Adam and Clement offered some Gaucho-style inspiration.

"Once we get a length or two lead," Adam said, "we'll take the rating down and sit on them. Should be no problem. These Irvine guys are happy just to have found the boathouse."

The Santa Barbara lightweights pumped their heads up and down in agreement.

"I have no doubt we'll be lengths ahead after two minutes," Clement said.

As my Gauchos continued to comment on Irvine's sketchy performance in past seasons, their questionable manhood, the odd Anteater nickname, I noticed one of the opposition coming down the dock. The Irvine man walked straight up to me and asked, "What time will the first race start?"

"Right away," I said. "Go ahead and launch."

At the same instant, Clement was saying, "Anteaters, geez, give me a break." The Irvine man glanced at Clement and then walked away. I could only hope that he was as deaf as my own rowers.

A medium-strong wind blew from the east, making the water bouncy and uneven. On my instruction, the crews warmed-up into the wind, so as to furnish a tailwind on the first piece. Lightweights love tailwinds. When both boats were finally warmed-up, heading in the proper direction and paddling together, I shouted in my best Harry Parker: "On this one!"

The UCSB lites blasted off, spray flying, heads down in deep power concentration, well above the prescribed limit of twenty-four strokes a minute. They were half a length ahead after twenty strokes, a full length in two minutes.

High rating or not, my boys were ahead. As I watched them flailing at the water, holding a boat length lead, I found that I needed every ounce of self-control to conceal a satisfied smile from my lips. Make no mistake, the heart of a coach sings with unbridled ecstasy when his crew is winning.

Four minutes into the piece, the tide abruptly changed. This baffled me since I knew that tidal fluctuations did not exist on landlocked Lake Cachuma. Sure enough, in front of my eyes, the Irvine crew began to come back, undoubtedly riding a faster tidal current. At the half-way mark, UCI pulled dead even - and they were understroking us by five or six beats. My heart abruptly stopped singing and I no longer fought the urge to smile. At ten minutes, I stood up and shouted, "Paddle." Actually, I shouted it twice, first to the Irvine team and then, after turning thirty degrees, I repeated the word to my crew. The Irvine Anteaters, the awesome Anteaters, certainly one of the best crews in the country this year, had won by three lengths of open water.

From a distance I studied my crew. Their heads lolled to the side as though they were semi-conscious. They were rowing only half-slide, with one hand on the gunnel to keep themselves upright. Basically, my team was toasted. The Irvine crew, as seen from a distance, was not.

The second piece, into the head wind, allowed Irvine to give us a thorough lesson. Lengths and lengths of lessons. The third piece was like two dogs in heat: a strong, well-conditioned attack dog forcing himself on a weary, defenseless fluffy poodle. We tried to scamper away at thirty strokes a minute. They chased after us at twenty-two spm, plowing steadily along. We soon fell behind but then fought back to within a length or two. At the eighth minute, Irvine jumped on it while the Gaucho lightweights slipped into a coma.

I sorely wished that I had tape recorded the pre-race comments of Adam, Clement and the others. Humility will be taught, whether you're in the mood to learn or not.

As the teams paddled toward the boathouse to switch crews, I happened to spot my first golden eagle. I had been looking around, studying the flora and fauna of the lake, when I saw what appeared to be a turkey vulture but with flatter, broader wings and heavily feathered feet, as though it was wearing Ugg boots. I checked my bird book. Sure enough, Aquila chrysaetus, golden eagle.

Eventually, after what seemed like years, the UCSB heavies and the Irvine B-boat found their way to the starting line. According to the Irvine coach both his A and B boats were of equal speed. I doubted it. Actually, I seriously hoped that Irvine's first boat had been stacked. No way his second boat was going to defeat my heavies. Or would they? Industrial grade doubt was spreading over the lake like an oil slick.

One hour later, my poor heavies had been battered, bruised, doored, floored and hammered into submission. After this series, I once more searched the crystal blue sky for golden eagles but none were to be seen.

The Irvine rowers, as it turned out, were exceedingly pleasant. Afterward both teams shared a box of oranges and compared supplicating blisters. Once the oranges were eaten and the Anteaters departed, I called my rowers together.

"When I was training," I told them. "I tended to learn more when

I lost than when I won. With that in mind, we just learned volumes. As far as the lightweights go, cautious optimism is good. Blatant arrogance is not. Before the race, Clement and Adam made some un-humble remarks, which may or may not have been overheard by an Irvine rower. Regardless, it was wrong."

The rowers stared at their feet. All they wanted to do was get down the mountain and into the Goleta IHOP.

"I wrote in Assault: 'You must purge yourself of all thoughts of self-importance and all inclination to judge either yourself or others. You must go to Power with humility and deep respect.' I learned this from Mike Livingston, the master of winning. He said the key is to treat everyone - your partner, your coach and most of all your opponents - with the same humility and deep respect."

"You think we would have won if we hadn't said those things?" Clement asked.

"Well," I said, "suppose that Irvine rower went back and told his teammates what you said. Maybe it got them good and angry, and as you may know anger is the strongest drug on the market. More likely you would have lost anyway. But at least you wouldn't have to suffer the double-whammy of getting your asses handed to you and wearing the fool's crown of arrogance. Being a champion is more than just crossing the finish line ahead of your opponents. A true champion behaves appropriately before, during and after the race."

Regarding the Gaucho heavies, I couldn't think of anything useful to say, so I adjourned the meeting with a curt, "Much work to do."

As is my usual custom, this morning I walked into the boathouse, my air pistol loaded, barrel up, ready to go. One shot. In the name of sportsmanship that's all I allow myself. As my eyes adjusted to the dim light, I saw King Rat running across the top girder. I aimed and fired. The pellet ricocheted off the steel and hit me in the chin. Lucky shot.

King Rat, followed closely by his queen, ran down the support girder and slipped out the small hole in the rear corner of the boathouse.

I put away my pistol and began mixing a sack of concrete in a five gallon plastic bucket. I poured the concrete liberally into the corner-hole where the rats had been making their ratty escapes. Forget UC Irvine, today my only purpose in life was to get rid of the rats. Perhaps I was creating a bigger problem by closing off the escape routes. Maybe the rats served a purpose. Did they eat the baby mice? Film at 11:00.

After concreting, I made my first attempt at repairing an outboard engine. As I removed the lid, I found myself wondering if all those years of working on my assorted Volkswagens would finally pay off. Fred Checks told me yesterday that his engine was cutting out. "Should I take it in?" he wanted to know. "Taking it in" means dragging the engine to a marine repair shop in Goleta and handing over $250, regardless of what the problem might be.

"No," I said, "let me look at it." I soon determined that the kill switch had been removed and the wires left dangling. Whenever one of the wires touched the inside of the housing, the engine died. I wrapped a little electrical tape around the raw wires, stuffed them out of the way and replaced the housing. Saved $200, minimum.

Down down down, home again, through a thin cloud that was pressed up against the mountainside. Beautiful in the late afternoon.

One of the best aspects of coaching at Santa Barbara was that it opened up the whole wonderful world of college life. Exciting things happen on a college campus - plays, concerts, effigy burnings.

Tonight I took advantage of this lively world by heading to Campbell Hall to see, in person, on-stage, actress-comedienne-former-Madonna mate, Sandra Bernhardt. She told a joke or two, sang a couple of songs - nothing, it seemed, worth the entry fee, although the audience enjoyed her immensely. During intermission I waved to the varsity women's coach, Terri Larson, who sat in the front row, but she must not have seen me.

After the show, I thought I'd apply Clement Nash's method for meeting young women to meeting famous people. I found the theater's rear entrance and waited for a few moments. Sure enough, Sandra Bernhardt soon came out and headed straight for her limousine. I took a deep breath, stuck out my hand and introduced myself. As I said the words, I felt a cherished, hot-nervous anticipation that I'd been seeking, the same wonderful sensation that I knew so intimately when I was racing. From the day I stopped competing, I've been on a never ending quest for similar emotions. Bungee jumping brought out the best duplication of pre-race excitement. The only down-side is that bungee jumping is fairly expensive. Meeting famous people might prove to be a low-cost alternative.

An ancient impelling force made her respond in kind. She stuck out her hand and said, "Nice to meet you."

Sandy - all her friends call her Sandy - signed my *Playboy* magazine, the issue with her on the cover, and promised to call if she ever wanted a ride in my coaching launch.

BENDER
Monday, November 8

Clear, cool November morning. We had the whole lake to ourselves. Not another person in sight. A light wind ruffling the water. The sun was just beginning to peek over the eastern hills. Steamy low clouds squatted deep in the canyons. We had arrived.

We rowed two eights, lites and heavies. After ten minutes, I had the rowers stop so they could take off their warm-up gear. During this break, I spoke to the troops: "I'm exactly where I want to be, doing exactly what I want to do. If you cannot make the same statement, then finish up the workout, get in your car and never come back. Today is the finest day of your rowing life. Acknowledge it and appreciate it, because it won't get any better. St. Catherine of Sienna said it best: 'All the way to heaven is heaven.' She was right."

"St. Elsewhere?" someone yelled.

"At frequent intervals you must be able to say that you are doing exactly what you want to do, being where you want to be. It's all optional at this level, so make sure you appreciate, enjoy, revel in the adventure."

Our first piece was five minutes at half slide. Then another. Then a ten minute piece at full slide. Then another. Lastly, we rowed a head race, down the fjord, around the coaching launch and back to the boathouse. Toward the end of the piece, I pulled my launch alongside the heavy eight and watched for a moment. From my vantage point, I noticed that the puddle belonging to the three man, Johnny Bender, did not have much turbulence associated with it. My perception was heightened by the fact that his oar was the only one of the eight that was unpainted.

"Bender," I yelled, "put some zip into it."

His immediate response was to deliver a blistering glare in my direction. At full power, he inevitably looked as though he was working hard. He had the appropriate facial grimace, followed by a hot 'n bothered expression when the piece was over. But I never saw much action at the end of his oar. If I didn't know better I'd say he was acting at rowing hard, as opposed to actually doing it.

Bender came up to me after practice and said, "Coach Lewis, damn it, I was rowing full power. I had plenty of zip. Don't ever tell me that I'm rowing at less than full." For a brief moment I thought he might be joking, but the fire in his eyes told me that he was damn serious. If Bender could manage to duplicate the same anger on the water, then we'd see some action.

"Well," I said at last. "Do your best."

Maybe rowing isn't his sport. Someone told me that Bender was a good enough tennis player in high school. A muscle biopsy might reveal that he's 98% fast twitch muscle and thus physiologically unsuited for rowing.

The great swimmer Matt Biondi, after winning several gold medals at the '88 Olympics, announced that he was switching to water polo. Biondi reported to the national team training camp in Newport Beach and began working out. A few weeks later a small announcement appeared in the local newspaper saying that Biondi was abandoning water polo and returning to regular old lap swimming, which he did with his usual success at the '92 Games. As I'm sure Michael Jordan, the basketball superstar turned mediocre Double A baseball player, would agree, it doesn't necessarily follow that success in one sport will lead to success in another. Yes, rowers benefit from practically all the hard work they invest, but it undoubtedly helps to have the right physiological make-up before proceeding too far down the rowing path.

Despite Bender's lack of zip, for the first time all season, the heavies defeated the lightweights. When the heavies returned to the dock, happy and relieved, you would have thought they had just won the San Diego Crew Classic. The lightweights, at the same time, were flustered and grumpy, pecking at each other with their razor-sharp verbal beaks. They held a quick team meeting and decided to row tomorrow instead of doing our usual land workout. After making their decision, Clement came up to me and asked, "Is it okay if we row tomorrow rather than erg-ing?"

"Yes," I said. "That's fine with me."

This proved to be a mistake on my part. It didn't really matter if we rowed or erged or went on a long, soft sand run. What mattered is that I changed my mind. I had demonstrated the lack of a cast-iron resolve. I was letting the inmates run the asylum.

All along at Santa Barbara I'd been far too agreeable and far too candid. Coach's Rule: never admit a lack of experience or knowledge. Carry on at all times as though you've guided a hundred champion crews. Honesty is not the best policy when leading a bunch of college rowers.

They are looking for strong, disciplined leadership and not a kinder, gentler coach. Once you've established a certain attitude and demeanor, it's nearly impossible to change to a different mode in mid-season.

TRAFFIC SCHOOL
Tuesday, November 9

A pure-white egret stood on our dock this morning, as still as a statue, hunting his breakfast. I watched him for a minute before the rowers arrived, his head tilted downward, his neck coiled like an S spring. Fish. Calling all fish. An egret might wait two minutes or two hours. He must be patiently impatient. He cannot let distraction break through. At last, with lightning speed and precision, the egret darted his beak into the water. A moment later he held a wriggling fish in his beak and then he swallowed it whole.

On a daily basis I preach to my rowers about the necessity for White Hot Concentration. All champions, I tell them, have the ability to focus on a specific task without letting distraction enter in. To an egret this concentration was not simply another Coach Lewis proverb. Rather, his life depended on mastering it to the fullest.

Beyond the dock, the lake was a foggy expanse, ephemeral, fleeting, untouchable. If you stared into the fog long enough, bizarre images danced inside your eyes. These images were often followed by a low-level vertigo that could make you taste last night's dinner. Whenever I drove my launch through this heavy fog, I found myself wondering if I was about to tumble off the edge of the earth.

Because of the fog, I told Fred Checks to keep his novice crew off the water. He stared into the fog for a few moments, considering the order I'd given.

Checks and I haven't been getting along too well lately - ever since his novice sculler almost drowned. I don't dislike him because of his ignorance. To a large extent, I'm equally ignorant. After all, we're both new to coaching. Rather, I don't like the way he repeatedly puts the health and well-being of his rowers in jeopardy. Too often over the last few weeks, I've seen Checks and his novice eights crossing the lake in a raging wind tunnel, a place where no rowing team has any business. When I mentioned to Checks that he might want to keep his crew off the water on these blustery days, he told me that Gauchos have always rowed on Cachuma, regardless of the wind.

All my squawking about safety must make me seem like a safety freak. No, not even close. But I have been around long enough to know that serious problems can happen. I know coaches whose rowers have drowned, and I know they will never really get over it. I also have more at stake that Checks. Ego and reputation are powerful motivations, specifically *my* ego and *my* reputation. I am the captain of the UCSB rowing ship. If one of Checks' rowers drowned, my name would be remembered in regards to the accident, not his.

This morning, after looking deep into the fog, Checks decided to keep his novices off the water. As a result they weren't squished by a crazed bass fisherman nor did they paddle over the dam nor were they sucked into the intake pipe. Rowing blind is not a good idea.

We stayed behind and played push-the-car, one of my favorite drills when I was training. Using identical VW Golfs, coxswains driving, I had two-man teams push the Golfs over a 500 meter course, a quad-burning, lung screaming exercise.

In the evening, I attended traffic school in downtown Santa Barbara. The ticket that I received while heading to the job interview had vexed me for months, first with a sizable fine and now in the form of this sloppy traffic school. The teacher fumbled with a videocassette player for a minute and then pushed play. Four hours later - after viewing such classics as *Blood Alley*, *Blood Freeway*, *Blood Off Ramp* - he pushed stop. Class adjourned. Tomorrow I must go back for another session. *Blood Parking Lot*?

The only interesting moment took place as the teacher was setting up the VCR. Each of us described the crimes we had committed. My violation was completing a pass after the passing lane had ended, as though I could somehow know the exact length of the passing lane on a road I'd never driven in my life, what the heck is the problem here, I'm a tax-paying, slow driving, tail lights working, self-actualized, Zen monkey, safety first, recovering Snickers addict, late for my interview, native Californian.

One young woman had been a passenger in a speeding car driven by her boyfriend. Just so happened her boyfriend was drunk at the time and his license was already suspended - for drunk driving. When the police siren started up, the boyfriend pulled over. Then the two of them quickly changed places so that the policeman thought she had been driving. This little deception kept her boyfriend out of jail, but she received the speeding ticket. The driving school instructor just rolled his eyes in dismay.

PICASSO AT 6:35
Wednesday, November 10

At the boathouse this morning, 6:35 A.M., I read to the rowers a quote by Pablo Picasso:

> Forcing yourself to use restricted means is the sort of restraint that liberates invention. It obliges you to make a kind of progress that you can't even imagine in advance.

"The UCSB crew," I went on to say, "labors under extremely restricted means. The most obvious restriction is the distance to Lake Cachuma - thirty miles from campus. We cannot row as many miles as we'd like. We don't have rowing tanks. We have only a few ergometers and we must share them with the women's team and the novices. Rejoice. All this restraint will liberate our powers of invention."

The rowers - the ones who were awake enough to hear me - said, "Huh?" Too early for Picasso. He probably never got up before noon.

Picasso was an interesting guy. I once went to a major show at the Chicago Art Institute based solely on his sketchbooks. Picasso spent hundreds of hours carefully planning his masterpieces. The sketchbooks were filled with ideas, bits and pieces, test runs, none of it meant to be seen by anyone. In a similar way, rowing practices are our sketchbooks, where we prepare our race-day masterpiece.

No fog this morning, although the lake surface went through ten distinct transformations during the course of our practice, windy to glassy to rough to whitecaps, and on and on. I've never seen a body of water change so quickly or dramatically. Lake Cachuma is warmer than the surrounding mountains, at least in the early morning, and the winds roar through the cold canyons and across the lake surface as though driven by huge whirling fans.

Lightweight Jeff Beldon came to practice this morning dressed in nylon shorts and a tank top T-shirt. "At least I wore my running shoes," he said, which was true.

"Like I said a few days ago, summer is long gone," I told them. "We're already having some cold weather. When we leave Isla Vista we have no way of knowing the weather at the lake. Might be warm. Might be a hurricane. So dress smart. Heavy cotton sweatshirts and sweat pants are fine for wearing to the boathouse, but when you actually row, put on long-sleeve polypropylene top and leggings. After the boats are put away, change out of your wet clothes for the drive to campus. In the words of the legendary drag racer, Don "The Snake" Prudome: 'Always keep your engine warm.'"

I had the wooden dowels out in force, working on the back end of the stroke. Five minutes arms only; five minutes arms and back only; five minutes half-slide. With their big strong arms, the heavies should have ruled the day, but in fact the lites won every piece except the first. All I can figure is that after their initial burst of energy, the heavies were exhausted. Not all of them were spent, but it takes only one or two men to bring the whole boat to its knees. I felt bad for the heavies, especially on the last piece when I gave them a fifteen-second lead. The lites caught up with about two minutes to go and then proceeded to crush the heavies into dust.

On the paddle in I told the heavies that their conditioning needed dire improvement. Once they were in better shape, they'd be able to maintain their technique for longer. Regarding a few of the rowers, I thought to myself: have they considered Ping Pong?

GALEN ROWELL
Friday, November 12

A persistent autumn wind blew all night long, rattling the windows of my apartment. As I drove up Highway 154, sycamore leaves scuttled across the road like lost crabs searching for cover. A huge Sta Puff marshmallow-cloud squatted on top of the San Marcos Pass. Scary driving, to say the least. Thankfully, the sky was clear at the lake. As I looked up, savoring one last moment of peace, a shooting star crossed my line of vision. So beautiful. So many stars. Given an eternity, will they all become shooting stars?

As I walked to the boathouse, I heard the rhythmic pulling of the generator cord, over and over. Checks wasn't getting it, the choke-aspect necessary to start our Yamaha 2000. Choke it, Checks, choke it. The generator finally started, abruptly shoving aside the lake's pristine silence. Like a jackhammer or jet engine or worse, a leaf blower, the generator shook the building to its foundation. Such was the price you paid for being in the woods. The noise meant power, and once the generator was running, an extension cord was plugged in and the overhead lights came to life, filling the confines with a dull brown light. I guess you could say morning had arrived.

We rowed in the fjord for most of the workout, two eights and a four-with, piece after piece, up and back the length of the channel. Before we began the last piece, I had the crews stop for a moment.

"Today's lesson is not for everyone," I said. "I want only future Olympians to listen up." I knew this comment would make each man pay rapt attention.

"My coach, Mike Livingston, told me years ago, 'You must prepare, not to die, but to battle for your life in each moment with every faculty and power available to you.' Everyone at the Olympic Games has an incredible will to win. Most people at the Olympic Trials have the same will to win. At the PCRCs, the Crew Classic, right down to the Christmas Regatta in Long Beach, nearly everyone has an identical will to win. The key is having the will to *prepare* to win. That's what Mike Livingston meant when he said that you must battle for your life in each moment. On the race course, that's easy. It's in November, when the wind is kicking up and race day seems a hundred years away - that's when battling for your life in each moment is hardest to master."

I lined up the two eights, let them paddle three strokes and then sent them on a head race, twenty-odd minutes, from the end of the fjord to the boathouse. Once they cleared the opening of the fjord, the crews encountered some of the roughest water I'd seen since the season began.

"Now is the time to battle," I yelled to the crews.

As soon as the words were out of my mouth, Andrew Moore caught a crab, the oar punching him full in the chest. He managed to recover and get back in sync, but a few strokes later he caught another boat-stopper. As the heavies rowed away, Andrew began cursing the way his seat was rigged. I could understand his cursing the bad water or the way he was rowing or even cursing me for having broken his concentration, but cursing the rig? I couldn't help but laugh. From now on, he can rig his own seat, and every other seat in the lightweight eight for that matter.

In the evening I went to see Galen Rowell at UCSB. He's an adventure photographer/naturalist/hiker/mountain climber. Campbell

Hall was packed to the rafters, everyone waiting anxiously to hear this master of the outdoors. The show started well enough. I was sitting next to a young woman who, although she was leaning toward her boyfriend, kept stroking my left thigh, by accident I assume.

Galen talked on and on about the similarity between going on a spiritual trek in Tibet and backpacking in the Sierra. In Tibet, some aspirants crawl on their stomachs around the whole circumference of a sacred mountain, twenty-one days. Sounded like a good workout, and I made a mental note to try it on my crew. The goal, Galen went on to say, both in Tibet and in the Sierra, is to recharge your spiritual batteries. We don't use spiritual-words in our lexicon because we live in a non-religious society, but the purpose is identical. Having spent many remarkable days backpacking in the Sierra, I found myself nodding in full agreement.

Then the slide projector broke. Interesting watching Galen Rowell, renowned naturalist/photog, come unglued. He had no contingency plan. Once the slide projector ceased showing slides, Galen started flopping around on the stage like a gaffed fish. I'd wager that he had endured freezing cold nights on lonely mountains with more composure than he demonstrated in front of 5007 unblinking eyes. The number of eyes soon diminished, a steady stream of mourners filing out of the hall. I joined them.

9 RESCUED AFTER ROWING SHELL HITS POTOMAC BRIDGE

Eight members of the George Washington University freshman crew and a coach were rescued from the chilly Potomac River late yesterday afternoon after their shell shattered on a pier of a railroad bridge. Police said more than 30 motorists reported the accident over their cellular phones from the nearby 14th Street Bridge, enabling rescuers to reach the spot in about 20 minutes.

11/23/93   Washington Post

After reading the article about the near drowning of the George Washington crew, I decided to postpone our 5000 meter erg test for a different sort of exam, a swim test. In theory, my rowers would not be doing any swimming at Lake Cachuma. They'd been instructed to stay with the boat should it tip over or swamp. But in real world situations, well-thought out theories quickly sink to the bottom. Boats break apart. People panic. You'd damn well better know how to swim.

We ran from the erg room, fifteen minutes, lites and heavies in separate lines, all the way to the Goleta Pier. We rested a moment at the pier and then ran another fifteen minutes, just to make sure everyone was warmed-up and ready to go.

"I should have done this on the first day and not two months into the season," I said. "It was a mistake on my part to put it off. Sometimes mistakes can be remedied. That's what we're doing today. If you don't know how to swim, then you have no business playing around in boats - any kind of boat, especially rowing shells. We all know how wild it gets on the lake, not to mention how cold it is. At Cachuma, no one can hear you scream. Off with the shoes. Here we go."

The sand under my feet was like granulated chips of ice. The Pacific

Ocean was as smooth as a glass marble and looked quite chilly. Since I am loathe to waste any time, I thought we could combine our swim test with an opportunity to practice keeping a straight face when all you want to do is scream and shout. I had everyone stand shoulder-to-shoulder, facing the ocean and then join hands - we are the world - and march forward, one long, continuous line of tip-toeing rowers.

"Yes, it's freezing," I said, "but don't show your discomfort. Make your face a mask. This skill might come in handy when you're nearing the end of a close race and your opponent looks over and sees your completely impassive face. Little will he know that you're only two strokes away from imploding."

Three more seconds and the coxswains began to scream as the water reached sensitive zones. At last we were up to the waists, then shoulders and finally overhead. Icy water leaked into my ears and up my nose. I started the timer on my watch: twenty minutes to go. The water was clean and clear and frosty cold. Shafts of sunlight danced across the ocean floor many feet below.

As we treaded water, Churchill took the opportunity to comment, "You guys know that a great white shark attack took place only a few miles away?"

"That's all right," Clement said. "I don't have to swim faster than a shark. I only have to swim faster than you."

About two minutes into our test, I noticed that one of the rowers was starting to sink a little low in the water. Yes, Herb Griffith, Herb the Humble, chunky little Herb, was definitely on his way down. Before he could slip completely under, Andrew Moore and another rower grabbed him under his arms and dragged him to shore. Once on the sand, Herb sprawled out like a beached whale. I'll be damned. Herb Griffith, one of the goofy guys I'd been sending out regularly in the single scull, couldn't swim. After we finished, I took Herb aside and told him to find another sport. What else could I do?

SMALL BOAT SUCCESS
Friday, November 19

Monumental morning! The whole team rowed in small boats. For the last few weeks I'd been repairing various singles and doubles, slowly gluing them back together, checking the rigging, getting everything ready. All for today.

First off, I called out the names of the single scullers. Rather than put the worst rowers into the singles, I put the best: Pressman, Shapiro, Moose, Mung. The next best rowers went into the four double sculls. Lastly, I called out the names for the quad-with. Once everyone was on the water, I had the whole squad paddle as a group from the dock to the entrance of the fjord, about two miles away. From a distance the collection of craft must have looked like a cloud of mosquitoes swarming slowly motion over the lake. Inside the protective confines of the fjord we began rowing a series of low rating, full power pieces the length of the channel.

"Great day!" I shouted at the end of the first piece. "We've accomplished something that few college crews have done, put our whole squad in small boats. From the first day, my ambition has been to shape the team into a band of elite warriors - like a rowing version of Special Forces. We're still months away from that goal, but by using small boats at least we're moving in the right direction."

Thinking back to my own college experience, I had loved rowing when Bob Ernst was the coach. He had us in small boats on a daily basis. What could be better than rowing in a straight pair with Bruce Ibbettson? One missed stroke on my part or a lapse in concentration and the pair would turn twenty degrees to starboard. When Ernst left for Washington and the subsequent coaches kept us in eights and nothing else, the whole process became tedious. Small boats had made rowing exciting when I was training, and with luck small boats would have the same effect at UCSB.

The toughest part of our inaugural workout was crossing from the fjord back to the boathouse. White caps were chugging down the lake by this time - even a veteran sculler would have found the conditions tricky.

"Stay poised," I yelled, as I zoomed around in my launch, shepherding the rowers like a mother hen. "Take only one small bite of water each stroke." Remarkably, they did maintain a modicum of poise and eventually everyone made it home. Not too bad.

Anger and Enemies
Saturday, November 20

Everyone kept their cool as we rowed small boats for a second day. Well, not quite everyone. Two of my heavyweights, Glen Mung and Philip Shapiro, don't care much for each other. Perhaps that's an understatement. Mung would rather walk back to campus, twenty-nine miles, than ride with Shapiro. Basically, Mung and Shapiro are enemies.

I don't know the details of their feud - something to do with comments Mung made to Shapiro's girlfriend, or maybe it was the other way around. Doesn't matter. The testosterone flows and words fly and before you know it, you've got an enemy for life. When I saw them shoving each other this morning, trying to claim the same single scull - despite the fact the boats are identical - I knew we were in for a bit of fun.

Like any good drug, anger can mask all reality. But anger is not an easy emotion to call up on demand, which is why an enemy is so wonderful. You're tired. Didn't sleep well. You have zero energy. Then you get lucky. You pull into the boathouse parking lot and see your favorite enemy. Celebrate. Your workout is saved. One look at that chowderhead can put you into the anger-zone. As you turn off your car, you can feel your whole physical being change. Respiration increases. The dull look on your face is magically transformed into the power-stare of a true rowing warrior. Now you're off to the races. With a sufficient dosage of anger coursing through your veins, you can move mountains, you can win races, you can do just about anything. If not for my own favorite enemies, and the anger they created within me, I'm sure I would not have gone far in the world of rowing. In one of my old training logs I have a quote by champion surfer Sunny Garcia:

> I need anger. I depend on anger to make me surf better. Without the anger I would be just an average surfer, going nowhere, winning nothing.

On the third piece, things got a little out of control. Shapiro went out high and hard. He earned himself a length lead and then slipped his single in front of Mung's. When Mung realized that his hated teammate had scooted directly in front, he went nuclear and jammed the rating to 39 strokes a minute. In short order he chopped into Shapiro's lead. Shapiro could not respond. Essentially, Mung proceeded to roll him over, the way you might run over a squirrel in the middle of the road. The good news: the boats aren't damaged. When they finally stopped yelling at each other, I talked to the whole team, although mostly I was addressing the two brawlers.

"Remember your physics," I told them. "No two objects can occupy the same space at the same time. And remember to be nice to the people you need. You need friends because they offer support. You also need enemies because they fire your bones. If anyone here is secretly dreaming of making it to the Olympics, I can tell you exactly how to do it, two words: Sustained Obsession. The obsession isn't so hard. But keeping it sustained is a tough nut to crack. A heart-felt enemy can go a long way to sustaining your obsession. Love your enemy."

As soon as I set them off, Mung and Shapiro renewed their battle, soon six lengths ahead of the next closest scullers. Thank God, they are both about the same speed. Mung has better technique, but Shapiro is bigger, stronger. Maybe they'll battle against each other all the way to the 2004 Olympics.

ANIMAL LANES
Monday, November 22

One month until the winter solstice. I'm afraid to speculate how much darker the mornings will get. The light comes up two or three minutes later each day and in the evening we lose another few minutes. Suppose this insanity never stopped. Suppose, instead, the days just kept getting shorter and shorter until the daylight vanished, never to return. Should that happen while I'm coaching at UC Santa Barbara, I will state ahead of time that practice is canceled.

Most beautiful of rowing mornings. The blue sky was overlaid with an intricate pattern of leaden gray clouds, a matrix of clean rectangular shapes that seemed to go forever. As I drove my launch past distant canyons, I saw the timid remnants of clouds left behind by last night's storm. The smell of fresh rain on the dark soil, on the oak trees, on the California sage, made for an intoxicating aroma. A family of deer stood at the base of the fjord, feeding on low bushes. When my launch passed they all raised their heads in unison, as though on cue from some invisible conductor. They watched me pass. I watched them watching me. No one said a word.

We rowed small boats again, the length of the fjord. For fun, I had them try a swimming-style workout: ten times the length of the fjord, on the eight minutes, 24 spm. The rowers had to hustle down the channel, turn around and be ready to go when the clock reached eight minutes. My two fastest scullers, who stayed on the outside of the channel in the coveted Animal Lanes, took only seven minutes to cover the distance and thus earned a minute's rest. Gordo needed nearly the full eight minutes - his few seconds of rest were consumed by turning around in preparation for the next piece.

I prefer tight workouts such as today's that specify the exact duration, rating and rest of each piece. You need disciplined rowers to make it work, at least when you're rowing small boats. This morning, to my great delight, everyone managed to stay on schedule throughout the workout.

After returning to the boathouse, I instructed my rowers to help the Gaucho women, who were unloading the van and trailer after having raced in the Bay Area over the weekend.

"Why should we?" Churchill asked. "We've never helped them before."

"That's exactly the problem," I said. "We've got one big family here. It can either be a happy family or a grumpy one. The next six months will be a lot more pleasant if we can all get along."

Unlike feuds between individual rowers, nothing productive can come from a feud between the men's and women's teams. So far, everyone has been getting along fairly well, in part because Moose's girlfriend is one of the better women rowers. The only complaint has come from those of my men who are anxious to mate with the novice women. Trixi Fujimora, the novice women's coach, is not too keen on the idea. Apparently, Trixi told her novice women that the varsity men have horrible venereal diseases. She's probably right.

ORION'S BELT
Wednesday, November 24

Clear and intensely cold. I looked for shooting stars for a long time, until the first light of dawn chased away the great mass of celestial bodies, leaving only the strongest stars to shine through. In these few moments, I pulled out my star book and tried to identify the constellations, Big Dipper, Little Dipper, Orion's Belt, Orion's Fat Ass. Perhaps the time is right for a '90s revision of the constellations, getting rid of Orion and introducing the Pamela Anderson constellation

Beyond these stars and constellations, what then? What exists at the far fringes of the universe? Would a Starship powered with unlimited fuel, headed in one direction, motor along for all eternity? At some distant outpost, another race of human beings has evolved, and no doubt they have VH1, plain M&M's, Coors Light and collegiate rowing. On this planet, at this very moment, the coach of a small college crew is cursing as he battles his outboard engine.

This morning I told my men to use the same boats they rowed on Monday. Then I retired to the adjacent dock where we stored the coaching launches. We had a curious collection of launches, two Sears 8' aluminum fishing boats and two tattered 13' Boston Whalers. One Whaler had a wheel and throttle while the other was a hand-held affair. Being the oldest coach, I had my pick of the litter and naturally I choose the Whaler-with-wheel. If nothing else I wouldn't be deaf by the end of the season.

After hooking up the fuel line and pumping a little gasoline through the hose, I prepared for a workout on the "coach's ergometer." If you can gauge the success of a program by the amount of time the coach spends starting his launch, then UC Santa Barbara would rank at the bottom, especially on these cold mornings when my finicky twenty-five horse Evinrude was downright rude. I began by pulling the starter cord a few times, just to loosen up - not the engine but me. Then I began pulling in earnest, again and again, 80 pulls a minute - choke in for 20, out for 20. Heart rate 175. Respiration maximum, temperature climbing. I was working at full throttle, approaching redline, but my Evinrude was dead to the world. Hibernating. Not even a casual cough told me that I was on the right track.

I removed the engine lid and squirted some Insta-Start ether into the carburetor. I pulled again and heard the engine catch. I stepped to the console and eased the throttle back slightly, before the engine revved itself into oblivion. Finally I toyed with the choke for a few moments to insure that the engine was now living on gasoline and not on fumes from the ether. Should the engine die at this point, I, too, would die. But once it had a little flow going, my engine tended to stay alive through the whole workout.

Now began the less pleasant part. After a vigorous effort on the coach's erg, and wearing seven and a half layers of clothing, I was soaked with sweat. As my heart rate simmered down, the perspiration became cooler and cooler until I felt as though I was standing naked in a meat locker. This chilly state of affairs usually continued for the remainder of the workout.

As we launched our flotilla of small boats, the Cachuma devil-fog rose from the surface of the lake. Slinky tendrils of steam took on bizarre shapes and then mimicked human movements. Quite beautiful to watch but dangerous for rowing. Since we were already half-way to the fjord, we kept going. By the time we arrived I couldn't see across the width of the channel. We slowly paddled to the end, taking care not to run into anything or anyone. As we waited for the fog to lift, I read a short article from yesterday's Los Angeles Times:

> Robert Wangila, boxer, 1988 Olympic Champion, fell into a coma while being pummeled in a professional fight in Las Vegas. He died without regaining consciousness. "He kept feeding off that gold medal," manager David Green said. "Even though he really didn't have the raw talent, he kept doing it for the money."

"Rejoice," I told my rowers. "Unlike professional boxers - or any professional athlete for that matter - rowers have little motivation to do it longer than necessary. With a modest amount of self-realization, you'll know when you've acquired the nebulous gifts that rowing has to offer, whether it's courage or a strengthened soul or a powerful body. Once you've got it, drop back ten yards and punt. Someone new will pick up the ball and run with it."

Because of the fog, our practice consisted of assorted low-speed drills: rowing in circles; rotating the blade 360 degrees on the recovery; clapping hands while on the pull-through. I also had the single scullers play, "how far can you choke before you choke?" This involves sliding your hands down the oar shafts, a little more each stroke, until you can't go any farther. Finally we paddled back to the boathouse. Just as we reached the dock, the lake became one hundred percent crystal clear. This foggy-phenomenon happened so often through the course of the year that I named it the "Cachuma Curse."

Tomorrow, unfortunately, is yet another holiday, Thanksgiving. Friday is the sacred Day-After-Thanksgiving Holiday, aka the Holy Day of Shopping. Saturday is the Day of Rest After the Holy Day of Shopping. Sunday is Snooze Button Ecstasy. Seems as though every time we get up to training-speed, a holiday shuts us down. I never realized how many holidays encroached on the collegiate training schedule. When I was training for the Olympics, only one holiday interested me, the Day After the Games.

BURGESS
Sunday, November 28

An on-coming driver flashed his lights at me as I crested the San Marcos Pass. Why the hell did he do that? I wondered. Three seconds later I had my answer: a CHP ticket-giver sat poised like a crafty tiger concealed in the foliage, waiting for fat, juicy speeders. As a matter of practice, I'm a slow driver, so I wasn't too worried.

Anthony Burgess died yesterday. He was a magnificent author, the creator of one of my favorite books, *A Clockwork Orange*. In his honor, I dug out my audio tape of this classic and listened to it on the drive to the lake.

> There was me, that is Alex, and my three Drugs, that is Pete, Georgie and Dim, Dim being really dim, and we sat in the Karova Milkbar making up our rassoodocks what to do with the evening, a flip dark chill winter bastard, though dry.

To be able to write even one solitary sentence that could match this phenomenal opening line - a writer could spend a lifetime and never actualize this dream.

I worked all day on boathouse chores, sorting about two hundred pounds of miscellaneous hardware - stainless steel nuts, bolts and washers. I inventoried the meager collection of tools, one excellent single-jack sledge hammer and a few rusty end wrenches. Not a 7/16s in the house. As part of my weekly ritual, I sprayed bleach on the floor and walls to counteract Hanta virus. Finally I got around to sorting the team's impressive collection of riggers, a few sturdy Pocock riggers, peculiar Matt Wood riggers from Great Britain that appeared never to have been used, aluminum Empacher riggers missing a few key parts, in particular the boat to which they should have been attached. I hung the usable riggers along the walls. The rest I dumped into a huge wooden box behind the boathouse. The only excitement came when I was high on the ladder - a bold mouse scampered from behind a post and stood at attention five inches from my nose. Nearly startled me to the ground.

A steady plinking of acorns falling onto the boathouse's metal roof kept me company all day, plink, plink, plink, another every few seconds. Took me weeks to become comfortable with the noise. Inevitably, I thought some kids were throwing rocks onto the boathouse. I'd look out the wide bay doors, trying to see who was pestering me. No one.

California Oaks - the source of these acorns - populate the whole of Cachuma park. Last year, a branch broke off one of these mammoth trees and crushed an eight-oared shell that was stored alongside the boathouse. This mishap provided a chunk of insurance money for the program. Acorns once made the world go 'round. Native Chumash Indians ate them by the bushel. The thriving population of squirrels, mice and rats still gorge on the acorns. Say what you want about my vermin, they had the healthiest, sleekest pelts of any animals in the forest. In preparing for the inevitable winter's day, the mice hid acorns in every possible nook and cranny. On most mornings, at least one rower would find a half-dozen handsome, shiny acorns tucked into one of the shoes of his footboard.

By the end of the day, for the first time since my arrival two months ago, everything was off the boathouse floor. Hooray! Celebrate. Bring on the FISA inspection committee. It's starting to look like a place where some decent rowing can be done.

I couldn't sleep beyond 2:30 A.M. Two-thirty is too damn early. It's smack in the middle, well after you've gone to sleep and hours before you wish to wake up. I dressed, made coffee and drove to the lake.

Dressing for coaching success, at least at this time of year, is like preparing to climb Mt. Whitney in the dead of winter. I wore layer upon layer, mixing synthetics with cottons, plaids with solids, expanding with each new addition until my girth rivaled the Michelin Man. No matter the conditions, I always topped off my wardrobe with my Timberland nine-inch high boots and black Patagonia parka, complete with a half-dozen fully functional pockets. Stroke watch, mini-notebook, boathouse keys, flashlight, a coach without pockets is soon overwhelmed.

The dark blue watch cap that I wore every day had the distinction of being the only piece of '84 Olympic team issue gear to have survived the intervening years. What happened to the rest of it? Even for a non-fashion person like myself, most of the clothes, with loud colors and funky fabrics, looked suspiciously clown-like. I hope some poor slum dweller in Bogota has found happiness wearing my velour USA parade uniform.

I arrived at the boathouse in plenty of time to watch a fat full moon sink into the surrounding highlands. As the moon disappeared, I hiked the length of a dirt path that runs along the shore. This mile-long path is about as remote as you can find at Cachuma, just me and the mountain lions bumping into each other on the windswept trail, overhanging oak trees rustling like in a scary movie, the not-too-distant howl of a coyote, the invisible rustle of a ??? in the thick brush. What did I hope to find on the path at this dark, involuntary hour? Nothing, really. Just looking for the source - the source of all truth, beauty, honesty, purpose, revelation. The source, from my experience, can always be found merely undertaking the search. Being up extra early has its advantages.

For all my preparation, dressing, coffee, driving, source-seeking, the wind this morning was too strong to allow for rowing. Instead we watched a video of Pertti Karppinen winning the single scull at the '84 Olympics. Pertti was remarkable. Big as a house and graceful as a ballet dancer.

As we watched a replay of Pertti's final ten strokes, Glen Mung said, "Yeah, he rows good, but couldn't we watch something a little newer, maybe from the '92 Olympics?"

After thinking a moment, I jokingly made him an offer I knew he'd refuse: "I'll make you a deal, Mung. I'll get new videos if you stop using 'well' when you mean 'good,' and visa versa. Well and good are not interchangeable. He rows well. He made a good stroke." Well and good never budged nor did I update my videos. I suppose some things are not meant to change.

Our workout this morning was not limited to watching TV or discussing the King's English. I had something new and exciting in mind, or at least this is how I presented it to my rowers. The day before, just by accident, I discovered paradise. Driving home from the boathouse, as I crossed Suicide Bridge, a favorite jump-site for failing students and mistress-harried professors, I looked down and saw numerous cars parked on the side of a small road. Curiosity took hold - what was down in that desolate hole that would attract so many people? Only one way to find out.

About a mile from the summit, on the inland side, I turned off Highway 154 and headed onto a side road, down, down, down until I came across the cars I had seen from the bridge. The car owners, I soon surmised, were patronizing an ancient watering hole called Cold Springs Tavern. Live music on weekends, drinking and food all week long - this establishment was a local legend. I had no interest in the Tavern but I was intrigued by the hill. I followed the two-lane track, Stagecoach Road, to its inception, several miles further down. Then I turned around and drove the whole length to the summit. As the tenths-of-miles rolled through my odometer, I knew that I'd stumbled upon something special, nearly four miles of steady, steep, uninterrupted uphill, 3.8 miles to be exact, with virtually no traffic. A flawless diamond, Stagecoach Hill. This morning's blustery wind made this an ideal Stagecoach day.

When I announced my proposal, the crew let out their usual collective groan. "What about the mountain lions?" Jeff Beldon wanted to know.

"Have you ever seen one?" I asked him.

"No," he said, "but they're around. Supposedly they stay near the tavern."

"If you get killed by a mountain lion," I told him, "I will personally make sure the lion is severely punished. I'll have his VISA card limit lowered to $500."

To some extent Beldon was right. Dozens of lions roamed the nearby mountains. One jogger had been killed by a lion, although that took place in a different part of California. Hell, if you started worrying about mountain lions, you'd never leave your house. After driving to the base of Stagecoach, I separated the team into corpulent buffaloes, grumbling weasels and spunky rabbits.

"Listen up," I said. "This is the sort of place where gold medals are won. Every champion has something special in his bag of tricks. One of the things I had was Spyglass Hill, in Newport Beach. By coincidence, Spyglass is almost the exact same length as this hill. Of course, this is better - no traffic, no hassles. Double knot your shoes because this is going to be fun." Fun is such a funny word. So many different interpretations.

The buffaloes started first, followed a minute later by the weasels and finally the rabbits. I drove behind the runners in the team van. A few of the lightweights, Clement and Rupert Foster, instantly fell in love with the Stagecoach. They appreciated the pristine beauty, the perverse simplicity, the intestine-twisting difficulty. Everyone else suffered. Several of the big men, Moose, Björn, had to be scraped off the pavement. Engine trouble. As far as I can tell, rowing is 80.6% engine. Most of my rowers would be better off running Stagecoach five days a week and rowing on the sixth.

The following week I borrowed a measuring wheel from the UCSB cross-country coach and carefully gauged the distance, painting the pavement every quarter-mile with 30 weight engine oil. As every juvenile delinquent knows, when it comes to leaving your mark on concrete or asphalt, engine oil is preferred over spray paint. Engine oil can never, ever be removed. The only way to eliminate the message is to pave over the road.

A POX ON FRED CHECKS
12:30 P.M., Tuesday, November 30

Captain's log, supplemental, as Picard would say.

Two weeks ago, after reading the Washington Post article about the George Washington crew's near drowning, I told novice coach Fred Checks that every person on his team had to pass a swim test within ten days. No exceptions. No excuses. The women had already conducted their own swim test as had the varsity men. Only the novice men remained.

My crew wasn't at the lake, and not until later did I learn the details from a few of the novices. The wind this morning was blowing with considerable vigor as the two novice eights paddled beyond the small cove that shelters the dock. At the same time Coach Checks was still trying to start his outboard engine.

One of the novice coxswains noticed that the water was too bumpy and turned around. He should be awarded a medal for showing a modicum of common sense: twelve-inch-high waves rolling down the lake, freeboard on our craft only ten inches high. Conclusion: we will soon be taking on copious amounts of water. Solution: turn around and head for home. You win the prize. The other crew was not so lucky or smart. They attempted to row across the heart of the lake to the fjord. A dozen waves splashed into the eight, causing it to sink low in the water. After enduring a few more waves, someone yelled that they should stop rowing and untie their shoes. Soon afterward the boat completely swamped and everyone tumbled out.

Checks' came alongside a few minutes later in his aluminum launch. On a calm day, these miserable launches can barely hold six people. In bouncy water they are worthless. Checks - already limited by having three passengers in his boat - was able to pluck only three rowers from the icy waters.

He made a serious error at this critical juncture, one that nearly cost several lives. Rather than head to the nearest shore and drop off the survivors, he drove his launch all the way to the boathouse, an extra mile each way. By the time Checks returned, three of the rowers were suffering hypothermia and were on the verge of drowning. Novice rower Tommy Thompson apparently saved one man's life by holding him above the surface until he could be rescued.

The lake rangers had been notified by this time and they used their powerful rescue boat to haul the abandoned eight back to the boathouse. Altogether, all the novice lost was seven seats - $1000. A rather expensive row by any measure. I'm still not sure if the oars made it back.

The novice rowers were exceptionally lucky. Lake Cachuma is an unforgiving rowing venue. You must err on the side of caution. You should not leave the dock when it's stormy. You should always have a coaching launch nearby. And all your rowers should be proven swimmers.

When I heard that none of his rowers had been given a swim test, I was furious. Ballistic is a more realistic term - I went ballistic. Adding fuel to this ballistic fire was my personal animosity toward Checks. After thinking it over, I called Ms. Pearson and explained the situation, concluding: "For the good of the team, clubs sports, and the school, I don't think he should continue coaching."

She said, "He works for you."

I said, "Adios, Fred Checks."

When I arrived at the weight room I told Checks to grab his gear and come outside. Once away from the room, I asked him, "Has everyone on your team passed the swim test?"

After a moment's delay, what police detectives call the liar's pause, he said, "Yes."

I said, "I know you haven't even given them the swim test."

As he stammered out a response - some bullshit about how he hadn't had enough time - I considered what Harry Parker or Bob Ernst might do. Most likely they would run his ass out of the boathouse. Finally I told Checks to shut the fuck up and find a new job. Checks immediately went to Ms. Pearson and literally cried in her office for an hour. As a result of his tears, she called me and asked that I think over my decision. I said I would. I did. I decided that I would rather not have a novice team than one coached by Fred Checks.

Made for good tension. Several novices have called me at home to say they will quit if Checks isn't allowed to coach. Good. I hope they do quit. Make the boathouse a lot quieter.

More Bad Checks
Wednesday, December 1

I stopped by the erg room on the way to Cachuma to formally announce to the novice team that Fred Checks was no longer their coach. They took it poorly, shouting at me that they wanted Checks and no one else. Then again, Charlie Manson had his supporters. Why is it that some rowers will follow their coach - no matter how lame he might be - to the ends of the earth? Certainly this phenomenon, this sporting version of the Stockholm Syndrome, deserves a government grant for further study.

I told the novices, "If you're rowing because you like Checks, then you're doing it for the wrong reason. Row because you like rowing." Hopefully, they will take up another sport, perhaps juggling chain saws.

As I drove to the lake, I considered an idea that Ms. Pearson presented to me late last night. She would prefer that Checks remain as the novice coach. She feels that Checks has learned his lesson, and to find a replacement coach at this stage of the season would be impossible. For better or worse, Ms. Pearson agreed to take all responsibility for him.

The most important person on any crew, especially ours, is the novice coach. Lake Cachuma is icy cold. The wind whips up hard and fast and blows steady at twenty-five knots. Novice rowers have no clue what they're up against and must rely wholly on the coach. Disasters happen at schools that have the wrong people coaching, schools such as UCSB. A tragedy occurs and people die and everyone calls it an accident. Yes, sometimes it is an accident. Other times it's negligence on the part of the coach.

Drenched sweatshirts were scattered around the boathouse this morning - the type of sweatshirt that weighs about seventy pounds when wet. It must have been a mess. Thank God no one was killed. Yes, I was furious. I'm still furious.

DUES DUE
Thursday, December 2

How quickly payday comes and goes. With all the excitement yesterday I didn't have a chance to enjoy it.

Along with my paycheck, Queen Wendy left a copy of the updated crew budget in my box. Written in the margin were these chilling words: "You're in the red." As I read the message I immediately felt another hair on my head turn gray. How could we be in the red? We haven't gone anywhere or bought anything.

The team's $100,000 budget proved to be a nightmare on paper, mostly because it lumped together the men's squad, women's squad, boathouse operations, all of it thrown into a confusing jumble. The women bought a new eight for $16,000. The men bought a plastic clip for holding the bow number for $1.60. I spent more than a few hours going over the line items, such as launch gasoline, $4,000. With even the most generous estimates, I couldn't see us spending half that amount. I suspect the old coach had filled his car's gas tank along with the outboard engine tanks.

The income side of the ledger was less confusing although plenty scary, relying on dues, erg-a-thon, cookie sales, winning the lottery and finding a sack of money on the side of the road while driving to the boathouse. To date, only Gordo and Adam had paid the fall quarter dues. The rest of the rowers are boycotting payment until *Twin Peaks* is put back on the air. Hey guys, it's over, so pay up. I hated having to impose dues. No dues were charged when I rowed at UC Irvine. Of course, that was before sliding seats were invented. Times have changed. But no matter how hard I tried, I could never instill the proper life-threatening tone into my voice when demanding their money.

After practice I called Ms. Pearson regarding Fred Checks and agreed to her deal. I loathed doing it. Nothing I hate more than the thought of returned Checks. Put me in a bad mood all day. I could only hope that she was right, that Checks had learned from his mishap. I felt I had an obligation to caution her. "Ms. Pearson," I said, "you have no idea of the mess you're buying into. At least come to Cachuma some morning and see what it's about." She never did.

We boated two eights. The lites had a novice woman in the bow while the heavies had Gordo in the three seat. I figured it evened out nicely.

We rowed a dozen lengths of the fjord at full-power, varying rating, all with feet-out-of-footboards. Of my hundreds of drills, feet-out-of-footboards is my favorite. The rowers are forced to balance, bow-to-stern, rather than simply port-to-starboard. Harsh motions within the boat are instantly visible - the offending rower's feet wave in the air like twin flags of surrender.

Afterward Adam came up to me and said, "I think the small boat work is paying off. It seemed as though the guys in my boat were rowing a little better." I asked him to repeat what he'd said, just so that I could feel these welcome words tumble over me. As he walked away I said a silent prayer for Adam and all his relatives.

Tomorrow is the Long Beach Christmas Regatta, one of my favorite races. It's optional, I told my people. If you want to race, great. Otherwise, stay home and study for finals, which begin on Monday.

Ten rowers decided to take the plunge. They de-rigged their racing shells, singles and doubles, and then left for campus. Seven hours later, I left. Rather than take the team's old blue trailer I had decided to build a double decker rack for the team van. In my mind I constructed the rack in a few minutes. In reality, I had a long day ahead. No breakfast. No lunch. No helpers. Scant electricity. Only a Skilsaw, an electric drill, scrap lumber and a handful of three-inch galvanized decking screws. First, I fabricated the bottom-layer and then loaded four double sculls onto it. Then I built the top layer, working around the boats. Once the top layer was in place, I loaded on five single sculls. When finally underway, the van creaked and groaned like a covered wagon, but at least it held together.

X-mas Regatta
Saturday, December 4

The races are only 850 meters long at the Christmas Regatta, which means you sprint like a demon the whole way. When I competed, I usually I had enough sprint-mojo for about 600 meters. The last 250 meters of a close race seemed to take forever, a slow motion dance of anaerobic   distress.

As my scullers rigged their boats, I couldn't help but notice that the Christmas Regatta had shrunk in size. If not for lightweight women and Masters, the regatta wouldn't exist at all. Old fashioned heavyweight rowers, especially collegiate men, seemed to be a scarce commodity.

The first race of the day was the novice men's single scull. We entered five men, Pressman, Kolbe, Mung, Björn and Gordo. They all managed to make the finals and they all promised me victory. Between races, as the rowers sat in my van and rested up, I talked to them about pre-race foods, glazed donuts versus tuna fish on rye, about pre-race motivation, *Playboy* versus *Penthouse*, about the meaning of racing life.

"On one level," I told them, "racing is nothing more than getting from the starting line to the finish ahead of the competition. But if you look a little deeper, racing is a great deal more."

"What the hell could be more than winning?" Mung asked.

"Racing serves as a formal demonstration of your ability to ride the three-headed monster," I told him. "The first monster is your physical preparation - lifting weights for strength, running Stagecoach for endurance, working on your technique. The second monster is your mental preparation - all our jabbering about humility, battling for your life, taking complete responsibility for the outcome. The last monster is your X Factor, your soul, your courage. Taken altogether, I call this three-headed monster the Process of Winning."

"You've got more sayings," Mung said, "than my dog has fleas."

"That's because I'm a left-handed, sculler-turned-writer-turned-coach," I told him. "It's my job to think up this stuff. It's your job to listen.

So listen up. The level of competition doesn't much matter, Olympics, Nationals, Christmas Regatta, right down to the Stinky River Sprints. What matters is that you successfully explore the process. Once you've mastered the process, you can apply it to another race, to another sport, to making money, to whatever interests you. If all you've managed to do is win the novice single at the Christmas Regatta, then all you get is a beer mug."

A short time later, as the blue and yellow UCSB shirts rolled down the course, I felt an unexpected swelling in my chest. Heart attack? No, simply a case of rapture of the coach. My scullers, my men, were streaming along, leading the pack. Made me wish I had a camera. Mung won, with Pressman second, Kolbe third, Björn fourth. Gordo was last.

Will Gordo ever regain the glory he tasted so fleetingly at last month's Newport Autumn Rowing Festival. Yes, at that event Gordo earned UCSB's only gold medal by winning the novice single. Amazing.

The best race of the day was the lightweight four-with. Not only did we win by a half-length but the whole squad, heavies, lites and Gordo, worked together in tight harmony. The lightweights leaped out of their straight pairs immediately upon reaching the dock and climbed into the waiting four-with, which had been readied for them by the Gauchos who were not racing at the time. Altogether a good bit of teamwork.

After claiming their beer mugs, we packed up our gear and headed to my favorite restaurant, Casa Sanchez, at the corner of Anaheim and Termino Streets. This Mexican-fast-food-dive was both the spiritual home of drive-by shootings and the perfect place to gorge on a post-race meal. Patio dining a must. As we devoured our burritos a grungy homeless man came wandering our way, making the setting even less appetizing than usual. Seeing our crew shirts, he told us he had rowed at Harvard a few years ago. I doubt it. Maybe just in the house boats.

Over our Casa Especials, Clement told me of an exchange that had taken place on the starting line before the lightweight four race, between him and an Orange Coast College rower.

"So, is Lewis a good coach?" the Coastie inquired.

"He doesn't just want us to be better rowers," Clement answered. "He wants us to be better men."

Give that man a Crunch bar.

PRICE CLUBBING
Monday, December 6

My rowers are in finals this week. Supposedly, they're studying or taking exams. Most likely they're sleeping late, watching copious amounts of Baywatch and Magnum P.I., eating Crackeroni & Cheese. At least that's what I'm doing. For the first time since taking this job, I'm enjoying a day off. I didn't go to the lake. Didn't go to campus. Instead I went to the Price Club in Oxnard, the poor man's Disneyland.

The forty-mile drive from Santa Barbara to Oxnard along Highway 101 rolls past the mansions of Montecito, the funky town of Summerland, the epic surf site of Rincon. I love this stretch of road. Always something new to take in, some little detail, the jet skiers playing among the pilings of the Muscle Shoals pier or the banana plantation on the inland side of the highway near Carpinteria.

As I approached Ventura, I saw a pod of dolphins swimming a few yards offshore. I pulled over and watched for a few minutes. The dolphins don't actually swim, they gracefully roll through the water as though eternally going downhill. Once, when I was surfing, a pod swam all around me. My first thought was, man, these guys are huge. Suddenly one of the dolphins leaped out of the water - a perfect arc - and then splashed down only an arm's length away. A dolphin won't bite your head off like a great white shark, but he could sure give a headache should he land on top of you.

When the dolphins rolled out to sea, I returned to the highway. Quite often, when making this drive, I think about the time I covered the same stretch of road during the '84 Games, riding in a school bus, the eastern European women beside me needing a bath in the worst way; or in our private van, Coach Parker at the wheel, taking the faster route through the back hills to Lake Casitas. I remember listening to my Walkman so I wouldn't be tempted to join in pointless and unproductive conversation. I can't say that it was a barrel of laughs, but it was an exciting time. Ten years ago. Time has passed quickly.

The Price Club, similar to Costco, Sam's Club or BJ's, brought me back from reminiscing. I parked my car, latched onto a big red shopping cart and marched through the gaping door, flashing my Price Club card like a movie star. I often go Price Clubbing without any intention of buying a thing. I go to watch the sweat-soaked chunky people push their sleds up and down the aisles, loaded to the breaking point with bushels of Huggies and seventy pound sacks of Hamburger Helper; I go to eat the samples, served up by old ladies in granny aprons, offering everything from sautéed abalone to jerked beef. No one has ever starved to death in a Price Club.

My shopping list today was rather short, a hundred feet of garden hose for the boathouse, five pounds of peanut butter and a carton of Crunch bars, 36 count, my prizes of choice. To date we've had some form of competition nearly every practice. Gradually I've manipulated the contests, sometimes subtly, other times in an obvious manner, so that everyone has concrete, or at least chocolate proof that they are winners.

I've told my crew that the only way to beat a better team is by being more proficient at racing, and that comes from practicing racing every day of the season. Ah, the season. With the arrival of finals, the season is now one-third over. The rowing season is too damn long. It should be limited to fifteen weeks. Rowers, and especially coaches, would be better off going high-and-hard for fifteen weeks and then moving on to new challenges. After finals we'll have a few days of Hell Week and then the crew will retire for Christmas vacation. According to the calendar, once they return from vacation, we'll have exactly four months until the PCRCs. Plenty of time to teach them everything-rowing.

To date, I've had a crash course in everything-coaching. I knew going in that "coach" was a powerful word, but I had no idea how difficult it might be to harness the power. And I still haven't put together a Gaucho newsletter, as I'd been instructed. Soon, Ms. Pearson, soon.

BLUE MARBLE
Tuesday, December 7

I had a chance to go on a solo cruise on the lake, long overdue. I took my time, motoring slowly, guiding my launch into every cove and cranny. Beautiful place, Lake Cachuma, particularly the side channels. I saw many birds of prey in these quiet retreats, including osprey and one golden eagle.

The osprey are my favorite. While a crow will eat anything from a squished rattlesnake to a week-old baloney sandwich, osprey eat only live fish. From its perch, the osprey watches for some unlucky fish to approach the surface. Once in range, the bird zooms in like a jet fighter, talons extended, ready to snatch its prey. The awesome speed of the osprey - from perch to water - is a blur of sheer energy. After a successful dive, a fish wiggling in its talons, the osprey sometimes flew near me as though to show off its skill as a hunter. Hey, check this out.

I turned off my engine at the top of the lake and drifted on the quiet waters. No other boats were near. No one interfered with my meditation. I stretched out on the bench seat and looked up at the sky. Clear, clear, clear. Warm and still. Every few minutes a jet on its way to San Francisco cut through the sky like tiny scissors, a white contrail in its wake, sharp at first, then widening and finally disappearing. The Blue Marble, for all its problems, hassles, craziness, never looked better.

After a good, long hour I returned to the boathouse and began working on a new project: a mammoth oar rack. Currently the men's oars were stored, handles down, in a dirt-bottomed pit on the right-hand side of the boathouse. For the last few decades, countless mice and rats have used this pit as their latrine. The women's oars were kept in a concrete-hole on the left side of the boathouse, leaning against the wall. For both men and women, several minutes were lost each morning as they tried to locate their oars in the mess. Most boathouses use a better system, with the oars suspended off the ground in rows of eight, hung upside down by their collars. I made it my mission to build such a rack. My first task was to dismantle the old racks, which had been designed when the oars were six inches longer.

When I least expected it, a heavy section of the old rack came crashing to the ground. No boats were wrecked, no major injuries. Working alone has its advantages. I salvaged about two hundred dollars worth of Grade 1 lumber, mostly clear two-by-six's, bone dry and pre-painted. The battle has begun.

These Count
Friday, December 10

Big competition this morning, but not for my rowers - for me. To help the coaches and staff get acquainted, the UCSB athletic department sponsored the Ultimate Gaucho, seven different competitions, including golfing, running, volleyball. I finished second in the mile race, 6:02. Not bad - certainly a lot better than I could have done two months ago.

We adjourned to the gym for the next event, 10 Free Throws. As I waited my turn, I watched the basketball coach warming-up, sinking shot after shot. The man could not miss.

"Okay," the judge said at last. "Now these shots count! Understand? These count!" The formerly flawless free thrower proceeded to miss every shot. Zero for ten. He looked a little tight in the neck and jaw area. Choke city, the big C, every athlete's worst nightmare. I took over and managed to sink seven out of ten. Now that my best events were out of the way I retreated to the golf course for a needed dose of humility.

After the Ultimate Gaucho I drove to Lake Cachuma, arriving just in time to see our new trailer being pulled into the parking area by a delivery truck. On top of the trailer was a brand new Dirigo eight for our women's team. Terri and her crew danced with joy at the arrival of their new baby. My interest was more with the trailer, which I knew I'd be dragging all over the state, from San Diego to Sacramento. The team had purchased a deluxe model, electric brakes, double axle, four-story racks. We could load every boat, oar, sling and mouse onto the trailer and still have room left over.

This incredible beast had been purchased with insurance money. The ability to wreck perfectly harmless equipment, otherwise known as the Gaucho Curse, was a continuing drama for everyone involved with UCSB rowing. While heading to the PCRCs the year before, the driver had become distracted while reaching for a cassette tape, left the roadway and flipped the trailer. Nearly every boat was ruined. One surviving shell was later destroyed at the regatta when a sling holding it gave way. If not for insurance pay-outs, the whole program would have disappeared.

The women untied their new boat and promptly set a world's record by having no less than eighteen rowers carry it into the boathouse. Rather than rig it up for immediate use, they carefully lifted their new boat onto the highest rack. Its maiden voyage would not take place until just before race season.

On the local TV news this evening, the weatherman was predicting a hurricane-force storm to hit some time tomorrow. Such tidings are not conducive to a good night's sleep, especially when Hell Week is scheduled to begin in less than nine hours.

HELL WEEK BEGINS
Saturday, December 11

By Gaucho and general rowing tradition, we were supposed to make up for the lost workouts of Finals Week, aka Heaven Week, by engaging in Hell Week, rowing twice a day, lifting weights, playing on the ergs, taking naps together. In this way everyone would become sick or injured or both - but at least we'd do it together. Hell Week soon earned its name.

Rained lightly on my way over the pass. Rained somewhat harder as I arrived at the boathouse. Rained with unbridled enthusiasm as I waited for the rowers. I stood at the boat bay doors looking out at the lake, marveling at the pelting rain and the way it seemed to blur the distinction between air and water. The heavy oak trees that surrounded the boathouse creaked and groaned as though they'd come to life. Tiny branches flicked off and scuttled across the roof, making weird screeching noises. The wind, just as the weathermen had predicted, blew like a hurricane.

Around 7:00 we abandoned any thoughts of rowing and headed for Stagecoach. The rain turned into a torrential downpour as we begin our hill running effort, the wind howling without pause. I drove the van, scooping up runners who simply could not make any progress into the wind. At the top of the pass, marble-sized hail came shooting out of the blackened sky. Everyone suffered, the fast runners shivering at the top while they waited for the elephants, and the elephants - well, they always suffered.

Clement Nash won the piece and despite the raw conditions he managed to set a course record, 28:33. Afterward, Clement's father, who was visiting from Manhattan Beach, treated everyone to breakfast at Cold Springs Tavern. While I was waiting for my pancakes, he discreetly handed me a donation check for $1,000. I told him that he could visit any time.

I returned to the boathouse after breakfast for a rigging session. Andrew Moore had been pestering me to rig the doubles as straight pairs, arguing that since we would be racing in sweep boats, sculling was not beneficial. Finally I said okay. I had learned by this time not to do the rigging myself. I set out any necessary tools and gave advice where needed. The actual rigging chores were performed by Andrew and Jeff Beldon.

As Andrew worked, I offered him some unsolicited advice. "Rowing should be like sex," I told him. "Become proficient in all aspects. Don't limit yourself to being a starboard, five-man, lightweight. Be competent at port, starboard, bow, stroke, sculling. You'll feel better about yourself. Everyone will be happier." As usual, only a grimace of a grin crossed his face. Andrew Moore, the More Man. Anxious, impatient, totally committed to the lightweight team, complete with built-in anger.

At last count, I had identified 8,732 different attitudes that a champion might possess. Some champions are nice people. Some are religious. Some are eccentric. Most are plain as oatmeal. Andrew's anger was one of the more common champion attitudes that I had observed. This particular anger-attitude was a pain in the ass for the coach, but that was my problem.

HELL WEEK, CONTINUED
Monday, December 13

As I crested the San Marcos Pass, I saw a stunning sight - the glittering white peaks of the Swiss Alps. Thanks to yesterday's cold weather and stormy conditions, the Sierra Madre Mountains on the far side of the lake were now covered in snow, more than any Gaucho veteran had ever seen.

I also saw my first dead deer on the side of the road. Cold weather in the higher elevations will be bringing them closer to civilization for the next few months. Crow's Delight. Turkey Vulture Treat. Deer parts scattered for an eighth of a mile. When Buick meets Bambi, it's not a pretty sight.

We rowed small boats from the floating outhouse, (I have yet to see anyone use the damn thing), around Arrowhead Island and back to the outhouse. Pretty good job of steering on everyone's part. Steering is the key: if one boat gets off course, all hell breaks loose. My Gauchos are prone to becoming distracted at the slightest provocation. A scrap of paper floating on the water might be enough to send one boat careening into another. I handicapped the start after the first piece, so that the slowest boats started ahead of the others. Once I had the proper handicaps sorted out, I said "Go" and then sat back and drank my coffee. Between the angry young men, the enemies, the lites who hated heavies, the heavies who would rather die than be defeated by lightweights, I think everyone had sufficient reason to grind themselves into a coma.

As the rowers marched through the last piece, Moose Morse suddenly stopped in mid-stroke. I came alongside and saw that he was in a great deal of pain.

"What's the problem?" I asked him.

"I just felt it again," he said.

"Felt what?"

"Something give way when I was lifting yesterday," he said, pointed to his lower back. "Just happened again."

"Why didn't you say something before we launched?"

He shrugged his shoulders but said nothing. Unfortunately Moose is typical of rowers: if you're injured, don't tell the coach. Wait until it gets really bad and then tell him.

With as much care as possible, considering that he weighed 225 pounds, I eased him out of his single scull and into the bow of my launch. I didn't want to leave the other rowers unattended so I gave Moose my parka, loaded his single scull into the launch and had him accompany me as I followed the others. When we finally arrived back at the boathouse I told Moose to head straight to the club sports trainer. Do not stop for breakfast. Get immediate treatment. Knowing Moose, he probably went to his girlfriend's house, cracked open a Bud and waited for her to come home.

In the evening, the whole crew - men, women and novice - went to Adam's apartment in the heart of I-V for a round of team bonding. On this rare occasion, I came along.

To what degree should a coach participate in team bonding? I'd considered that question many times since arriving in Santa Barbara. Apparently, the previous Gaucho coach had bonded to the max, partying with the rowers on a regular basis. I had purposely limited my involvement to the practice sessions. Excessive bonding serves only to humanize the coach, making him one of the gang and costing him valuable respect in the bargain. Certainly if a rower has some sort of dilemma, a personal problem for which he needs advice, then the coach should make himself available. But in general, to maintain any sort of discipline, I felt I should keep a healthy distance.

I arrived at the crew commune on Trigo Street around 7:15. Despite the early hour, I saw that Moose was already asleep in a corner, oblivious to the noise and commotion that raged around him. Adam told me that Moose had excessively self-medicated himself with the usual hops-drug. We ate a surprisingly good pot luck dinner and then settled down to watch videos of famous rowing races and a video of our own team that Adam had shot the day before, using his dad's camcorder.

To me the Gaucho men looked much better on video than they had in person, as though their flaws had been cleverly edited out. I tried to make a few points - faster hands away, slower on the slide - but I doubted that my words would be remembered on the water many hours from now.

The mentality of rowers never ceases to amaze - here we were, several dozen seemingly healthy people, cramped into an over-heated room, watching with utter concentration the same solitary stroke over and over in slow motion. Rowers are a strange breed. The very best rowers have the fierce competitiveness of a Green Beret soldier, the artistic temperament of an old world master, the control and patience of a Zen monk. They are not driven by dreams of glory or money. They are selfless and sturdy. They will cooperate with people whose company they don't much enjoy in order to achieve their goals. Strange, wonderful people.

When the crowd finally grew weary of CREW-TV, I suggested we switch to Channel 7. Downhill Racer, the classic ski racing saga starring Robert Redford, was on tonight. A few good lessons are buried somewhere in that movie. I once read that the Italian ski champion Alberto Tomba used it as a how-to primer.

Maybe we could organize an Athlete's Film Festival. I'd include the obvious ones, Chariots of Fire and the original Rocky. I might suggest a few off-beat entries such as the hockey movie Slap Shot and baseball's Bull Durham. "Don't think," the veteran Costner tells rookie pitcher Tim Robbins. "It only hurts the team."

I'd include the first segment of New York Stories, where the grizzled veteran artist, played by Nick Nolte, is asked by the aspiring young Rosanna Arquette if she should continue her artistic struggle. Nolte tells her, "If you were a real artist, it wouldn't matter what I thought." An aspiring rower might do well to employ a kindred sentiment. The advice of family, friends, teammates and especially the coach is flawed at best and should only be followed when it corresponds with what's in your heart. If you are a real champion, it doesn't matter what anyone thinks.

HOUR OF THE PEARL
Tuesday, December 14

I parked my van a hundred yards from the boathouse, facing east, and searched the pitch blackness for the first scant morsels of dawn, the "hour of the pearl" according to John Steinbeck, an everyday miracle that I've come to love with all my heart.

I've noticed that if you sit very, very still, you can actually feel the inexorable rolling of the earth, like an ant riding on a wooden top that's spinning at 2000 miles an hour. This morning I sat extra-still and looked straight ahead. Suddenly I saw a small, faintly glowing triangle of light directly in front of me. The top of the triangle was defined by a low, thick cloud - the sides were shaped by two mountains. In less time than it took to write this sentence, the triangle turned a hundred different and distinct colors, as rapidly as flipping through the pages of a book. I gripped the steering wheel and stared straight ahead. Had I really seen that? So stunning and unexpected. Then the clouds filled in, the triangle vanished and it was over. In its place, a lighter shade of gray told me that dawn had arrived. Rain was probably not far behind, maybe snow in the higher elevations. No matter. Let a tornado lift the boathouse off its foundation and carry it to Lompoc. I had seen the birth of a day.

An old cliché claims that National Park rangers are paid in sunsets rather than in cash. In a similar way, I was graciously rewarded during my coaching days by these indefinably beautiful pre-dawn infusions of power. Until I took this job, I'd never lived in a place where city-lights didn't rob me of this drama. Perhaps I could have seen it when backpacking in the High Sierra, but in that rugged setting, the 5:00 a.m. hour would not find me awake. Thanks to my coaching at UCSB, I witnessed this magic over and over.

We rowed the outhouse-Island loop for an hour-and-a-half in small boats. In the course of the workout, two straight pairs ran into each other and Johnny Bender flipped his single. I didn't mind his flipping over but I was annoyed that he hadn't brought any dry clothes to practice.

After the boats were put away the boats, I noticed the men were messing around on the dock.

"What are you doing?" I asked them.

"A little team bonding, as you call it," Mung said.

I looked more closely and saw that the men were tying the novice women's shoes together. Then they tossed the string of shoes around the upper branch of an oak tree. "Here they come," someone yelled. The varsity men ran to their cars and raced out of the parking area, throwing dirt and dust into the air. Upon seeing their shoes dangling from a high branch, the novice women began cursing and gnashing their teeth with such fury that it could be heard in the town of Los Olivos, ten miles away. They swore vengeance and I had no doubt they'd get it.

My half-wits had no other choice: They needed to get the attention of the novice women. Rowing naked, honking at them in the parking lot, being obnoxious in the weight room, every tactic of theirs had been ignored. Each day the varsity men failed to be noticed was a blight on their record. The purpose in all this attention-seeking? It's an old story.

In the afternoon we met at the erg room for a long awaited 5000 meter test. Once everyone had spun the erg, I brought out a box of Crunch bars and a case of Hansen's soda.

"Time for a quick team meeting," I said. "A few days ago I took part in the Ultimate Gaucho, and through the course of the competition I had a chance someone choke."

"Did you do the Heimlich?" Churchill asked.

"Different sort of choke," I said "the sporting kind. Before we get to race season, I thought it might be a good idea to talk about choking."

After describing what I'd seen a few days before, I went on to say, "Let's agree on the terms. To choke means not doing your best on race day. Rest assured, on occasion it happens to everyone. For some people it happens all the time. These people live sad, miserable lives and then die lonely deaths." The heavies and lites nodded their heads in full agreement.

"How to keep from choking? For starters, what is the opposite of choke? Triumph! Deep down, we all live to triumph. It's a natural quest, one that transcends time, setting, sport. If I had to choose between triumphing at the Olympics and a hundred million dollars, I'd take the Olympic triumph. Money comes and goes. Triumph lasts for eternity.

"From this launching point, start by setting realistic goals. Don't ask more of yourself on race day than you can produce on your best practice day. That would not be realistic nor would it be fair. Nor is it altogether necessary. At the Barcelona Olympics only one world record was set in 37 individual track and field events. Thus a sub-world record performance won the gold in all other events. If it should happen - a race day performance that goes beyond anything you've done before - consider yourself blessed. You can kiss God on all four cheeks when you meet him." Michael Kolbe, the only religious guy in the group, laughed at the thought of kissing God.

"Second, in the course of your training, make special note of all little victories. A killer hill run. A personal best on the bench press. That's why I want each of you to keep a training journal. You must fill your journal to overflowing with these little victories. In each instance, you did not choke. You were a champion. You did it right. You triumphed."

My rowers stared at the floor. I knew none of them had bothered to keep a journal.

"Leading up to the big race, you must practice triumph-ing. Practice it the way you'd practice making a quick catch or a powerful drive. Experiment. In some manner, we've raced almost every day this season. If you were out of college, I'd recommend that you compete in lots of obscure events - running races, swim meets - any legitimate competition. Become as comfortable with triumph as you are with brushing your teeth. Know that you can do it, on demand, sunshine or rain, head wind or tail, east coast or west, good night's sleep or up all night." I stopped and drank my soda and grabbed another Crunch bar.

"Now, on the day of the big race, imagine that you're carrying a five-gallon bucket filled to overflowing with both your proper expectations and your numerous little victories. Add to this bucket a few drops of faith. Faith is the catalyst. Faith is necessary to make the final leap. All champions have faith in themselves. Faith is tough. It requires a leap of imagination, of trust, of confidence.

"Before you can win your first Olympic medal, you must have faith that you are capable of doing it. Not everyone can make the leap. You must have faith in your X Factor, faith that you will respond at the critical crossroads in a way that satisfies your soul. Through your efforts - perhaps years in the making - you will create the appropriate setting for a performance that will completely fulfill your athletic promise. Afterward, after you have triumphed, make sure to say your prayers of gratitude so that you can do it again. Class over. See you tomorrow."

Choking can be one of the most bedeviling aspects in sport, or in life, for that matter. Nothing is worse than spending hundreds of hours in preparation and then failing to deliver at the big race. On the other hand, nothing is better than spending hundreds of hours in preparation and then triumph-ing. It's a risk, but a worthy one.

The 7
Monday, January 3

New Year, new quarter, new day. I am anxious and ready. The Christmas break was so damn long, it seems as though we'll be starting over. The last training day was December 15, a full nineteen days ago. Will the rowers remember how to row? Will I remember how to coach?

Flushed with excitement at the thought of returning to my coaching ways, I arrived early at the lake. Immediately I saw that the novice men were already in attendance. In fact, they had launched their eight. This meant they would spend the next thirty minutes rowing by Braille. No other way to describe it. This wasn't city-darkness, with assorted street lights and Citgo signs to guide the way. This was old-fashioned country dark.

I hoped the novice men had their radar cranked to the highest setting because a few days ago I noticed that Santa Claus gave the lake rangers a truck load of new buoys, a couple dozen at least. The buoys stood three feet out of the water with an equal mass below, cylindrical in shape, sturdy, made of steel, white with little numbers painted on them. The rangers dropped the buoys in a seemingly random manner, although to a passing airplane they might have spelled out "Cachuma."

Fred Checks, thank God, now had only one boat to coach. The other novices quit after the near-drowning, and thus his chances of killing anyone had decreased by half. Still, the well-being of nine rowers was a huge responsibility. One could only pray and be prepared to help out at a moment's notice.

When my rowers finally showed up, each in turn took a moment to stare at me: I'd re-grown my beard over the long break. Then they stared at the former oar pit, which I'd filled with dirt and covered with a layer of concrete. Lastly they stared at the new oar rack, which I'd finally finished. With all ten sets of oars suspended off the ground in neat rows, the rack proved to be a revelation to Adam. Speaking to no one in particular, he said, "So that's how you're supposed to do it."

I had them run ten times around the quarter-mile loop next to the boathouse until the light came up. Then we took out two eights, although one boat had only seven men.

The curse of a small program is the 7. The ghost in that vacant seat is like a harbinger of evil. He grins at you and mouths obscenities. He'll stand up in the boat, turn around and drop trow just to distract you. He berates you for having signed up to coach such a funky program where only seven heavyweights show up the first day after Christmas break. Of course, only the coach can see this vacant-seat ghost, which makes it all the worse. On occasion, he'll take up a ghostly-oar and help the cause. This morning, he lent a hand on the last piece and he didn't look too bad. His erg scores aren't going to scare anyone, but I'll give him credit, he's light as a feather on the recovery. All told, he's quite adept at pulling his own weight.

About ten minutes into our last twenty-minute steady state piece, the ghost kicked in and before my eyes, the heavyweight 7 worked ahead of the lightweight eight, one length, two, and finally three lengths of open water. I didn't know what to say, so I used Harry Parker's tried and true method: I stared at the rowers with hard intensity and said nothing.

BEACH TAR
Tuesday, January 4

The Goleta shoreline next to campus is famous for having suffered a huge oil spill in 1967. Photos of oil-soaked sea birds were flashed all over the world. You'd have thought the shoreline would be ruined for eternity. No, just a few months.

Oil is old news in this area. A century ago, Richard Henry Dana, in his book Two Years Before the Mast, wrote about the strong smell of oil when his trading ship sailed into the harbor. Not much has changed since Dana's time, certainly not the natural seepage from the ocean floor, which fouls the beach at a rate of two hundred gallons a day. Even a short stroll on the wet sand is enough to collect a quarter-pound of tar on the soles of your feet.

Because of this morning's rare, minus three-foot tide, we were able to run along the beach the whole way to Santa Barbara - five miles - and then back again. Unfortunately, as we were heading home Antonio slipped on a seaweed encrusted rock and banged up his knee.

I'm beginning to see why a coach might limit his workouts to the straight-and-narrow. Get too creative and people will inevitably hurt themselves. Spin the ergs, lift light circuits, row in eights - and everyone will to get through the season in one piece. I suppose that's the difference between training only myself and coaching others. When I rowed, I sought fun-tough-challenging workouts. If I were coaching just Clement and Pressman it might be different, but with Clumsy, Sticky Hands and Short Stack along for the ride, I must use caution.

When I returned home, I found a treat in the mail: My brother had sent me a video - Howard Stern's New Year's Eve Party. It was vintage Howard, the utter antithesis of politically correct. At one point, he offered John Wayne Bobbitt $15,000 to show his severed/re-attached member on live television. You could see Bobbitt sweating like a wheel of cheese under the hot studio lights as he tried to make up his pathetic, wife-beating mind. Howard baited him: "Fifteen thousand dollars buys a lot of reconstructive surgery." To my surprise, Bobbitt backed off, declining the money. He'd live to regret that decision. Hell, he was probably regretting it before the show was over.

Howard is an acquired taste, much like sniffing glue. Howard's New Year's video was the largest-grossing pay-per-view of all time. By comparison, the Triple Cast for the 1992 Olympics was one of the lowest.

Weight on Head
Wednesday, January 5

A mirror broke in the erg room just as practice was getting going. Was it another omen, some premonition of bad luck? To hell with luck. For fun I had my rowers try a new drill: I instructed them to place a 2.5 pound weight on their heads and then row using the regular handle-flywheel apparatus. Right away they saw that the slightest slam into the catch caused the weight to fall to the floor.

Some of the rowers could not manage even one stroke without the weight tumbling off. Not surprisingly, the better rowers spun the erg as speedily with the weight on their heads as without it.

Ergometers - I hate them. They don't factor in body control, balance. Zero penalty points are deducted if you slam into the catch like a madman. If you were to make that same slam-catch in a single scull or straight pair, the boat would stop dead in its tracks. Clement is a good example. He's our best athlete by lengths, and yet in a single scull even Gordo has his number. Perhaps I would feel differently about riding the iron maiden had I reached even a modest level of success. By any measure, however, I was sub-par on the ergometer and not even a ten-year massaging of my memory can alter the facts.

After practice I visited Queen Wendy to discus the UCSB rowing world. I had barely taken my seat in her little cubicle when she asked, "Are you familiar with the facts of life?" Before I could answer, she continued, "If your rowers don't pay their dues, your program will cease to exist."

"Oh, those facts of life."

"Because the dues haven't been paid, you're deep in the red."

Ouch. One more gray hair. Could this be the omen?

"Also the crew newsletter is now several months overdue."

Damn that newsletter. When my turn came, I mentioned to her that I needed money for bow and stern lights for the eights since we were now rowing in the pitch black.

She countered by pointing out that Gaucho rowing had survived for years without bow and stern lights.

"Think of it like this," I said. "NASA launched the space shuttle a few dozen times without a problem. Then Challenger exploded. Turned out, the other launchings had just been lucky - they all could have blown up. In relation to our little world, I don't want to survive just by being lucky. We should be prepared."

Queen Wendy nodded her head and said, "If you want lights, collect the dues."

After my meeting, I stopped by Marvac Electronics in Goleta. My old megaphone, a standard 1880s dunce cap model, was starting to unravel and my lungs weren't faring much better. The time had arrived to buy a power megaphone. I tried every model in the store, looking for the right blend of power and price. I soon concluded that nothing is more fun than testing megaphones inside an electronics store - people jump out of their boots when you turn up the volume. One Fanon-brand megaphone, the display model, was half-priced. The plastic had faded from baking in the window for innumerable months - now it was as white as a bleached skeleton - but it still worked well. Big range. Eight C batteries. The Riot Stopper by Fanon. I had to buy it. My crew won't know what hit them. Hell, I can chat with Michael Jackson at his Neverland Ranch from my coaching launch.

I now have all the necessary coaching toys. Stroke watch, megaphone, wool cap, Hobie sunglasses, heavy parka. Since our coxswains all had Cox-Boxes, I rarely used my own stroke watch, a pre-digital model that needed four catches to calculate the stroke. I wore it nonetheless, more as a fashion statement than for any real function.

The Riot Stopper
Thursday, January 6

Before we began our practice, I told my rowers a brief story. Back when I was training, quite a few of my fellow scullers fell by the wayside because they couldn't crack the monetary nut. Many of these guys were superior to me in terms of their athletic ability. Nonetheless, money did them in. Adios. They became firemen or real estate agents or itinerant bums. You simply cannot ignore the financial side of campaigning a single scull.

Along the same lines, you cannot ignore the costs of being a UCSB rower: $120 in the fall, $80 in the winter, plus another $300 worth of erg-a-thon money in the spring. If you can't find any erg-a-thon donors, you must pay it yourself. At this point, I unveiled my new Riot Stopper megaphone. I took great pains to show them the price tag on the side of the box, which did not reflect the 50% discount. I told them I didn't actually want this megaphone but as the coach I had an obligation to buy the damn thing. Essentially this was how I paid my dues.

"So now it's your turn," I said. "Pay up!"

I would rather battle a herd of rabid mountain lions with both arms tied behind my back than demand money from my rowers. After I got the dues-blues out of my system, we ran a series of seven minute pieces, from the cliff around the Goleta pier and back to the cliff. Good, hard effort by everyone, one of those welcome workouts where you feel more energized at the finish than when you began. We ran one more piece, just to "Beat Cal!" Won't be long now. Only a few weeks until our first race and only three-and-a-half months to the PCRCs.

As I walked from my car to the boathouse, I knew immediately something was wrong. I searched my jacket, my jeans, my brain. Where were my boathouse keys? I'd left them at home, next to the coffee maker. I kicked at the door in frustration, which made me feel better but got me no closer to getting in. Checks finally arrived, unlocked the door and we got underway.

The bulk of our practice was reserved for drills and technique, lots of eyes closed, (the rowers not the coach), trying to instill a sense of swing into the effort. The last part was reserved for our usual end-of-week finale, a 5000 meter race.

Early in the practice I engaged in a classic bit of coaching. I couldn't figure out why my new megaphone was acting up. Batteries weak? Not likely. But the damn thing just didn't have the range it did a few days ago. Did I drop it? Get it wet? Andrew finally yelled over, "Take the foam out of the front." I turned it around. Sure enough, a thick piece of Styrofoam packing material was wedged in the bell. So that's why I wasn't getting any volume.

Back on the dock, Michael Kolbe called to order an impromptu team meeting. "Race season is almost here," Kolbe said. "The time has arrived to start cutting down on late nights, excessive drinking, crazy partying."

"That's easy for you to say," Churchill said. "You don't do that stuff anyway."

"Wrong," Kolbe said, as offended as if someone had insulted his mother. "I am this team's Chug King and you know it." Kolbe was reputed to have a cast iron stomach, and not just involving alcohol, either. Supposedly he once drank the unfiltered contents of a Shell gas station window washing tub. Ouch.

When I left they were still on the dock, sorting out the do's and don'ts of proper Gaucho life - yes to novice women, no to heroin. I drove to Malibu, where I met a friend for an early lunch. We ate at Patrick's Roadhouse, on Pacific Coast Highway. The new mayor of Los Angeles was in attendance - not at our booth, but a few seats away. Afterward we walked to the beach and watched Wilt Chamberlain play volleyball. Who needs a map to celebrity homes? They're everywhere in Los Angeles.

As we dug our toes into the sand, I noticed a huge guy wearing a USA Olympic rowing shirt cruising toward us on rollerblades. I introduced myself and we talked for a few minutes. Robert Shepherd, five-seat in the 1992 Barcelona eight-oared shell. Pretty cool guy.

Whether you're walking down a dangerous back alley in Cali, Columbia or window shopping down the Champs Elysée - you see a person wearing a rowing shirt and suddenly you have an instant friend, or at least common ground on which to strike up a friendship. Pretty cool, the brotherhood of rowing, and much underrated. Long after the shirts you've won have been eaten by moths and all the shiny medals covered in rust, the brotherhood lives.

In the evening I went to another show on campus, a lecture by mountain climber Greg Child. He told a wild story of having spent a night at 26,400 feet, by himself. His mountaineering party had been trying for a month to reach the top of a hairy Himalayan peak. With the summit only a day's hike away - but out of food and with bad weather on the horizon - his companions gave up and went back to base camp. Only Greg stayed behind, huddled in a snow cave, sleeping fitfully, wondering if he'd survive until morning, thinking about how incredibly difficult we make our lives. From his description, I couldn't help but feel that he was recounting an all-night test of his X Factor. The next day Greg Child climbed the peak and then returned safely to base camp.

Certainly a computer generated analysis of the situation would have arrived at the conclusion reached by the other climbers - go home, get warm, be safe. At great risk Greg went his own way. Jung said it so perfectly:

> Each man is his own savior. The fact that many a man who goes his own way ends in ruin means nothing. He must obey

his own law as if it were a demon, whispering to him of new and wonderful paths.

IMAGES
Monday, January 10

Pitch black images on this early Monday, a slight breeze rocks my van as I enter the park, glancing up and seeing stars by the billion, peering straight ahead and seeing the varsity women jog toward my van, their gray, ghostly shapes vaguely illuminated by my headlights, walking toward the boathouse, the generator running but no one around, getting my launch in order, seeing Fred Checks trying to change the spark plugs on his Suzuki outboard by flashlight, using an adjustable end wrench, while at the same time his crew rows into the void, laughter in the distance as my rowers arrive, the Port-o-Let door slamming shut over and over, an unnerving sound that is both sharp and dull at the same time.

We ran ten warm-up laps next to the boathouse and then launched our flotilla of small boats for a double-Arrowhead Island row.

Besides Adam the coxswain, a photographer from the school newspaper rode in my launch. For some reason, a man with a camera infuses a special significance into the workout. Everyone sat up straighter, put a little extra bend in the oar, took uncommon care with catch timing. Maybe I could get the photographer to come out every day. I told him to take lots of pictures of Johnny Bender, who was rowing with Moose in a straight pair.

Watching Bender row was like watching a wounded bird try to fly. For the last three months I've been telling Bender not to drop his hands toward the finish. In the straight pair, at the finish of each stroke, the boat fell heavily down to his side as Bender dropped his hands. Bingo.

127

Problem identified. Figuring out the problem, however, is quite different from fixing it. You need relentless determination to make lasting changes. This morning I simply sat back and sipped my coffee as the straight pair did all the coaching.

Make the right faces and you can hide in an eight-oared shell, but you're naked and exposed in a straight pair. Bender, a sturdy heavyweight, didn't care much for losing to several lightweight combinations. As Bender cursed me under his breath, I offered up these philosophic words: "If any shithead could do it, there'd be no challenge."

About halfway through the morning I realized that one of the better lightweights, Rupert Foster, was not at practice. Quiet guy. Steady. Exactly the sort of rower you need to hold things together. I wondered where he was? Sick, injured, or did he simply not get back in time from the Toad the Wet Sprocket concert?

The highlight of the morning came on the second piece. We were following the boats around Arrowhead Island, keeping a little distance so they could tussle among themselves. Adam was telling me about past years when the water level at Cachuma was so low they had to carry their boats half a mile - each way - to reach the water. For seven long years, ending in early '93, this area endured a terrible drought. At the height of the drought, when every reservoir was nearly bone dry, a plan was conceived to build a massive de-salination plant, similar to the plants used in Saudi Arabia. At a cost of millions, the plant was built. The timing, however, could not have been worse. A party to celebrate the completion of the de-salination plant had to be canceled on account of rain, lots of it, enough to fill the reservoirs.

When we reached the backside of the island, Adam said, "You're a little close to shore, aren't you?"

"I've scouted this area pretty thoroughly," I said. "I'm certain no rocks are below the surface."

As the last word left my mouth, our propeller struck a rock and we careened heavily over to port. Fortunately, the prop didn't snap off. Adam and I laughed like crazy. The timing could not have been better.

This afternoon at weights, as I was attempting to impart one of my life lessons, I found myself battling a difficult foe: the Gaucho near-graduate ex-rowers. These near-grads had rowed at UCSB in the not too distant past and were now trying to earn a university diploma to complement their modest collection of rowing shirts. As a concession to Gaucho history, I'd been letting them lift during my private time, and once or twice I'd let them take out a straight pair or four-with. Today their jabbering distracted me to the point where I shouted, "Shut up or leave!"

One quieted right down and the others left, so I guess they got the message. My toughest critics were these near-grads, about six men altogether. They'd show up at regattas, drinking beer at 9:30 A.M., heckling the other crews, never hesitating to point out how well the Gauchos had done in previous years. I thought of them collectively as the "Yeahbuts."

"Yeahbut, we won the Crew Classic two years ago," they'd remind me. "Yeahbut, the old coach would let us take out any boat we wanted. Yeahbut, I don't see why we should fix the boat. I didn't see that tree floating in the lake."

SUBTRACT KOLBE
Tuesday, January 11

For fun, I rowed a single scull, three Arrowhead Island loops. Adam followed behind in my launch, in case someone tipped over. Fortunately the water was a little bouncy, so my better technique allowed me to stay ahead. No matter how out-of-shape I might be, I didn't want to finish behind any of the rowers. Bad for the coach's image.

I found out today that the Gaucho men's basketball coach makes $125,124 a year. I knew he was well paid, the third highest employee on campus, but I had no idea he was making so much. I suppose it's the prestige that makes him so worthy. Gaucho football disappeared a few years ago, making basketball the king of UCSB inter-collegiate sports. Great insight was shown by getting rid of football. All those wrecked knees and torn rotator cuffs, you'd think small college football was sponsored by the Orthopedic Surgeons of America.

The basketball coach is a funny guy. I see him on campus fairly often. He's always rushing around, meeting with recruits, talking on his cellular phone, hurrying from one place to another. Yet for all he's paid and all his rushing, the team is awful and it keeps getting worse. Each week I read in the school paper that another top player has quit. Maybe I could interest those ex-basketballers in rowing.

When the basketball coach is fired at the end of the season, I might put in for his job. Amazingly simply: no driving to the boathouse. No worrying about howling winds or bass boats or Hanta virus. Every man on the team has been playing basketball since before he could talk. Compared with coaching crew, it'd be a breeze, and he gets a free parking pass.

My second favorite rower, Michael Kolbe, called me at home this afternoon to say that he was going to need a few days off.

"I went back to my high school over the Christmas break," he said, "and wrestled a little, just for fun. During one of these matches I pulled some intercostal muscles. Nothing serious, I hope."

A week's rest and he'll be okay. Or he might be out for the rest of the season. Being ill is one thing - you'll probably get over a cold or the flu. Being injured is far worse. That nagging little pain in your ribs might never go away.

As Kolbe described the incident, I found myself biting my tongue to keep from saying, "What the hell were you doing wrestling? You're a rower." But I'd already said several times that our rowing team exists under the umbrella of real life. Does wrestling come under that umbrella? Unless I'd specified otherwise, it probably did.

I am as fond of cross-training as the next coach, but not wrestling (Greco-Roman, freestyle, mud), boxing or full-contact karate. Alpine skiing is another bad idea and so is bike racing. In 1981, Scott Roop won the World Rowing Championships in the lightweight single scull. While training the next year, he fell during a bike race and separated his shoulder. The subsequent loss of training cost him about 1% of his speed, enough to drop him from first to third place at the '82 Worlds.

Life, in general, is much harder but much more simple when going for the highest prize. While he was writing Madame Bovary, Gustave Flaubert wrote to a distant girlfriend, saying: "I am leading an austere life, stripped of all external pleasure, and am sustained only by a kind of permanent frenzy, which sometimes makes me weep tears of impotence but never abates."

Clearly he makes no mention of extreme skiing, street luge or snake handling. One must lead an austere life to reach the pinnacle of success. I suppose that's one reason so few people reach the top. It can be an exceedingly dull pilgrimage.

TONYA HARDING, KNEE WHACKER
Wednesday, January 12

We rowed a few hard pieces on the ergs and then played card tricks. My life's goal is to teach Clement to make a catch without his lunging forward as though he's climbing into the coxswain's lap. I considered hammering some 16 penny nails through one end of a 2X4. Adam would hold the board at Clement's eye level, at exactly the place where his head should stop when making a proper catch. Decided against it. Instead, I held a playing card at the catch-end of the stroke.

"Okay, Clement," I said, "roll forward, slowly, take your time, now grasp the card." In slow motion Clement tried to punch me in the nose with his outstretched hand. I instructed Adam to hold Clement's shoulders in place.

"Once more, Clement," I said, "here we go, roll forward, slowly." With Adam restraining Clement's shoulders so that he couldn't lunge, Clement neatly took the card from my hand.

"Perfect," I said. "Exactly right."

We repeated the drill fifty times with Adam still holding Clement. The catch is funny. Unlike some parts of the stroke, trying harder at the catch does not make the boat go faster. Instead, more effort only serves to brake the boat.

"If you're keen on trying harder," I told Clement, "do it at the finish where you can reef on the oar with complete abandon and have it improve your boat speed."

I told Adam to step back and watch. This time Clement rolled forward and neatly took the card from my hand. Success. Not a solitary wasted motion. Victory. Let's call it a day, a season. Let's get out of here.

To celebrate a catch well made I bought both Clement and Adam breakfast burritos at Freebirds. As we ate, we talked about a controversy that's on everyone's mind, the Tonya Harding, knee-whacking saga. Apparently figure skater Tonya tried to disable her main competitor, Nancy Kerrigan, by having an associate strike Nancy with a steel baton.

Once again real life has proven to be stranger than fiction. Tonya puts an interesting twist on the poor-girl-makes-good cliché. In her case, poor girl shows herself to be a complete loser. In a popular book, The Ultimate Athlete, the author suggests that when the rewards in a sport become high enough, some people will inevitably cheat. They simply do not have the character of a true champion.

"Yeah, Tonya's a sick puppy," Clement said, "but I find her sexy in a trailer-park-trash sort of way. I wouldn't mind sharpening her skates."

Clement, I'd come to know, could find any female on the planet sort-of-sexy. Hormones to the max. As unbelievable as it might seem, he once had to stop rowing on the ergs in mid-piece because he was becoming aroused.

"She's just your type," Adam said, "like Rosanne, Cher, Madonna, Lassie."

I was awake anyway, 4:30 A.M., debating whether to get an early jump on the morning or go back to sleep. At that moment, an hour of doze seemed far more appealing than seeing another dawn-rise.

At 4:31, I heard someone tapping on my window. This seemed a bit strange, considering that I lived on the second floor. No mistaking that noise, though. Then I realized that the sound came from the venetian blinds on the inside of my apartment, striking the window glass. Tick, tick, tick, like the opening for 60 Minutes. What the hell? A tingle shot up my spine as the word formed in my brain: Earthquake!

The floor began shifting back and forth, one corner up, the other corner down, rock and roll. A potted plant crashed off the top of the refrigerator. Pictures fell off the wall. My whole apartment flexed and creaked like an accordion.

Sure enough, a meaty little tremblor, 6.7 on the Richter scale, was in the process of scaring the doodle out of eleven million people and their relatives. An earthquake this size tends to last quite a while, a half-minute or more, which gives you plenty of time to regret not having bought batteries for the portable radio. You have time to wonder if this is the dreaded big one, 8.8 range or more. Everyone in California, rich or poor, famous or infamous, is just one good earthquake away from being homeless.

Immediately I did the only sane thing: clicked on the television. The news teams were just getting up to speed when the power went out. That's when I dressed and prepared to leave, just in case this tremblor was a warm-up pitch for a fastball earthquake, the kind that squishes whole blocks like dominoes.

Surprisingly, no one was around when I went outside. As I stood in the parking lot, turning a slow, steady circle, I saw that the power outage extended as far as I could see, extinguishing street lights and all other sources of artificial illumination. For the first time in decades, the potent country darkness of Lake Cachuma was paying a visit to the big city. Looking up at the sky, I saw eleven trillion stars. So beautiful. The quiet was broken by the sound of police sirens in the distance and through several windows I saw my neighbors lighting candles. I didn't smell gas leaking - otherwise we would have had a giant crater instead of an apartment building.

I sat in my van and listened to the frightened Radio 1070 All News newscasters beginning an account of the damage: National Guard called out, gas lines ruptured and lit and boom, apartment building collapsed in Northridge, parking structure collapsed in Burbank, freeway overpass collapsed in Simi Valley, which sadly killed a policeman on his motor-cycle. He must have been scared beyond belief as he took that last, long arcing flight through the air.

Many damaged roads. Highway 154, according to the radio, had some fallen boulders. I went back to my apartment and tried the phone. Yes, it was still working.

"Moose," I said, "You alive?"

"Barely," he said. "My fish tank took a tumble. I've got fish flopping all over the place. Looks like sushi bar in here."

"Do me a favor, will you? As soon as you get the fish under control, call your heavies and tell them to meet at the erg room. Driving to the lake's too risky."

"No problem," he said.

I called Clement and told him the same thing. Then I drove to the base of Highway 154 and stood for a while, hoping to flag down any rowers who might not have gotten the word. None passed me, although the light was insufficient to be certain.

We had a decent workout on the ergs, six times five minutes, all at high ratings, full-tilt, kick ass effort. Not surprisingly, only a handful of rowers showed up, and those who did were distracted by the events of the day. Every rower on the team had relatives in other parts of southern California, and many had not been able to get through on the gridlocked phone lines. The only news we had came over the radio, which said that somewhere to the south a firestorm was raging.

Later in the day, I went on a run through the deserted streets of I-V. No dueling stereos, nothing. We need more quakes, just to keep the noise level in check.

On a different morning, as I was running through Isla Vista, I stopped to watch an interesting exchange on the front porch of an apartment building. A student was rhythmically revving his Ninja 1000 CC motorcycle. The noise, at full RPM, was beyond deafening. His neighbor, another student, was shouting at him to quit causing such a racket. The guy with the Ninja shouted back: "No!" He'd rev it anywhere, anytime he pleased. This little story is an parable for the way world wars get started. As I jogged off, the two men were starting to slap-fight each other.

The novice men rowed at Lake Cachuma on this earthquake morning. As it turned out, the boulders on Highway 154 were not a problem, the Bradbury Dam didn't burst and the water was beautiful.

First we had forest fires, then violent rain storms and now a 6.7 earthquake. I think we've pretty well exhausted the natural disasters, and it's too soon for another riot, aka Free TV Day. We should be okay until the end of the school year.

Since classes were canceled, I thought a little diversion might be in order. At 3:30 in the afternoon the whole crew met at the sand volleyball courts next to Storke Field and chose up teams. Of all sports, I figured sand volleyball was the least likely to cause injury. Wrong. Within fifteen minutes, both Moose and Philip Shapiro had hurt themselves diving for balls.

But the game did give me with an opportunity to offer a life lesson. Each time Adam served the ball, he smacked it into the net. Then he'd promptly say: "I'm lousy at volleyball."

During a break between games I told Adam and the other rowers, "Watch your language, guys. By saying, 'I'm lousy at volleyball,' Adam is creating a negative self-label. If he repeats that label often enough, he'll think it's true, both on a conscious and subconscious level. The self-fulfilling power of these labels is remarkably potent."

"But he is lousy at volleyball," Clement said.

"Relative to Karch Kiraly we're all pretty lousy," I said. "The point is - you'll never reach your fullest capability if you keep telling yourself that you're lousy."

"You're supposed to lie to yourself?" he asked.

"No, you don't need to lie," I said. "Nor do you have to paint a happy face on every event, good, bad or otherwise. Simply call it like it is: 'I made a lousy serve.' Let it go at that. I've seen this self-labeling phenomenon quite often in rowing. A man will finish fourth in a single scull race and promptly say, 'I'm a loser.' At this point he might as well sell his boat because once he's saddled with the loser-label, he will never triumph. All he had to say is 'I finished fourth.' That's the whole story. For that matter, champions say nothing at all."

Cruel and misguided parents are renowned for labeling their kids as losers, which creates assorted neuroses the children will battle until the day they die. Coaches have the same power. Who can ever forget Kris "You-Row-Like-Shit" Korzenowski? He was a nega-labeling nightmare for those rowers who did not have the knowledge or strength to fight off his destructive spell. Whether self-imposed or brought on by others, anyone victimized by loser-labels should seek professional therapy. The debilitating effects are not to be underestimated.

On my way home from campus, I stopped for a moment and looked over the ocean. A mile offshore, a patch of sunlight cut through the heavy hanging clouds, creating a circle of gold-plated water. In the shore break below me, in the aftermath of the earthquake, waves still rolled in and surfers still surfed.

Back home, images of massive destruction pre-empted every program on TV. The local news showed that Santa Barbara - county, city and campus - had been extremely lucky. We were only sixty miles from the quake's epicenter, yet we'd escaped any serious damage. Most of the harm was done to people's sanity. Nerves on edge, to say the least. A week or two would be needed to quell the queasy feeling in the pit of our stomachs.

Spin
Tuesday, January 18

We tried an interesting workout on the ergs. First piece, six minutes, 20 spm, at a modest effort of two minutes for each 500 meter split. Second piece, six minutes, 30 spm, same exact effort. Third piece, six minutes, 36 spm, same effort.

I wanted my rowers to sense the quickness necessary to hold a high rating. Quickness, of all aspects of the stroke, is underrated. Some of the men tried to solve the stroke-per-minute challenge by applying more force. But then their split times dropped below the prescribed two minutes per 500 meters. No good. For this workout, I wanted them to solve the stroke challenge by adding more quickness, particularly quick-hands-away at the finish.

As our practice was winding down, I offered a supplement to yesterday's life lesson on labeling.

"Along the same lines," I told the team, "whenever possible you should spin your comments in a positive direction. When I sailed in the America's Cup - in the middle of a brutal tacking duel - one of the veteran crewman inevitably shouted, 'Don't fuck up this tack.' In the commotion, noise, howling wind, with adrenaline flowing, our subconscious might hear only a portion of the message, in this case, '…Fuck up this tack.' Like it or not, our subconscious tends to obey what it's told. Finally I told this crewman to say, 'Let's make this a great tack.' Essentially it's the same message, but spun in a positive way."

To the coxswains I made a special plea: "Whenever you give a command, try to use positive spin. Rather than saying, 'Don't fuck up this start,' say, 'Make this our best start.' When you consider the thousands of orders you'll give through the course of the season, the way you phrase your commands can make a huge difference." They promised to at least think about what I'd said.

To a large extent, the way we phrase our daily lives is a function of habit, and habits are hard to break. Lately I'd been trying to change some of my own habits. When I began coaching at Santa Barbara, I used the traditional strategy known as "error detection and correction." A few weeks ago, at the Amateur Athletic Foundation library in L.A., I came across some literature on new coaching techniques. One method I found appealing was called "strength enhancement." For example, I'd say to Kolbe, "your catch is excellent, fast and sure. You've got it wired. Now press with your legs a little quicker to take advantage of that great catch." The key is to build on the existing strengths of the athletes rather than merely criticize their flaws. I like it. Now, if I can only break my old habits.

CRUNCH TIME
Saturday, January 22

We boated one eight and two quads this morning, for three times twenty minutes. First piece easy, second piece full power at 20-22 spm, third piece full power at any stroke rating.

Moose Morse re-injured his back on second piece and I took his place in the quad. Poor guy. Sculling, more than sweep rowing, seems to aggravate his problem. In rowing, your body is like an archway made of stone. The keystone is your lower back. Should it fail, all crashes down.

The women and novice men launched their boats after we had returned to the boathouse. I prefer to row early, especially on weekends. Get in and out as fast as possible, even though the water is actually better in the late morning, once the wind vectors have simmered down.

Today, for the first time, the varsity women rowed their brand new boat. They were so excited, carefully carrying it down the dock, patiently lowering the shiny hull into the crystalline waters of Cachuma, cautiously setting the oars into place. Yes, the first row of a new boat is a special occasion.

As I mentioned earlier, the rangers had recently deposited a sizable number of buoys around the lake. These buoys sat low in the water. At the same time, a coxswain's range of vision was limited by the eight rowers sitting directly ahead. Countless times, I'd said to Adam, "Do you have that buoy?" Usually he nodded his head yes. One time in twenty, he'd abruptly crank the steering cables to avoid a collision.

Toward the end of their workout, the women were chugging along at three-quarter power, not a care in the world, loving life. Suddenly, BAM, they slammed to a stop. Their brand new boat had marched dead-on into a brand new buoy. Crunch time. For the next hour, their moans and anguished weeping were like something out of a horror movie. The poor varsity women's coxswain had to take refuge in her car and lock the doors or else be lynched by the mob.

I inspected the damage - obviously minor. I inquired if anyone was injured - no, everyone was fine. I shrugged my shoulders. I opened my hands, making the universal sign for bummer.

"Well," I said finally, "it could be worse." Then, involuntarily, I smiled.

Upon seeing my smile, the women's varsity coach, Terri Larson, entered into a state of sheer convulsive hysterics. "How dare you laugh at our misfortune" was the essence of what she was trying to say, minus the cursing, screaming, arm waving, foot stomping. You had to give Terri credit, she had plenty of energy. I followed the coxswain's lead and retreated to my car.

I hadn't spoken to Terri much since arriving in Santa Barbara. We tried to keep our teams on opposite schedules, to take fullest advantage of our meager erg equipment. Once, after seeing her pour gasoline into the generator as it was running, I suggested that she turn it off first, or else we'd be naming our humble shed the Terri Larson Memorial Boat-house. My suggestion, for some reason, seemed to offend her. Perhaps Terri would have done well to switch to decaffeinated coffee. When I mentioned to Clement about Terri's short fuse and on-going distress, he nodded his head as though familiar with the subject. "Let her suffer," he said. "It makes her happy."

As I drove home I thought about how everyone acts about the same when things are rolling along well. The human animal becomes quite interesting when a monkey wrench is thrown into the works, or a buoy pops out of nowhere, or you're suddenly presented with some crisis that jars your sense of normalcy. That's when a person's character is tested. You get a peek into their soul. Quite revealing. Sometimes scary, as in this case. Other times refreshingly reassuring.

CONN, THE LEGEND
Tuesday, January 25

This week marks the half-way point of the season. Half of our work-outs are behind us, most of our races are ahead. We have several dual meets coming up in the next few weeks, against Stanford, Orange Coast College, Cal Poly SLO. Our two biggest events, the San Diego Crew Classic and the PCRCs, are months away, in early April and mid-May.

I still have plenty of time to teach them everything-rowing, but will I have enough students? At the final practice leading into the Christmas break, I had made a point of congratulating my rowers for having persisted through the darkening dawns. At that point only one rower had quit the team, a troubled young man with a brief history of suicide attempts. I had wanted him to continue - to use rowing as a refuge against the world. He tried for a while but the medication he was taking made him sleep twelve hours a night.

Over the interminable Christmas break we lost several more men. The combination of cold weather, lousy grades and a new-different coach discouraged the marginal rowers, so that now we're down to nine lites and nine heavies, which includes two novice heavies, Tommy Thompson and Bob Lowe, whom I liberated from Fred Checks. Actually, Fred didn't know what to do with them because his other novices were all lightweights. Tommy Thompson is an exceptional young man, one of those rare, gifted athletes who can quickly master any sport. He saved a fellow rower the day the novices swamped. The other novice, Gentle Bob, is a good runner but not as coordinated as Tommy.

We also lost one coxswain, Eileen. Or was it Elaine? I hated to see her go. Eileen and Elaine had seemed more like identical twins with each passing week. Now, with Eileen gone, at least I'll no longer struggle to differentiate between the two.

Due to early morning classes, illness, pulled muscles, annoyed girl-friends, not everyone shows up each morning. I do my best to juggle the boatings depending on who appears, but I'm not good at it. A few days ago Johnny Bender became enraged when I was unable to recall which side he rowed, port or starboard. I told Johnny that he was so talented he could row either side. Unfortunately he wasn't in a buying mood.

As we launched our eights this morning, a little drama took place overhead: a crow was harassing an osprey, dive bombing, squawking, gen-erally making the osprey's life miserable. Whenever possible, the osprey tried to poke its talons into the crow's beady black eyes. I told my rowers that this was an allegory for lightweights harassing heavyweights. The osprey is more powerful, the crow more agile. They will continue to do battle for eternity. George Orwell said it all, "A state needs an enemy. If it doesn't already have one, it will invent an enemy." Within our Gaucho rowing state, we had an ongoing battle, heavies versus lites, which was annoying at times but also created a degree of warfare motivation. On occasion I found myself fanning the flames of this animosity with a few well-chosen words, 'Hey heavies, the lightweights are laughing at you.' This would make the heavyweights rage and tear at the water until their anger was spent. If only they could rage for six and a half minutes - then we'd have something special.

We worked on body swing this morning, with lots of flat slide, swinging from the hips, trying to hold onto the water until the bitter end of the stroke. During a break between pieces I read to the rowers a recent article from the L.A. Times:

Several male weight lifters in former East Germany developed large breasts after taking steroids and had to have them reduced surgically, Stern magazine reported. Some female athletes grew beards and left athletics after having to shave.

"This is related to the Tonya Harding incident," I said. "Winning at all costs is wrong, plain and simple. Certain basic, universal rules exist, and to be a true champion you must live by these rules. The consequences of doing otherwise might take a physical toll - a 34C cup size - or it might take a soul killing psychological toll. Both consequences are devastating."

As usual, when I made my pronouncements, the rowers listened with one ear and glanced at me with one eye. Any left-over sensory organs were employed in whispering to each other or staring into the limpid waters of Lake Cachuma or tearing away a piece of dead skin from a busted blister. If nothing else, since taking on the coaching mantel I'd learned to keep my epistles clear, concise and to the point.

After I finished my squawk I looked at Robert Churchill, our in-house comedian, and nodded my head. As per our agreement, this was Churchill's cue that he was now permitted to speak. For the hundredth time, he did not disappoint us, shouting at the top of his lungs: "Why didn't they just get endorsements from Wonder Bra and Schick razor?"

Around noon a well-worn Ford Galaxie rolled into the parking area. At first I thought another fisherman had come to use our dock. As the lean, 6'7" man unfolded from the driver's seat, I knew this was no ordinary fisherman. Conn Findlay, a true rowing legend, gold medalist in the pair with coxswain, had come to Lake Cachuma. Conn waved hello, grabbed a bucket of tools out of his Galaxie's trunk and headed into the boathouse.

Conn had been invited to Cachuma for a specific repair job, to fix the women's brand new eight. Since the accident, Coach Terri had been convinced that the boat was ruined, the impact into the buoy permanently twisting the bow like a spiral corkscrew. Whenever she made these claims I nodded my head up and down, kept my hands clasped tightly behind my back and a dour look on my face. To myself I would think, Terri, you've flipped out.

As I knew would happen, Conn took one look at the damage and pronounced it as ultra-minor. Using a piece of cardboard as a palate, he mixed-up a few ounces of Bondo and began smoothing over the wound.

Having Conn visit our boathouse, regardless of the reason, was a welcome event. In 1974, he had come to UC Irvine to repair a boat that the Irvine crew was renting from him. I remember it clearly because he had lifted the heavy Pocock four-with, full-rigged, off the racks and into the slings by himself. I found it reassuring that twenty years later, little had changed. As always, Conn was doing what he chose to do, repairing a boat, making it whole, in general living a free-spirited, unencumbered life that suited him to perfection.

As he worked, I spoke to Conn about my coaching experiences thus far at Santa Barbara. I told him that I was worried that my rowers didn't seem to be getting much out of it. Conn, who had once coached at Stanford University, told me about one of his rowers who had returned for a ten-year reunion. The man said he remembered with great fondness the long car trips to regattas, and the friendships and camaraderie the trips created.

"Don't be discouraged," Conn said. "Everyone gets something different out of the sport. Your rowers may be getting things you can't even imagine."

DAN JANSEN, THE SPEED SKATER
Monday, February 14

I was so sleepy that I sat in my car for several minutes, eyes closed, trying to marshal my energy for another day of coaching. I blame my fatigue on the Olympics. I stayed up late last night and watched the '92 Winter Olympics for hours on end.

When it comes to the Winter Olympics, the particular event doesn't much matter. Luge, ski jumping, biathlon, bobsled - I inevitably find myself watching them all with an intensity normally reserved for Die Hard and Traci Lords movies.

The Olympics presents a wonderful how-to on being a champion. Downhill skier Frans Klammer careened down the slopes at the 1976 Olympics, pushing himself to the extreme edge of his ability. In 1992, Picabo Street managed the same exact miracle. With each Olympics comes a new batch of stories, essentially a blueprint for all aspiring athletes, along with several cautionary tales thrown in.

Speed skater Dan Jansen showed how hard it is to perform in front of 80 million people, how difficult it is to be the reigning world record holder, how much pressure is added by having had two chances and not delivered. Nerves. Slight tightening of the jaw and neck muscles. Often followed by an over-production of adrenaline, which then jars the carefully balanced equilibrium of your psyche and physique. Then you lose again and it appears as though you're destined to be known as the best speed skater never to have won an Olympic gold medal. How would that look on your business card?

For a solid hour the pairs ice dancing held my attention, in particular the Soviet pair, gold medalists in '88. About half-way through the program, the Soviet man caught the tip of his blade in his pant leg. He then showed remarkable poise by recovering his balance and going on to finish the program without another flaw. The television commentator mentioned that the Soviet coaches require their skaters to perform the whole routine a thousand times before it is considered competition proof. This morning, before I called out the boatings, I described the event to my rowers along with an accompanying rowing lesson.

"Don't let a bad stroke distract you from the next," I told them. "Nearly every race has at least one bad stroke in it. Champions manage to win regardless. Further, we need a thousand races before we are regatta proof. That's why we compete against each other on a daily basis, on the water, on the ergs, when running, even while lifting weights."

I commenced a new project after practice: rolling slings. From the first day, I've seen the need for two pair of rolling slings, so that an injured boat could be rolled around the boathouse rather than being stuck in one place like an anchor. The scissors-style slings, which we have by the dozen, are fine for regattas but poorly suited for inside the boathouse.

The design for my rolling slings came from inside my head, a conglomeration of a hundred different models I'd seen over the years. Using scrap lumber, including the '84 Olympic map, I slowly pieced together a prototype.

STEVE SCOTT, THE RUNNER
Tuesday, February 15

As we ran to the beach, I had the team stop at the bluff overlooking the ocean and take a long moment to watch the dawn coming up, the brilliant colors, red and alive.

"I'd rather see it from my bedroom window," Churchill said.

"Not the same," I told him. "Not the same."

At some point during each workout, I make a point of stopping the whole team and having them take a deep breath. I tell them to appreciate their good fortune at being able to embrace the day with strong, healthy arms, to see it with good, sharp eyes. Allowing these days to slip past without acknowledging them, without appreciating our fortunate place in the universal spectrum, is to miss the essence of life.

We ran the cliff-Goleta Pier-cliff loop, five times. Between pieces, I told them about Steve Scott, an amazing middle-distance runner who was a friend of mine. In training and in racing, his work ethic was beyond reproach. Eventually he set a national record in the mile that still stands, 3:47.

"Steve had a characteristic that all champions possess," I said, "sustained obsession."

"That seems counter to what you've been saying about maintaining priorities," Johnny Bender said.

"Yeah," I said, after thinking a moment, "I suppose you're right. I should have explained that for the most part, Steve became obsessed after he graduated. We lifted together in the weight room at UCI, and that's when I saw his obsession at work. Keep in mind, too, that each sport is different. If you were doing women's gymnastics, your Olympic life would already be over. If you were a yachtsman, you'd hardly have begun. Every blue moon a rower comes along who can compete at the Olympics while still in college. Pretty rare. The rest of us mere mortals must take a slower road."

Back home, I read in today's Los Angeles Times that Steve has cancer. Rather an odd coincidence, since until this morning I hadn't thought about him in years. Eric Hulst, who was also on that great '76 UC Irvine cross-country team along with Steve Scott, died of brain cancer a few months ago.

JOHANN KOSS, THE CHAMPION
Wednesday, February 16

Speed skater Johann Koss of Norway set a world record last night in the 1500 meters as part of the first pairing. Every skater for the rest of the night tried to better his time but to no avail. Koss, I can tell already, is the one athlete from these Games who will use his Olympic fame for something beyond selling Wheaties. He seems like a good guy.

Without a doubt, speed skating is one of the most exciting TV-sports. The splits are clean, the camera angles are excellent, the motions of the skaters are fluid, almost hypnotic.

Dan Jansen once again stumbled around the track during his race. One more chance for Dan. If he doesn't pull it off, he goes straight to post-Olympic hell.

Our main workout this morning was walking our new trailer from the boathouse to the storage yard, about a mile away. In 1977, at the World Championships in Amsterdam, I saw the East German national team walk their fully loaded trailer into the boat bay area. The DDR insignia on the blades was like the royal crest of an all-powerful, black knight. As they walked, the Easties sang their national anthem.

I could not interest my rowers in singing. Afterward, we put two eights on the water for a solid hour of catch drills. Sit at the finish, oar buried, on my command come to the catch and set the blade at full reach. Ready? Hut! Simple drill. The heavies got it - the lites didn't. I had the lightweights come in early due to Robert Churchill's near-homicidal melt down. Give that man a sedative.

After practice I built three more rolling slings, cutting the bottom pieces, the side pieces, the 2X6 uprights. I stacked everything neatly and checked to make sure I hadn't forgotten anything. Then I went on an assembling blitz, using my power drill to drive home the decking screws. Now that the rollers are bolted in place and the canvas straps secured, I realize that my slings have one slight flaw. I designed them so that I could comfortably work on various shells. But when the diminutive novice men, essentially an army of dwarfs, try to take a boat out of the slings, their noses will be about level with the gunnel. Next project: footstools.

A violent thunderstorm rolled into Santa Barbara last night, ten hours of serious rain and kettle-drum thunder. Because of the storm only five lites and three heavies showed up at the erg room. After contemplating my next source of employment, I found myself wondering - what the hell went wrong? Where was everyone? No doubt they were at home, cowering under the covers.

I was beginning to feel like Goldilocks. I had a few super-dedicated guys, so hot to conquer the world that they often out-distanced me. I had some cold bowls of porridge, who only dabbled at training and would have been better off investing their dues in a new VCR. In the middle were the just-right guys, who I felt were properly invested. Taken alone, any of the three groups would have been fine. But when blended together, nothing tasted right.

I am the first to admit that part of it is my fault. From the beginning I simply haven't been strict enough with the rowers. Discipline - I took it for granted. When my college coach said practice was at 6:30 A.M., everyone showed up at 6:20, just to be on time. No questions asked. If you weren't feeling well, you showed up anyway. Sometimes a hard workout was exactly what you needed to make yourself right with the world. I had assumed, incorrectly, that once I announced the starting time everyone would show up, sober, serious and ready to roll. Not quite. Some of the men needed to be threatened, heckled, pestered, reminded again and again. No thanks. Adding to the confusion was our club sports designation. Ms. Pearson had made it clear that if they paid their dues, they were on the team. At the Olympics it's so straightforward. Everyone charges full-speed ahead. Programs such as UCSB - where interest levels varied with the tide - were far more difficult to run.

Five times five minutes on the ergs at increasing rating was our workout. Novice Tommy Thompson turned in some excellent numbers. Otherwise it was a damn dull day at the erg room.

On the way home, to cheer myself, I bought a copy of The New York Times, national edition. As always, buying the newspaper from a box on the street was a gamble. Quite often I'd been forced to stuff my boot into the box's plastic window after it ate my quarters but failed to deliver. This morning, after only a few minor threats, the box relented and I retreated to my cocoon, paper in hand. Over breakfast, I read an article about the New York Knicks and their famous coach, Pat Riley, formerly of the L.A. Lakers.

RILEY SENSES PRESENCE OF CONCENTRATION GAP
It was more of an overall lack of discipline and emotional stability that cost us the game yesterday, Pat Riley said. There was a lack of control, a lack of discipline going down the stretch.

Discipline and self-motivation are elusive at every level, from club sport rowers to multi-millionaire basketball players.

DAN JANSEN, PART II
Friday, February 18

As my van labored up the pass, I heard on the radio that Dan Jansen had set a world record in the men's 5000 meter speed skating. Involuntarily I shouted out, "Right on, Dan!" Yes, I was ecstatic. But immediately I began to worry. Would his time hold up throughout the competition? I'd have to wait to find out.

Absolutely beautiful morning. Golden sunlight on the lake. Snow on mountains. Water smooth as silk. Everyone showed up. My launch started on the third pull. Amazing, and with no "go juice." We rowed five times ten minutes at 20, 24, 28, 32 spm, and rower's choice. The heavies won the first three - lost the last two. Good hard racing. Little victories for coach and crew.

Not until the last rower had departed was I able to turn on the radio and find out the results. Sure enough, Dan Jansen had won the gold. Hooray for Dan. The curse is lifted from his soul. I felt like crying. When I met him in Albertville two years ago, he looked defeated even before he'd been issued his team gear. That's all history. Champion Dan.

ACCIDENT
Saturday, February 19

This morning, a mile after cresting the San Marcos Pass, I saw a car straddling the middle of Suicide Bridge. This bridge spans an immense, deep gorge, and is only two-lanes wide. A car abandoned in the middle is a serious hazard. As I pulled alongside, I noticed that the front end of the car was slightly mangled as though it had struck the bridge and bounced off. I saw a man standing nearby and asked if he was okay. Yes, he was fine. I offered to call the Highway Patrol using my trusty cellular phone. He told me the CHP had already been called. I waved and drove on.

About a half-minute later, I began to worry. Perhaps I should park my van and then try to slow traffic as it approaches the accident. I could imagine a less cautious driver - a young rower, for instance - speeding onto Suicide Bridge and ramming into the obstacle.

I drove on. When I arrived at the lake twenty minutes later, I was shaking, in part because it was extremely cold this morning and also because I was worried about the accident. Unfortunately, my worries were well-founded. When my rowers finally arrived, half an hour late, I asked them, "What the hell took you so long?"

"We had to detour down Stagecoach Road," Clement said.

"Why was that?" I asked, already fairly certain of the answer.

"A car full of novice women crashed on the bridge."

An ambulance had been called. One woman was banged up and lost several teeth. Clement suggested that the accident had been caused by black ice. I doubt it. I had driven the same road only minutes before and had not encountered any ice. Later I learned that the novice woman was cited by the CHP for speeding and not wearing a seat belt.

The accident put a shroud over the whole workout. My launch wouldn't start. The rowers looked awful. My megaphone kept cutting out. My mind was elsewhere. When I drove across Suicide Bridge on the way home, I saw the white chunks of flare residue left over from the accident. I should have stopped. No excuse not to. I'd been around them long enough to know the truth. Yes, according to their chronological age they were certified, voting, draft-registered adults. But I knew better. Regardless of the cause, twenty-odd weeks into the program my worst nightmare had been realized. Inevitable. Driving sixty miles on a twisting mountain road in the dark - do it often enough and you'll have an accident.

TEN THOUSAND MILES
Monday, February 21

This morning as I drove to the lake I made a startling discovery. Just after cresting the pass I saw that the whole inland valley had been magically replaced with an ocean, one that rivaled the great Pacific.

Certainly that's what it looked like from the driver's seat of my van. I pulled into the view point and stared long and hard. No, it wasn't an ocean but rather an endless flat fog cloud. The light from a full moon glistened off the top of the cloud, so even and thick and smooth that I wouldn't have been surprised to see a sailing ship cruising across.

Miles later at Lake Cachuma only a thin fog covered the water, light and translucent, like steam rising from a hot bath. Not too good for rowing although fantastic to see. When the fog lifted, we launched our flotilla of small boats, seven single sculls, a few straight pairs and a four-with. As the scullers worked toward Arrowhead Island, I stood up in my launch and bellowed through my Riot Stopper, "The strokes must be connected as though by an invisible thread."

My words bounced off the canyon walls and then skidded away. I repeated it several times, the strokes must be connected, hoping that each of the men could hear me. Then I sat down and sipped my coffee. Of the seven scullers, five were probably too deaf from excessive Walk-manning to understand what I'd said. I could imagine them thinking, "The chokes must be rejected as though by a squishable Fred. What the hell does that mean?"

Of the two remaining scullers, one man considered my every utterance to be ludicrous. He no doubt ignored me and continued plotting my assassination. Once I thought I saw him tampering with my brakes.

That left one solitary sculler, the novice Tommy Thompson. Yes, sure enough, Tommy heard me. Not only did he hear, he managed to apply what I said, soon connecting his strokes as though by an invisible thread. Remarkable transformation. His strokes began flowing from drive to release to recovery to catch, one stroke after another, on and on. He looked damn good, flowing easily from the different segments of the stroke, flowing as though the parts complemented each other. When properly executed, a rowing stroke is exquisite to behold.

I followed behind the scullers for a good portion of the workout, watching, saying little. I've learned over the months that excessive chatter by the coach serves only to break the concentration of the rowers. Too much talk can even have a reverse effect, which I called the red-faced monkey phenomenon. When someone says, don't think of red-faced monkeys, your immediate response is to think of these exact red-faced monkeys. In the coaching world, when I said, "Tommy, keep your head in the boat," more often than not his immediate response was to turn and look at me.

After we returned to the dock, I told Tommy, "Now that you've got the basics figured out, any minor problems with your stroke can be cured with ten thousand miles of practice."

"Ten thousand miles," he said. "Holy shit. That'll take forever."

"No, not at all," I said. "My college coach told me the exact same thing: 'Ten thousand miles, Lewis, and you'll have it wired.' He was right. But here's the secret: ten thousand miles can take three years or three lifetimes, depending on how intensely the fire rages in your hair."

"What fire?" Tommy asked, patting his head.

"That fire in your hair," I repeated. "Don't tell me that you can't feel it? You look like a two-hundred pound kitchen match walking around." He shook his head, not comprehending.

"You must concentrate and consecrate yourself wholly to each day, as though a fire were raging in your hair," I said. "That's the Zen-warrior philosophy. Works quite well in rowing, too."

Yes, good advice is timeless.

Besides seeing a rare display of skillful sculling, I had another reason to feel good about life - my hero had come to town. Everyone needs a hero. Mine happens to be Peter Matthiessen, who I considered to be the greatest author alive today.

Matthiessen was giving a talk this evening at the Santa Barbara Museum of Natural History. I arrived early and sat in the third row. Within minutes the hall filled with five thousand fans, sycophants, literary critics and environmental activists. Apparently I wasn't the only one in Santa Barbara that thought of Peter Matthiessen as a modern master. When he finally walked on stage, the place hushed with incredible respect and awe.

I had never seen, in person, a really accomplished author. I've got to say, I was hypnotized. He'd actually done it - written beautiful sentences, paragraphs, pages and books. He'd created stories that had a greater purpose, and he'd done it with style, patience and poise. Peter Matthiessen, a gold medalist writer.

Tall, lean, weathered face, graceful stride, Matthiessen latched onto the podium with a strong grip and began a long discourse on the power of writing to bring environmental issues to the fore. Not surprisingly, as a speaker he was average. You don't spend all your time rowing and then expect to be a good swimmer. The same holds true in writing: staring at a computer screen for ten hours a day does not make for a great speaking ability.

Afterward I stood patiently in line to have him sign my tattered copy of his classic work The Snow Leopard. When my turn arrived, I said "I'm Brad Lewis, the UCSB rowing coach. Some years ago I rowed with your nephew, Henry Matthiessen, on the US national team."

He looked up for a moment, glanced back down, ran his pen in a horizontal line for three inches across the title page, closed the cover, slid it toward me and said, "Next."

I'm not sure of my point. Perhaps it is not to expect anything from famous/busy people. No, that's not relevant nor is it necessarily true. The point is that famous/busy people are often uninterested and to expect otherwise is wrong. No, I'm sure some are quite interested. The point? It's buried inside. I'll find it.

NEGA-COACHING
Wednesday, March 9

Against my better judgment, I put Gordo into the lightweight eight this morning. Big mistake. Royal Canadian coaching mistake. Everyone, including Gordo, would have been better off had the lites simply rowed a 7.

We were attempting a new workout that I borrowed from national team coach Mike Spracklen - a castle series of pieces, high rating for a segment, dropping to low rating, then back up to high rating - all at full power. Repeat as necessary.

Unfortunately our sturdy castle soon deteriorated into a crumbling apartment building. After the initial hold-your-breath piece, the crews slowed way down, lightweights especially, their speed at the high rating roughly the same as at the low. On the last piece, as the heavyweights proceeded to crush the lightweights-con-Gordo, I heard some prolonged noises coming from the losing boat - this despite my exceptionally loud outboard engine. I slowed my launch to better hear what was going on.

"Fuck this!" Andrew Moore was screaming over and over at the top of his lungs.

When he stopped yelling to take a breath, I said, "That's right, Andrew, let go of your anger."

"Let go of your anger" instantly became a mantra for the crew. When in doubt, when lost for an answer, shout it out: "Let go of your anger." Well, I've heard worse mantras. Too bad Andrew didn't take my words to heart, letting go of all his anger before the workout was over. Back at the dock - before the boat was even in the house - he came up to me and demanded that I offer more negative coaching.

"We just don't try hard enough without someone yelling at us," he said. "For God's sake, no more lava lamping."

"Lava lamping?" I said, laughing, "What's that mean?"

"You know those lava lamps," Andrew said, finally cooling down a little. "They look really mysterious and all, but when you get down to it, they just sit there. We need yelling, lots of it."

"Andrew, I'm no screamer," I said. "I don't engage in put-down fests. I don't nega-coach. In a competitive workout like today, you should have all the motivation you need."

He hates me, of course, because I'm not the coach of his dreams. He wants a nasty parrot who would ride next to his eight and scream non-stop into his ear. No thanks. I never liked those theatrics when I was rowing and I'm sure as hell not going to do them now.

I stopped by Ms. Pearson's office in the afternoon and saw an interesting exchange. A former novice woman sat in front of Ms. Pearson, tears cascading down her cheeks. Months ago, during fall quarter, the novice had rowed for a few weeks, decided she hated it and quit. Subsequently she stopped payment on the check she had written to cover her crew dues. Her rationale was simple: why pay if she wasn't going to row?

Now the novice woman was being denied entrance into UCSB for next semester until she made good on the check. Ms. Pearson listened to her story, waited patiently for the ex-novice to wipe away her tears, and then said, "Pay the dues."

As I waited for the woman to take the hint, I noticed a copy of The Amateurs on Ms. Pearson's desk, with a few markers strategically placed within the book. I made a mental note to get her a copy of Assault. Finally the novice departed and I took the now vacant chair directly across from Ms. Pearson, literally the hot seat, the pad having been warmed to the scorching point by the previous occupant.

"So, how are you coming on that newsletter?" Ms. Pearson asked.

"The newsletter," I said. "Oh, yes, it should go to press on Friday."

"Are you sure?" she replied tersely. "Friday is day after tomorrow."

"You are right, sir," I said. Thanks to Churchill and his incessant imitations, the silly voice of Ed McMahon occasionally made a guest appearance in my skull.

"How are things going in general?" she asked, thankfully ignoring Ed. From the bumpy tone of her voice, I suspected that one of the lightweights had already visited Ms. Pearson and chatted her up.

"I couldn't be happier," I said. "I'm having a heck of time." That was true. I'd lost eleven pounds. My VISA bill was almost paid off. Everything was relatively okay.

"The team," she said, "how's the team going?"

"The team's great. Everyone is alive and well. The lightweights are as frisky as ever. We're all psyched up for the Crew Classic."

"No problems?" she asked.

"Nothing we can't handle."

"And the newsletter will be out on Friday?" Was she trying to trick me into using Ed McMahon again?

"Day after tomorrow."

As I stood up to leave, I though of one thing I'd been wanting to ask her: "I'm curious how it came that UCSB has a rowing team?"

"Why do you mean?" she asked.

"Well, I've been here long enough to know that in a practical sense,

Gaucho rowing is simply not practical," I said. "I welcome a healthy challenge. I know adversity is part of the drill. But a sixty-mile commute to the lake? It seem outside the realm of realistic, not to mention the wind is so strong that we can't row half the days."

After thinking a moment, she said, "I honestly don't know how rowing started at UCSB. It happened before I got here. All I know is that for three decades UCSB has had a crew team. That makes me think it can't be too bad."

For an instant I considered correcting her. "Crew team" is a redundant term. I decided against it.

BUKOWSKI
Saturday, March 12

One of my favorite authors, Charles Bukowski, died yesterday, and in his honor I read a few of his poems.

> When you're young
> a pair of
> female
> high-heeled shoes
> just sitting
> alone
> in the closet
> can fire your
> bones

Yes, Bukowski drank too much, but he also had an awesome work ethic, slaving away for years as a mail sorter - one of the worst jobs in America - while continuing to write his amazing poetry. The name of his books was enough to fire my bones, *The Days Run Away Like Wild Horses Over the Hills*.

After sleeping on it or maybe because Bukowski was on my mind, I decided to step out of character this morning and harangue the light-weights during practice, ninety non-stop minutes of error detection and correction by the coach from Hell. What the heck, I figured, it wouldn't kill me. Who knows, I might enjoy it.

Toward the end - perhaps because I was over-caffeinated - my berating slipped into the province of outrage: "Jeff Beldon, if your catch was any slower a seagull would perch on your blade. Robert Churchill, why are you breathing hard? You haven't been pulling. Andrew, I think the women's team is looking for someone to row in the bow." A few more gulps of dark roast coffee and I tossed civility overboard and commenced blasted invectives with a 50 caliber verbal-cannon. "Wimps, losers, liars, drunks, drug addicts, perverts, bastard children of commercial real estate agents, future night managers of McDonald's, pikers, shriners, wombats, spears." I concluded with the worse possible indignity known to man: "Egotistical wankers!"

Afterward they left without saying a word. Not even a thank you. Something is up with these lightweights. More grumbling than usual, more pecking at each other than is healthy. Perhaps they're simply dieting in anticipation of the upcoming San Diego Crew Classic. I've heard that dieting can make you a little testy. I have no personal experience, so I can't say for sure.

Today I finished the EMT training that I'd begun months ago after Clement's fake death. This final part required that I spend ten hours in the St. Francis Hospital emergency room. At first I simply stood off to the side and observed the arrival of blood-covered, bullet-riddled near-dead customers. Gradually, as the hours passed, I found myself helping out, taking blood pressure, vital signs. At the end of my shift, after I lifted a five-gallon Sparkletts water bottle onto the dispenser, the head ER nurse gave me the honorary degree of AAD, Almost A Doctor.

For improving your outlook on life, few experiences can compare to a day in the emergency room, especially when you're just passing through and not a patron. Here's what I learned in ten hours: 1) Don't drink to excess; 2) Don't drink and drive; 3) We're all going to die eventually, so have your organ donor card with you at all times.

Broadcast Peak
Tuesday, March 22

"Forcing yourself to use restricted means is the sort of restraint that liberates invention." I read that quote by Pablo Picasso back in November and I'd thought of it many times since. Its applicability to the Gaucho crew cannot be underestimated.

A howling wind at the lake this morning was our restricted means. I took advantage of it to instigate a team hike to Broadcast Peak, 2000-odd feet high, the tallest mountain in the Santa Ynez range.

On a clear day the summit is plainly visible from the boathouse, bristling with antennas and relay dishes, its very presence serving as an open invitation to find the trail head and start hiking. Naturally I assumed that my rowers had climbed it at some time, but no, not a single one had visited the summit.

I told the men to grab a jacket, a water bottle and any food they could find - we were going hiking. Starting from the boathouse we crossed Highway 154 and walked up a dirt road that led to an abandoned Boy Scout Camp. Another quarter-mile brought us to the trail head. The sun had not yet found its way to the east-facing slope as we marched double time up the narrow, switch-back trail. Clement led the way, through deep undergrowth and occasional stands of California oak trees. After five miles uphill, through prime mountain lion and black bear terrain, we made the summit, coxswains included.

The temperature was near freezing at the top and the stinging wind made unpleasant whistling noises as it played through the antennas. Altogether not a place to linger. Below us, when the clouds parted, we could see our favorite haunts: Goleta Pier where we ran our soft sand runs, Freebirds in Isla Vista, the Black Lagoon on campus. Looking the other way, Lake Cachuma, our boathouse, the harbor, Arrowhead Island, all stood out in perfect relief.

For a brief moment we huddled together for a team photo. At our first workout in September, I had studied the rowers who comprised our team. Back then they had appeared almost indistinguishable to me. Now, months later, they all had personalities, quirks, girlfriends, likes and dislikes. I could pick them out a half-mile away by the sound of their laughter. I'd spoken to their parents and counselors and doctors. The evolution of a team is quite magical. It's not sudden or dramatic like in the movies, just a gradual building of relationships, a subtle transformation until they stopped being the rowers and became my rowers. I don't mean this in a literary way - I always referred to them as my rowers - but in a feeling way. Now they felt like my rowers. On this mountain top, seventeen remaining oarsmen, two coxswains and one coach stood still, everyone smiling, arms looped around shoulders, a solitary speck of time preserved on light-sensitive 35 millimeter film. Perhaps in ten years the rowers and coxswains will look back on this hike as the highlight of the season. Perhaps in ten years, so will the coach.

Once we returned to the boathouse, the rowers headed home while I stayed to repair our heavyweight eight, the Carrie On. The main knee at the two seat had cracked clean through. I had assumed the knee was made of plywood wrapped in carbon fiber, but after poking around a little, I discovered the knee was essentially hollow, carbon fiber wrapped around a light foam core. No wonder it broke.

I trimmed two thin aluminum plates until they fit snugly on either side of the cracked knee. Then I through-bolted them into place, above and below the crack. Finally I glued the mess with Goop-on, aka Goughon Brothers resin. Once the resin dried, the knee would be bombproof.

Zen practitioners have a saying: "The gong, well struck, always sounds." For boat repairmen, the Goop-on, properly mixed, always hardens. This may not sound like much, but when I was younger and used resin to repair my surfboards, it often never progressed beyond the jelly stage because I hadn't mixed the right ratio of resin-to-hardener. Only then do you learn to appreciate a resin that always petrifies to perfection.

The best place for cooking up a batch of Goop-on was toward the rear of the boathouse, in the early afternoon, after the west-facing wall had heated up like a microwave. The Goop-on would sputter and smoke and dance like an angel when kicking off, not to mention the smell, an ambrosial combination of clover and napalm that was certain to deaden a few brain cells. In the world of rigging and boat repair, an ample supply of Goop-on was second only to a handful of 7/16s end wrenches.

With my chores completed, I indulged in a project that I'd been wanting to do for some time. In an empty corner of the boathouse, using scrap lumber, I constructed a speed bag platform.

Once finished, I celebrated my creation by beating the shit out of my speed bag for twenty minutes. The act of whacking a speed bag is wildly underrated as a means of dealing with anger, melancholy, despair - all the usual coaching emotions. In Zen lore, you're not supposed to give anyone the power to make you angry. Regular sessions on the speed bag can help you reclaim the Zen-anger-power that is rightfully yours. Cheaper than psychoanalysis, safe, legal, muscle toning. Long live the speed bag.

SHORT CUT
Saturday, April 2

Easter. Great holiday. One of my favorites. Chocolate, chocolate everywhere. At Lake Cachuma I soon found out that Easter meant more than chocolate bunnies. It meant bass, bass fishermen and bass boats.

Now that spring had sprung, the bass fishermen were arriving by the hundreds, dragging with them the worst of southern California - Bud, smokes, AC/DC, belligerent attitudes. Their $30,000 bass boats, (where do they get the money?), are as quick as a snake, leaping from Cachuma harbor to Arrowhead Island in a matter of seconds. No speed limit on Lake Cachuma. No traffic signs. Rooster tails like thunder boats on Mission Bay. Behold the American Sportsman: pop the top, flick the lighter, jam the throttle and blast off.

We'd been warned by the lake rangers that a big bad bass tournament was scheduled for today, but I hadn't considered that it might keep us off the water. My mistake. The three hundred participating fishermen were madly chasing after Barney the Bass, a specially tagged fish that was worth $5000. The faster a fisherman might arrive at his favorite hole, the more likely his chances of catching the money-bass. If that hole proved to be empty, the fishermen would roar to another place. As seen from the space shuttle, these half-drunk fishermen bouncing around the lake must have looked oddly amusing. At water level, we weren't laughing.

Only a few minutes from the dock, I had a scare that rivaled the time I thought Clement had died. A low-slung bass boat zoomed out of the light fog, coming straight toward my heavyweight eight. The boat seemed to be going a hundred miles an hour - more likely it was only half that number, but still, on a foggy day, the speed was clearly beyond anything reasonable. I stood up and waved my megaphone in an attempt to get the driver's attention. The bass boat's hull was lightly skipping across the water, on a certain collision course. I was unable to do a damn thing except brace myself for disaster. With only fifty feet to spare, the driver cranked a hard turn to port and went zipping off in another direction.

We were all so shocked that no one said a word. Finally I sat down heavily on my bench seat and said, "Let's go in." Practice adjourned.

My brother, Tracy, who was visiting from down south, told me that he wanted to see something of the countryside. What better way than to hike to the top of Mt. Santa Ynez, the mountain next door to

Broadcast Peak. Off we went, Tracy and I, following the same trail that I had traversed a few days before with my crew.

Once we reached the summit of Mt. Santa Ynez, I noticed an unused trail that seemed to lead directly back to Lake Cachuma. I suggested to my brother that we give this shortcut a try. Reluctantly, thinking of all the unwise shortcuts I'd led him on over the years, he agreed.

My shortcut was superb, allowing us to drop rapidly down, down, down. My only concern was that given the steep angle and poor footing of the trail, we'd never be able to climb back out. But as long as we kept moving, we'd be okay. Then the bed broke. Four miles into our descent, the trail disappeared and Bramble Town began. Ouch all over. My legs were soon cut to shreds. Extremely harsh going. We climbed on top of brambles and through sticker bushes in search of our missing trail. Profound pain was waiting every step of the way. After a long hunt and much blood lost, the trail finally reappeared. Five minutes later, it vanished again. More crawling over razor blade shrubbery.

By the time we finally limped back to the boathouse, blood oozed from deep, open wounds on my legs and arms, and a dozen bloated, blissful ticks were embedded under my skin. My shortcut had been a disaster.

POISON OH
Wednesday, April 6

In the middle of the night I dreamed that a million fire ants had found their way into my bed and were gnawing off my flesh, one ant-sized bite at a time. I pulled back the covers to see... poison oak.

From the bottom of my feet to the crown of my head, blistering poison oak. Between my toes and behind my ears, searing poison oak. Lodged in my lungs and spilling into my spleen, venomous poison oak.

Saturday's hike with my brother, the short-cut aspect, had taken us through a giant quagmire of the virulent stuff. We had literally been up to our ears in it. After a few days had passed and I showed no symptoms, I assumed that I'd escaped unscathed. No such luck. The poison had been germinating inside me like a time bomb. Tonight it exploded. I soon found out that my brother had it too - perhaps even worse than I did. At least I could wear walking shorts and continually douse myself with pink Caladryl Lotion. I am literally caked in the pinky stuff as though it's my hard shell exterior. Tracy, my poor brother, must wear business suits that aggravate the poison to near flammable levels.

Never before had I endured anything like poison oak. Never had I felt the extreme discomfort of those horrible welts and acid-filled blisters. Poison oak gives a whole new meaning to pain and suffering. A tightly cinched pair of handcuffs securing my arms behind my back could not keep me from scratching every square inch of my body.

This morning's excitement - besides my scratching like a mental patient - was a big accident that closed Highway 154. I had to detour onto Old San Marcos Road, the same stretch of highway where I thought Clement had died. It proved a difficult passage at the pre-dawn hour, especially with my new itchy-addiction. The accident on Highway 154 turned out to be a semi-truck that had driven over a cliff. The driver, now dead, probably didn't see the road's hairpin turn in the thick fog, at least not until it was too late.

A mock 2K Race was on tap this morning, 2000-meter pieces, complete with start, predetermined moves and a sprint at the finish, all at half power.

"Before we begin the first piece," I told them, "I want you to don the sacred Face of Anger."

They looked at me with the face of bafflement.

"The face of anger is like a hockey player's mask," I continued, "intense, hard-eyed, a fighter's scowl. Every winner uses the face of anger. Some winners trot it out only on race day. Others wear the face 365 days a year. Regardless, the face of anger is an essential piece of the champion's psyche, and like everything, it must be practiced until perfected. So let's try it."

The rowers contorted their face into different poses, face of pursed lips, face of jutting chin, face of shock and dismay. Finally I stopped laughing and started the piece. They rowed four mock 2Ks, a piece for the heat, the semi-final, the final and then one more because it was too early to come in.

Heading South; San Diego Crew Classic, part I
Thursday, April 7

No Kolbe. No Gordo. Thus the heavies rowed a 7. Can you imagine the University of Washington rowing a 7 right before the Crew Classic? No frigging way. I couldn't help but feel discouraged that the last practice before our biggest race of the year should be half-assed.

I was in a bad mood all day, due mostly to my incessant itching. A steady diet of scratch & itch can cloud your judgment and make your life seem hardly worth living. Rather than bore the reader with my torment (how many different ways can you say ouch?) suffice to say the pain didn't let up throughout the endless Crew Classic weekend.

Our only hard work this morning was a 500 meter piece simulating the first 500 meters of a race. The lites looked good. Maybe they'll turn a few heads in San Diego.

In a steady rain, we soon began loading the new trailer with every decent racing shell owned by the Gaucho crew. Throughout the drill, the usual confusion-cloud stayed poised overhead. The combined team - men, women, lites, heavies, novices, coaches - searched for more bungee, more line, more straps. Each crew hurriedly loading their boat onto the trailer without much concern as to whether it was centered or not. Then they strapped it down so that the buckles cut deeply into the hull. Not a pretty sight, especially for someone who values good boatmanship. Once the rowers were finished, I went through and re-positioned the boats and re-tied the straps.

Then came the tough part: hooking the trailer to the truck. Luckily, I had a knowledgeable ally to guide me through this tricky terrain - Richard the Gaucho Master.

Richard, a veteran rower who occasionally came by the boathouse to take out a single scull, was the exact opposite of the Gaucho Yeahbuts. Richard was only too willing to lend a hand. When he wasn't helping out, he offered me a welcome ear as I railed against the demons that confront all coaches. In general, Richard was a pleasant addition to the program, asking nothing in return for his efforts except a few words of sculling instruction when convenient. Being an equestrian, Richard was well versed in trailer lore from having hauled his horses around the state. This morning he quickly showed me how to hook up the trailer. To a new driver like myself, a boat trailer is a complicated, scary animal, torsion bars, safety chains, trailer height, tow ball diameter. As we worked, I began to miss the bad old days: strap your single scull onto the roof and adios.

Just before leaving I topped off the truck's gas tank using the generator gas can. Hopefully this would allow me to drive all the way to San Diego without a stop. Unless you've also had some experience dragging around a boat trailer, this modest accomplishment may not sound important. But trailer driver's know: a gas stop can be a traumatic experience. You need enough clearance on every possible side. You can't cut the turn too sharp or you'll clip the gas pump. Getting back on the freeway can be as challenging as sending a man to the moon. A simple gas stop presents a thousand way to ruin your trip. Avoid at all costs.

The hardest mile happened to be the first, from boathouse to park exit, a stretch of super-slow going, twists and turns through the park, kids on Big Wheels scooting in front of my bumper, old ladies tottering on their walkers. By the time I reached the park exit my blood pressure had climbed several notches and I was thirsting for water, not unlike the start of a 2000 meter race.

Finally I was on my way, driving down Highway 154 to the 101 Freeway to the 405 Freeway to the 5 Freeway to San Diego, all in record slow time. Whenever I ventured over 53 miles an hour, the trailer began swaying back and forth like the tail of a happy dog. My only companions on this marathon drive were my assorted books-on-tape, *Art of War*, *Book of Five Rings*, *Dispatches*, all my favorites. As I drove, my stomach worked overtime digesting those foods invented for people driving long distances, Fig Newtons, (the poor man's Powerbar), peanut M&M's, raw carrots and tons of chewing gum.

As I rolled across the San Diego city limits I tried to recall the exact route to the Crew Classic site. By the time this weekend ends, I'll know it better than my own name. Next year I'll likely have forgotten again.

Around 4:00 in the afternoon I eased into the Crew Classic parking lot. Upon setting the brake and turning off the ignition, my immediate desire was to stretch out on the ground and take a nap. Pressure city. I had concentrated so hard that I forgot to scratch.

STARING, GLARING, SPITTING; CREW CLASSIC, PART II
Friday, April 8

My heavies rigged their eight and went for a pre-race row. Who was that chunky guy in the three seat that kept missing water? He looked a little old to be in college. It was me.

Michael Kolbe would not be arriving until later in this evening, so rather than forgo a chance to row over the course, I took his place. The feeling was somewhat unsettling, rowing in a collegiate eight on the Crew Classic course. The last time I had done it was in 1975. At this rate I won't do it again until the year 2013. I should be well rested by then.

As part of my continuing coaching education, I went with my lightweights to their weighing-in ceremony. Immediately upon entering the weighing-in zone, I sensed an oppressive tension in the air, the lightweights staring and glaring at each other, snarling like lean, frenzied dogs. Extreme hunger has a way of creating these emotions in even the most mild-mannered people. I know this from observation only - heavyweight rowers, even those ten years retired - would rather wear a muumuu than diet. Off to the side I noticed the teams had stashed several hundred pounds of junk food for the moment they made weight. Snickers seemed quite popular along with Double Stuff Oreos and my own favorite, Milky Way Dark, the crack cocaine of candy.

"Will your guys make weight?" I asked Clement.

"Pretty sure we will," he said. "On the drive down we had the heater cranked up and each of us spit a quart."

Spit a quart? Once again I'd been stumped. I asked Clement for an explanation.

"That's what we always do," he said. "We spit saliva into a quart container. If everyone does it, the crew drops five or six pounds. Pretty cool."

Next up, blood-letting.

Every member of the Gaucho lightweight crew weighed in at less than 160 pounds. I figured we were home free. "Let's eat," I said, reaching for a MWD. Clement pushed my hand away and reminded me that besides being under 160 pounds the crew still had to average 155. Oops. Sorry about that, guys. True to Clement's word, they managed to average just under the limit. When the all-clear signal was given, nary a second was wasted before a second command was screamed: "Gentlemen, start pigging-out."

The Gaucho lightweights, to a man, gained five pounds within fifteen minutes. A litany of what they ate - Cheetos, corn dogs, burritos, pizza - was enough to raise John Candy from the grave. My lightweights gained seven to ten pounds before the day was over. What, exactly, is the purpose behind lightweight rowing? Seemed to have slipped my mind.

With the heavyweight squad plus Gordo, I retired to the mansion of Mrs. Carrie Morse, the mother of heavyweight team captain Moose Morse and frequent benefactor of the crew. Good ol' Mrs. Moose. At her mansion overlooking San Diego harbor we feasted like lightweights on a catered five-course meal that had been prepared exclusively for our dining pleasure. Then we unrolled our sleeping bags and took over the floor.

I hope every under-funded college crew has a Mrs. Moose to call its own. Without her we'd have been sleeping in leaky tents at the race course, eating uncooked hot dogs and drinking Sunny Delight. This regatta cost us a mere $280, for entry fees and gasoline. Compared with most schools, we were winning the money-race by lengths of open water. Too bad our frugality couldn't be factored into the equation, thereby earning us a handsome handicap in tomorrow's race.

As I was scratching off to sleep, I heard on the news that rock singer Kurt Cobain had blown his brains into tomorrow with a shotgun. Forget artistic, drug-ridden angst, I'd wager that the cause of Kurt's distress was a bad case of poison oak.

CAL CUP; CREW CLASSIC, PART III
Saturday, April 9

Fred Checks must have been very bad in another life because he sure is getting spanked in this one. Last week the outboard engine was dropped off the stern of his launch by someone trying to steal it. On Wednesday he accidentally locked his keys in the boathouse after everyone had left. Yesterday he was fired from his job at the shoe store.

This morning Checks called to tell me that his Jeep Cherokee had been stolen overnight. It's probably halfway to Mexico City by now, along with several perpetual San Diego Crew Classic trophies that were inside. The Jeep can be replaced. The lost trophies - that's going to be a problem. Are they insured by the Crew Classic committee? What's the next step? Yo, Fred, get out your checkbook!

My team's first race, a heat in the California Cup, was scheduled for bright and early this morning. The Cal Cup was designed especially for schools such as UC Santa Barbara, crews that had no chance against the big boys, UW, Harvard, Wisco. Through and through, we were Cal Cup material. In fact, if another division existed beneath the Cal Cup,

169

perhaps the Mid-State Between Coalinga and Oxnard Cup, I'd sign us up in a blind second.

As the heavyweights gathered around for our pre-race meeting, I opened my notebook, turned to the appropriate page and read these carefully crafted racing instructions: "Milk, eggs, butter, bread. Sorry, wrong page."

The only true consequence of most pre-race meetings, in my opinion, is to make everyone even more uptight than before.

"Is anyone nervous?" I asked. Like justice, nervousness is blind. It can ravage a world champion as easily as a novice rower. In the pole vault event at the '92 Olympics, Sergey Bubka - world record holder and undefeated since 1983 - failed to clear any height. He said later, "I was just too damn nervous."

"Yeah," Glen Mung said. "I'm nervous as hell."

I immediately stepped forward and slapped him sharply in the face. His nervousness vanished. Magic. Without another word, although Mung glanced back at me several times in fear that I might run up and give him another whack, they launched their boat and headed for the starting line.

As soon as they left, I began a slow walk alongside the race course, a saunter, a stroll, a purposeless meander. I had nowhere to go and nothing to do except wait. In a definitive coaching manual, several pages might be devoted to a coach's comportment while his crew is racing. I tried to avoid other coaches, mainly because I didn't want to answer the toughest question: how did I think they'd do? I considered changing into the regatta clothes I'd brought along, pressed shirt and khaki pants. No, the grunge look is the height of fashion for coaches. I walked to the UCSB alumni tent. It was deserted except for a lone Winchell's Donuts box on the table. I peeked inside - a sad shredded coconut donut looked back at me. If a tavern had suddenly appeared alongside the race course, I would have found my way to a quiet booth and downed a beer or two. If nothing else I could have used a good slap in the face myself because I was damn nervous. At least Mung and the others had an outlet for their agitation. I was stuck in nervous-mode like a broken record. Please, please, please,

I kept repeating, just finish in the top three. I didn't care if my heavies won the race, but I definitely wanted them to make to the finals.

Some endless minutes later, my heavies, looking a tad ragged around the edges, finished second in their heat and thus advanced to the finals. Hooray. Success. Flushed with the satisfaction that comes from achieving their goal, they talked of winning the whole damn thing. I nodded my head and smiled. No harm in dreaming, boys.

In the collegiate lightweight eight, my rowers placed fifth in their heat. Too bad for Adam, Clement and company. No grand final this year. At first I was surprised at how poorly they finished. Then I remembered that the heavies have been crushing them lately and I know the heavies are slower than slow.

After the lightweights landed and were washing their boat, I saw, off to the side, Robert Churchill having a fit, yelling at the coxswain, carrying on like a spoiled brat. This is exactly what I disliked most in a competitor. The time to be upset is during the race, when you can actually do something about it. Nothing could be done now. A thousand times I'd told them: the key to racing is to come off the water regretting nothing.

"Yes," I told him, putting my arm around his shoulders, "you should take racing seriously. Racing is serious business. You should take it so seriously that you invariably race well. That way, win or lose, you'll come off the water like a human." He pulled away and marched into the parking lot, flailing at the grass and cursing. That boy needed a good spanking.

The Brotherhood of Rowing; Crew Classic, part IV
Sunday, April 10

In Sunday's finals, the heavies finished fifth. Having watched them for many months, I felt that fifth place was just about right. Afterward, they had a chance to race again, in the Cal Visitor's Cup, petite finals. Some of my rowers didn't want to race, but I insisted. It wasn't as though they had something more pressing to do. Tijuana, the Bodyshop and Les Girls would still be waiting.

"You need to practice racing," I told them, "and the Crew Classic is the ideal place." They finished fourth out of five boats.

Our lites won the petite finals, defeating a few of the crews who had beaten them the day before. They spent the afternoon eating copious amounts of fatty foods and kicking the dog.

As we were loading our trailer, I saw Antonio stuff something into his duffel bag. "What have you got there?" I asked him. From out of his bag he brought a roll of vinyl cloth - when he unfurled the cloth, I saw that he had stolen a regatta banner.

"Antonio, you jerk," I yelled. "I told you: do not take anything that does not belong to you. Do not take banners, signs, posters - nothing."

I made him carry the banner back to the regatta organizers and apologize for his stupidity. I am beginning to wonder if some of my rowers belonged in the slow learners' class.

After the last boat was strapped down, I visited the Rower's Bookshelf booth and signed a few copies of Assault. One man who bought the book had four arms, a budding Buddha. Turned out his girlfriend was standing directly behind him.

People I saw at the Crew Classic while at the Rower's Bookshelf booth:

Bob Ernst, of University of Washington and my old college coach. He always asks the same question: "How's your dad?"

Harry Parker, Harvard coach - our annual nod, wave and brisk walk away. Gotta make sure the truck has enough air in the tires.

Johnny Walker - one of my UC Irvine teammates, now a FISA official.

Dan Louis - my training partner. For the first time in years we had a chance to catch up on life's great adventure. He's happily married with kids.

Charlie Altekruse - I waved and yelled hello, but he must not have heard me because he kept walking.

Paul Enquist, my Olympic double scull partner, was not at this year's Crew Classic. I know from talking to him that he's married with a family and a house in Seattle, all of which he earned through plain old-fashioned hard work.

As I stood in the booth chatting to people, it occurred to me that besides good racing, the Crew Classic provided an ideal setting for the brotherhood of rowing. The brotherhood connects real rowing people. Teammates who haven't visited in years come together, and so do former opponents who once battled like mortal enemies. Suddenly they discover they have much in common. The brotherhood lives.

Missed Practice and Half-Fired
Tuesday, April 12

Today marked the first and only practice I missed all year. My poison oak had taken an unbearable turn for the worse. I simply could not function. I filled my bathtub with ice and pinky lotion, and sat in it all day.

For the most part, I'd faked it over the long Crew Classic weekend, stealing away on occasion to splash more lotion on a hot spot. The regular infusions of adrenaline that I experienced, whenever one of my rowers disappeared just before his race or some other crew-calamity transpired, served to counteract the poison. Now that the fun was over and the adrenaline withdrawn, the fire in my pores raged unabated.

My only visitors came late in the afternoon. Upon hearing a knock I stumbled to the door and peered through the peep hole. On the landing stood Clement and Adam, no doubt coming by to cheer up their ailing coach. Not quite. As Clement and Adam shuffled into my place, I retreated to the kitchen and began applying more lotion. From the living room, in a serious tone, Clement said, "The lightweights want to begin working with Fred Checks."

I stopped what I was doing and asked, "Really?"

"Yeah," Clement said. "The guys don't think we're going to win at the PCRCs the way things are going."

"Did you clear this with Ms. Pearson?" I asked.

"Yeah," Adam said, "Elizabeth said that it was okay with her."

My immediate thought was, "Geez, they're on a first-name basis with my boss." The bottom line: my coaching style had simply not been cruel, aggressive or angry enough to suit the lightweights. The previous coach had given them their money's worth of castigating. I had not. Fred Checks, they hoped, could deliver.

"Best of luck," I said, as I hobbled back to the bathroom. They slammed the door shut and, except for one brief exchange some weeks later, that was the last time I spoke to any of the Gaucho lightweights.

Did I have a built-in bias against lightweights? I don't think so. Two of my best friends were former lightweights. I had battled lightweights my whole sculling career. I had the utmost respect for them. Granted, I didn't know much about the differences between training lites and heavies. I wasn't even sure a difference existed, nor had I made an effort to research the subject. Rowing is rowing. Perhaps I erred in that assumption.

As I relaxed in my pinky lotion and ice bath, I thought back to something I wrote in Assault, about how I wanted to retire from training so that I could stay up late and watch the Johnny Carson Show. That's exactly what I did. One night Johnny's guest was Joan Embry from the San Diego Zoo. She talked about the best way to train animals, concluding that they learn best when they're rewarded with food or some other positive reinforcement, as opposed to being beaten over the head with a club. But once you've established a mode of training, you can't change it. I had opted for the Crunch bar reward system, which seemed to work fine with the heavies but not with the lightweights.

As Tolstoy said in Anna Karenina, "All happy families resemble one another, but each unhappy family is unhappy in its own way." The Gaucho rowing family had unearthed yet another way to be unhappy. I could only hope that the divorce would be in everyone's best interest.

From now until the end of the season, one month away, I would work with only the heavyweights. I'd be remiss if I didn't mention the feelings of disappointment that broke through my poison oak stupor, in part because Adam and Clement were two of my favorite rowers. I wished Andrew had delivered the news. It would have been much easier to take from him. Being fired, rightly or wrongly, is one of the most humbling experiences known to man. I've yet to hear of a US Postal worker getting a job and then shooting up his workplace, but it's a different story on the flip side. Overall, I could endure the disappointment, so long as my paycheck wasn't adversely affected.

FRED CHILL
Friday, April 15

Couldn't sleep last night. Wide awake, itching like crazy. This morning, as the heavies rowed two four-withs, I followed alongside in my launch, saying little, squirting copious amounts of pinky lotion down my legs. For once I was thankful for the chill Cachuma breeze that served to numb my diseased skin.

When I returned to the boathouse, I saw Fred Checks diving off the end of the dock. Keep in mind, it's a $500 fine if the lake rangers catch you swimming in Cachuma. I soon learned that he had dropped his key ring into the lake. Good-bye to his car, boathouse and apartment keys. The water was freezing cold and quite deep where he was diving, twenty feet at least, and by the time he pulled himself out, his face and hands had turned a dull blue color. Checks' one stroke of luck was in having escaped detection by the rangers. I offered him a ride to campus. He looked at me for a moment, the faintest hint of fear and loathing in his eyes. He loathed me because I'd tried to get him fired. I'd like to think he feared me just on principle.

"Come on," I said, "There's no other cars in the parking lot. You can either ride with me or walk home." That wasn't quite true. His car was in the parking lot, a new BMW with a peculiar splat of orange paint on the left rear panel, lent to him by his parents until his stolen Jeep could be replaced. The Beemer's key, however, was at the bottom of the lake.

"How 'bout a little heat?" I asked, as he climbed into the van, hoping it would to break the ice.

Teeth chattering, he nodded his approval. I cranked up my van's heater to maximum and started toward the park exit.

"The only way you're going to get those keys back," I said, "is to borrow a strong magnet from the dive shop in Goleta." I waited for Checks to say something back, but he seemed not to be listening.

After a barely a mile on Highway 154, we found ourselves stuck behind a slug-powered tour bus. These enormous buses frequently traveled the highway, carrying Japanese tourists to-and-from the picturesque town of Solvang, twenty miles to the north.

At last Checks spoke, saying, "I think you can pass him now."

"We're okay," I said. "The turn-out is only seven miles ahead." Checks shook his faintly blue head in dismay, no doubt distressed at my lack of aggressive driving. In his chilled-out state, seven miles must have seemed like seven hundred.

"What's wrong?" I said, with a laugh. "You don't like diesel fumes?"

"I just don't like going this slow," he muttered under his breath.

"You know, Fred, my theory is that some people like to go fast, like race car drivers, and other people like to go slow, like rowers. I'm a rower."

"No," he said, "you're just weird."

Our superficial civilization doesn't allow many opportunities for a good old-fashioned man-to-man chat. Just as well. For such a chat to occur, it helps to be locked within the confines of an Econoline van while hurdling down the highway.

As I zipped around the tour bus, I asked, "Are you still mad because I tried to get you fired?"

How should I interpret the sound of Checks' teeth grinding? After a long stretch of silence, just when I was about to turn on the radio, he said, "Damn right, I'm mad."

Now it was my turn to be quiet. As we neared Goleta, I said, "At the time I was pretty mad, too, so let's just say we're even."

As he climbed out of my van, I called upon every ounce of strength to offer an olive branch of reconciliation: "Listen up, Fred. Only amateurs stay angry. We've got barely one month to go. Let's put any hassles behind us and start fresh. Okay?"

We shook hands. Better late than never.

Around noon, I met the Cambridge University lightweight crew from Great Britain. They had raced at the Crew Classic and were now making a brief tour of southern California.

As part of the ongoing brotherhood, I took them on a tour, starting with the best coffee in town, Santa Barbara Roasting Company, on State Street near the 101 Freeway. With double cappuccinos in hand we found chairs inside the high-ceiling cavern and read day old copies of The New York Times. Besides good coffee and old newspapers, we were able to enjoy firsthand the funky, nutty atmosphere that pervades this part of town.

Santa Barbara Roasting Company, or RoCo as the natives called it, is on the leading edge of the Bean Revolution. The mere smell of their dark roast was rumored to have pulled musician David Crosby, a local mountain man, out of a drug induced coma.

After RoCo, we drove deep into the Los Padres National Forest to Red Rock. I'd been wanting to visit Red Rock since I was in high school. Naked women were rumored to swim in Red Rock's deep, clear pools. After a short hike, we found the natural pools, deep and clear, but unfortunately we were the only naked swimmers.

Freebirds in Goleta was our last stop. The brief walk from my van to the restaurant took us past a fraternity house where a party was in full swing. A hundred young men and women - all of them lean, suntanned, bathing-suit clad - were crowded around the frat house, playing volleyball, tending the barbecue, drinking beer, posing. I stopped and stared. The Cambridge rowers stopped and stared. The living, breathing California Dream, so prevalent on beer commercials and MTV, stood only an arm's length away.

NATIONAL TEAM TRYOUTS
Monday, April 25

We arrived on time. Score one for the Gauchos. As I looked around, I gradually realized that no other crews were in attendance, just us and the national team rowers who trained on Otay Lake. Then I noticed the wind was blowing twenty knots, straight down the course, direct headwind. As my rowers slowly climbed out of the van, I was amazed to see them shrink ten inches in stature as they came face to face with their prestigious competition. I was a tad nervous. I could only imagine how they were feeling.

Way back in 1974, the national team coach Allen Rosenberg paid a visit to southern California. He was conducting workouts all over the country, searching for rowers to fill out his team.

On the appointed morning, Coach Bob Ernst, his van filled with excited UC Irvine rowers, drove to the UCLA boathouse in Marina del Rey. The Irvine rowers - the only undergraduates in the lot - jumped into different four-withs and took part in the national team tryout. I was lucky enough to be among those Irvine undergrads. During the workout, I observed that the older rowers, some of whom would certainly go on to make the national team, were not doing anything radically different than I was. Yes, they tugged a little harder on the oar and sat up a little straighter, but overall I felt that given enough time I could match their mojo. And although I was not selected for further trials, I did acquire a small kernel of confidence, which along with a hundred other such kernels, contributed to my later success.

Now, twenty years later, national team coach Mike Spracklen was having open tryouts at his Otay Lake training center, a few miles east of San Diego. The only difference from the '74 tryouts was that this racing would be conducted in straight pairs. When I saw the announcement, I knew that I wanted my rowers to compete. My crew had rowed straight pairs dozens of times and I was confident that my six best heavyweights could keep a relatively direct line down the course. Obviously we wouldn't win, but perhaps one of my rowers would find the experience as enlightening as I had two decades before.

This morning, after a few brief preliminaries, the first race got underway. From my vantage point near the finish line, I immediately saw that the two Gauchos entries were having a terrible time. Their course was as serpentine as a snake in heat. Spracklen's rowers, on the other hand, were pounding out precise, perfect strokes, while keeping an arrow-straight course from start to finish. I put down my binoculars and prayed to God that the next race would go better. To some extent, it did. Michael Kolbe and novice Tommy Thompson finished fifteen seconds behind the last national team crew. Not too bad for Tommy, who had been rowing only a few months.

Another series of races was planned for later in the day. With luck and a major miracle, over the next six hours we could improve fifteen to twenty seconds. When we returned to Otay Lake in mid-afternoon, the wind had escalated to hurricane proportions and was complemented by a pounding rain. With no end of the storm in sight, the races were mercifully called off.

Five hours later, after countless freeway miles, a flawless double-double burger from In & Out, further investment in Shell Oil Company, a blow-by-blow account of Glen Mung's date the weekend before with a novice woman known affectionately as the Natural Dolly Parton, we rolled into Goleta. By this time my rowers had convinced themselves that given another chance, they could have defeated at least one and possibly two of the national team boats. Dream on, boys, dream on. Dream long enough and train hard enough and it just might happen. I have yet to meet the champion who had the success and then had the dream. No, it doesn't work that way. The dream must come first.

We boated seven single sculls and a straight pair this morning for six times 2000 meters. On each piece I gave a huge head start to Gordo and Björn, less of a lead to Kolbe and Tommy. Finally, I started the remaining scullers, Mung, Pressman and Shapiro, along with the straight pair of Moose and Johnny Bender. Everyone hustled like crazy to finish first.

This particular workout was one of the best of the season. With fewer men under my care, I could again use small boats. Every rower by this time had a functioning knowledge of pacing, rating, technique. By handicapping the start, they kept fighting throughout the workout. Halfway into the morning, I saw a weird monster swimming across the fjord. Big knobby head, little sticks poking out. A baby Loch Ness? Turned out to be a young deer taking a shortcut across the channel.

"Listen up," I said as they prepared to start the last piece. "Today's life lesson might be the final one of the season. It comes from *Zen Mind, Beginner's Mind.*"

The 100 mile journey is only half over at 90 miles.

"Repeat it to yourselves," I suggested, "the 100 mile journey is only half over at 90 miles. We are at the season's proverbial 90 mile mark. Don't start thinking that it's over. Maintain the same warrior's sharpness from the first mile to the last. We have less than three weeks to go. Let's make good use of every minute." This life lesson was as much for my own benefit as for the rowers.

Later in the day I met with my boss, Ms. Pearson, to tell her that I was going to pursue other challenges at the end of my contract in June. I figured that by telling her now she'd have plenty of time to find a qualified coach for next season.

"I hope you're not quitting because of your problems with the lightweights," Ms. Pearson said.

"No," I said. "I'm leaving because I don't think UCSB should have a rowing program. Sailing, yes. Surfing, yes. Rowing, no."

My decision to quit might seem odd, given that we'd just had one of our best workouts of the year. But in the big picture, I felt that Gaucho rowing was poorly conceived. Yes, I'd been reminded several times that the crew had been in existence for decades. Who knows? Maybe the situation had changed over the years. All I knew were today's facts: the program was dangerous and impractical. No thanks. If it were up to me, I would sell the boats and give the money to UCSB's nationally ranked women's ultimate Frisbee team, the Burning Skirts.

As I stood up to leave, I extended my hand to Ms. Pearson for a farewell handshake. Then I said, "I hope we can part as friends."

"Why?" she asked. "We're just acquaintances."

VARSITY FOUR
Monday, May 2

The last race of the season, the Pacific Coast Rowing Championships, has finally arrived. Well, not quite. We still have this week of training and next week, too. Altogether we have ten more workouts on Lake Cachuma. But who's counting? (Hundred mile journey, hundred mile journey.)

This morning I discussed with my heavies an idea that I've been contemplating for some time: instead of racing the varsity eight at the PCRCs, perhaps we should race the varsity four-with. Clearly, we won't win the eight. Most likely we wouldn't make the finals. But a Gaucho heavyweight four-with could do pretty well, a medal perhaps. Who knows - we might even win.

Feelings were mixed. Moose and Pressman, who would certainly be in the four-with, are in favor of it. Björn, at the other end of the scale, is dead against. One man, Shapiro is uncertain. He might be in the boat or he might lose out. The decision must come made soon, as entries are due by the end of the week.

Even before asking their opinion, I'd made up my mind - race the four-with. I can't see any reason why we should contribute to a Husky rower's T-shirt collection. If we had eight decent athletes, then we could expect to be competitive in the eight-oared shell. But since we don't, our options are limited: race the four-with or get our collective asses kicked.

With that in mind, only one small task remained: deciding who would row in the four-with. While we have four starboard rowers, Pressman, Kolbe, Bender and Björn, I'm certain that Pressman and Kolbe are superior to the other two. The port side is a little trickier since we have four qualified men, Moose, Mung, Shapiro, and Tommy. To solve this brain teaser, I told the rowers to prepare themselves for some good old-fashioned, Harry Parker-style seat racing.

For this first try, we had exceptionally good luck with the weather, no wind, perfectly smooth water, as inviting as milk chocolate. Despite the flawless water, our seat racing quickly turned into a coach's nightmare. The slow boat - I know it's the slow boat because I've been watching them for thirty-three weeks - won the first piece by a full length. Then the fast boat won the second piece. And so it went for the next four pieces, back and forth. Conclusion: I hate seat racing.

THE BIG CUT
Friday, May 6

On my way to the boathouse, a mountain lion leaped in front of my car. I slammed on the brakes to keep from tagging him, and then a moment later he disappeared into the brush. The lion was huge, as big as a saber tooth tiger or a snow leopard. Regardless of the brand, an evil omen was contained somewhere in this errant cat crossing.

After several days of horrible weather - bashing around, getting nowhere, muddling along until we were all ready to scream - we finally had a chance to conclude our seat racing. Throughout the pieces, the boats kept falling apart, the rowers complained of being tired, injured, generally out-of-it. Also, we had to borrow a coxswain from the novice team. For some reason this coxswain insisted on exploring an uncharted polar route across the lake. Clearly, this was not our finest hour.

When it was all over, the results were more or less as I knew they would be. The coxswain component was fairly obvious. Adam had gone with the lightweights, leaving Elaine as our sole cox. She steered straight, said little and dated only one rower at a time - my idea of the perfect coxswain. To me, the other four seats in the boat were equally straightforward, although my opinion was not shared by everyone. Back at the dock, I called the team together. Time for the big cut.

"Listen up," I said for the millionth time. I do believe I prefaced every statement with those two words, listen up. "Everyone did a great job. I want to thank you for being so diligent. Whether you're in the boat or not, you should take satisfaction in knowing that you performed well." With the public service announcement out of the way, I named the boat: "Okay, in the four-with we'll have Moose, Pressman, Mung and Kolbe. I'll announce the quad tomorrow. Any questions, see me afterward."

The other names - the unspoken ones - were the source of my discomfort. I felt bad for them. They'd trained hard, paid their dues, all but one. It did not seem fair. In the distance I heard someone yell, "Fucking bullshit!" Apparently someone agreed with me. My first experience with the big cut - on the skinny end of the megaphone - had been even more discouraging than I had imagined.

We still had an ace in the hole, one more boat to select for the PCRCs, an event that I was counting on to be our salvation: the quad-with. As I was putting my launch away, Johnny Bender came up to me and said, "I have good news for you."

"What's that?" I asked.

"Here's a check for my dues," he said.

"Great day. That's it for the dues. Everyone's paid up."

"One more thing," Johnny said. "This is my last day of rowing."

"You must be kidding," I said, completely caught off guard. The look on his face told me that he was damn serious. "Why quit now when you've come this far? If you stick around, you can race in the quad at the PCRCs."

"I hate sculling," he said. I knew this to be the case, although it seemed unfortunate to bail out so close to the end. (Hundred mile journey, hundred mile journey.) Even a bad season must be seen through to completion.

As he walked away I glanced down at the check. He'd made it out to "Reagands [sic] of UC." Close enough. After everyone left, I pounded my speed bag for fifteen solid minutes. Stress reduction at its finest.

THE LAST FEW STROKES
Tuesday, May 17

"The Moose is out of our hair," Shapiro said, and then he began laughing like a madman.

I climbed out of my van and stared out him. Could I be hallucinating? Maybe I'd accidentally put a generous helping of Peruvian coffee creamer in my cup. What the hell was going on? A moment ago, when I'd pulled into the parking area next to the boathouse, Shapiro had been waiting for me, grinning an unusually mischievous grin, even for him.

"Moose is finally out of our hair," Shapiro said again. "God, I've been waiting all season to say that."

I considered giving Shapiro a short kick in the groin just to make sure I wasn't dreaming. "What are you talking about?" I asked.

"Yeah, Moose is in the student health center," Shapiro said. "In fact, he stayed overnight. Blew out his back last night lifting beer kegs. The guy is toast."

What a way to start the day. I soon found out that Shapiro was more or less telling the truth. Moose had re-injured his back at his part-time job unloading beer trucks at SOS Liquor in I-V. Of course, he hadn't called to let me know. Typical. And of course Shapiro was only too pleased to spread the word of Moose's demise. Philip Shapiro, besides being an enemy of Glen Mung, was also a foe of Moose-man. Perhaps most importantly, it meant that Shapiro might now race in the four-with.

Robert "Moose" Morse, our resident muscle man and heavyweight team captain, gone. Just like that. His back had been giving him trouble all season, and although he tried resting, rehabilitation, rowing-with-pain, massage, manipulation, his girlfriend walking on his back in stiletto heels, nothing seemed to fix the problem. The beer kegs finished him off. The bottom line: he will definitely not be racing at the PCRCs this weekend.

Without Moose, we now had an open seat on the port side. I could fill it with either Shapiro and Tommy. I'd prefer that Tommy the novice to take the seat. Despite his lack of miles, Tommy has shown time after time that he is a poised, competent oarsman who can go the distance. Shapiro, although a veteran and a good rower, is a little short on endurance. Nonetheless, he's certain that he should take Moose's place. A more experienced coach would have called out the new boatings without hesitation or remorse: Tommy, Pressman, Mung and Kolbe. But to some extent, I felt that Shapiro deserved a final chance, not to mention that I liked him. He was a decent guy. He was left handed. He had pursued sculling with a rare vigor. Also, his father was a big-time power lawyer who might bring legal action should I condemn his son without a thorough trial.

Certainly one solitary seat race would clear things up and set everything right. The job of coaching becomes especially unpleasant at these times. No matter how you cut it, you're forced to disappoint people, anger them and generally wreak havoc with their lives. Ten years from now, when the shunned rower is blasting away with an AK-47 from the roof of a book repository, only his former rowing coach will know the true reason.

Too bad Johnny Bender quit. We could have used him today. Even without Johnny we still had eight heavyweight rowers but one is Gordo, who generally had a negative net effect on a boat's speed.

As we worked our way to the fjord, a relentless rain soaked rowers, coach and coxswains. Between the pelting drops, I watched Shapiro's four-with. They were rowing so poorly that I found myself involuntarily lowering the hood on my rain suit to obscure my vision. What the hell was going on? Were the other rowers, who generally disliked Shapiro, trying to ruin his chances? What should I do? The answer came quickly in the form of a loud, resounding crack. Through good fortune, a rigger on Shapiro's boat snapped in half and thus we were forced to return to the dock without having rowed a solitary piece. Try again tomorrow.

After they left, I stayed at the boathouse and repaired the four-with. Fortunately, we won't have to use this boat at the PCRCs. Instead we'll be borrowing a four-with from Stanford University. Thank God we lent them our truck at the Crew Classic after theirs broke down. It's much easier to ask for a favor when you're owed one.

I'm also hoping to rig the Stanford four-with as a quad-with. To achieve this mission, I'll bring four riggers off the Carrie On and a slew of extra bolts, shims, blocks and oarlocks. Should be a true coach's challenge, rigging a four-with as a quad-with in three hours or less - and without having practiced ahead of time.

At 10:50 P.M. the phone rang. I fumbled with the receiver, finally getting it right-side-up to my ear. The Nordic-twang of Björn, or a very good Björn-imitator, came over the line and told me he was quitting the team. Had Björn called at a decent hour or had I been fully awake, I might have tried to talk him out of it. Instead I said, "Good." Then I hung up and fell back asleep.

BLIND SEAT RACING
Wednesday, May 18

Pre-dawn questions frequently asked by coaches: did I get a phone call late last night? Did Björn tell me he was quitting? Yes and yes. With Björn gone, we can no longer seat race, head-to-head. How about a new format, one that I conceived while the drive to the boathouse: Blind Seat Racing.

One boat would race against the clock for a specific distance. I purposely made this distance about five minutes in length - too drawn out for Shapiro to hold his breath. Then I'd switch the affected rowers, Tommy and Shapiro, and the boat would race over the same stretch of water. Blind seat racing is aptly named since no one can see what's going on. Everyone must agree to try their hardest on each piece (fat chance). The coxswain must keep the same true course (maybe). The wind must not fluctuate too much (pray). The ratings must be similar (that we can do). Overall, no one can play favorites, (except the coach).

With Tommy in the four-with, the time from buoy-to-buoy was 4:54. After Shapiro switched for Tommy, the time was 5:15. They rowed three more pieces to confirm the results. Fortunately, the water was calm and the riggers held together. As I watched them row, I couldn't help but think back to my own seat racing experience in the spring of 1984, the nadir of my rowing career. I hoped Shapiro was gaining as much character building insight through this grueling process as I had.

Back on the dock, I confirmed my observation with Pressman. He said the difference had been quite dramatic, in Tommy's favor. I thanked him and went looking for Shapiro. A quick search of the boathouse and parking area told me that Shapiro had already departed for campus. I guess he figured out the results on his own.

Only the quad-with remained. I decided to put Shapiro into the quad, along with Kolbe, Pressman and Mung. (Rowers at the PCRCs were permitted to row in the quad and another event.) With two seats between my dedicated enemies, Shapiro and Mung, I felt they could survive 2000 meters without killing each other.

For a brief moment I considered putting Gordo into the quad. Yes, that would make a wonderful, fulfilling conclusion to this season in the drink. Go for it! Front and center, Gordo. Spit out that taco and grab a pair of sculls. Then I came to my senses. I wanted my rowers to win something this season, and although I would have loved to reward Gordo for his diligence, I wanted even more to have a UCSB heavyweight crew cross the finish line in first place. They might still win with Gordo, but if they lost, I'd have to jump off the bridge.

LAKE NATOMA
Friday, May 20

No shortcuts, short of flying. We all piled into my van for another brain-numbing drive to Lake Natoma near Sacramento, the site of the PCRCs. I'd seen this stretch of road twice before over the last few weeks, driving to the State Schools regatta and the regional championships.

Waiting for us when we arrived at Natoma was our four-with, an excellent boat. I was so relived at seeing the boat, shiny and new, that in celebration a solitary gray hair on my head reverted to it's natural brown color. My rowers went out for a short practice and then off to Elaine's parent's house to eat the spaghetti that was left over from our last visit. More money was saved - tons more money - by not staying at a hotel, and it was more fun. Elaine's parents were well prepared for the rower-invasion with forty pounds of spaghetti and all the Kool Aid we could drink.

I remained at the race course and contemplated how I was going to turn this four-with into a quad-with in short order. The heat for the four-with was the first event tomorrow. The final for the quad was mid-morning. I'd have about two-and-a-half hours to make all the necessary changes. My preliminary measurements told me I was going to have trouble getting the right spread at the bow position. The skinniest riggers off the Carrie On were simply too big for this boat. As the sunlight factory shut down for the ten trillionth time, and I started fading after another endless day, I could conceive of only one solution: Sleep on it.

THE FINAL REGATTA
Saturday, May 21

I found a secluded place to watch the heat of the varsity four-with, away from the modest, early morning crowd. I had my coffee in hand, binoculars and stroke watch around my neck. I considered myself to be exceptionally well outfitted, the very picture of coaching competence.

As the race got underway I immediately tangled my stroke watch with my binoculars. Then I spilled coffee onto my shirt. I didn't need it anyway, not with my heart rate zooming higher and higher with each passing second. Is it cool for a coach to yell from the sidelines? Damn straight. How else can we vent our tension? My rowers finished first in their heat, rowing beautifully. I was ecstatic.

Then the rigging fun started. Off with the sweep oarlocks, on with the sculling locks. I bolted the quad riggers into place and adjusted for height, spread and pitch. As I thought might happen, the bow seat of the quad would not cooperate - it had too much spread. The only practical solution was to borrow a pair of riggers from the Gaucho lightweight eight. Two slight problems presented themselves. The lightweight's heat was only a few events before our quad final. Even more daunting was the fact that the Gaucho lites had no interest in assisting the heavyweights or me. To put it mildly, relations between the two weight classes had been strained since they began working with Fred Checks.

With time running out, I took Clement, Adam and Andrew aside and related a few key inspirational words: "We are all Gauchos," I told them, "and Gauchos never die and Gauchos always help other Gauchos and if you don't let me use the riggers I will sneak back here tonight and cut your boat in half with my Skilsaw. Go Gauchos."

The lightweights saw the light and agreed to let me use their riggers. They raced their heat - finished second - took an inordinately long cool-down and finally returned to the dock. As they carried their boat to the slings, I began spinning my speed wrench to unbolt the riggers. Within five minutes I had stripped the riggers off the lite-eight and secured them onto our quad. With sculling oarlocks in place and the rigging close to correct, my heavies hustled the boat to the water and prepared to row straight-away to the starting line.

My pre-race instructions came in the form of one word, repeated three times: "Hurry, hurry, hurry!" Off they sprinted to the start. If nothing else, they'd be well warmed-up.

Finally, an eternity later, the quad race came down the course. Sculling quite nicely, with adequate timing and decent rhythm and strong finishes, the Gaucho quad maintained a one-length lead across the finish. Fantastic! They had earned the first PCRC victory for a Gaucho heavyweight crew in a long, long time.

FINAL REGATTA, CONCLUDED
Sunday, May 22

Grand Final of the varsity four-with. I had raced in this event back in 1974, finishing third behind two University of Washington boats. Could my Gauchos better my results? Time to find out.

As they approached the half-way mark, I could tell that my rowers were about a length behind the lead crew. Scream as I might, they finished second behind the University of San Diego.

At this moment, as I sit at my computer typing up these notes, O.J. Simpson is slowly cruising down the 405 Freeway in a white Ford Bronco, a gun to his head. As so often happens in L.A., O.J. is lost. I'm especially glad to be sitting here, safe and sound in my Motel 6 apartment in Goleta and not driving the Gaucho boat trailer down the same stretch of road.

Guilty or not, O.J. seems to have ignored many life lessons. Too bad he took up football instead of rowing. I can guarantee that he would never be in this predicament had he sought salvation through crew.

The story of a rowing season at any school could easily fill a thousand pages, each workout worthy of a chapter. The time I had to leave Gordo on the dock because it was too windy for sculling, he stood stock still, watching us, looking so terribly sad. Or the time Moose took out a racing single for the first time, saying the classic words, "Why is it so tippy?"

My journal entry for one day was simply, "Hawk takes coot."

Omens and Curses might be a suitable subtitle for this story. Perhaps the Gaucho boathouse was built on an sacred Indian burial ground. Certainly the program endured more than its share of mishaps. Just when I was beginning to wonder if I'd gone completely over the deep end, I met a well-respected coach who had been hired by the school some years earlier to analyze the program. His conclusion: rowing has no place at UC Santa Barbara.

Eternal questions I never solved: where to hide the boathouse key? A TB outbreak on campus put a scare into everyone, myself included. The rats were finally banished to the forest where they belonged - the mice stayed put. The novice women eventually got their revenge by throwing the varsity men's shoes into the Port-o-Let. I found out with two weeks to go that my coxswain had a congenital heart problem. Maybe that's why she always kept her cool during races. To do otherwise would have killed her.

Highs and lows by the hundreds, having to meet with Bender's parents when my poison oak was at its absolute itchy-worst. They must have thought they were talking to a crazy man, the way I kept bouncing out of my chair to scratch.

As I thumb through these pages, I realize that I've got a mishmash of ideas, recollections, incidents. Welcome to small college rowing. It is a mishmash, the coach wearing a hundred different hats, from rigger to fund raiser. I remember going to sleep one might wondering if I'd be able to remember how the outboard engine I'd taken apart earlier in the day would fit back together.

We all survived, a feat not to be taken lightly. We raced a dozen times, dual races, Newport Regatta, home and away. At the home regattas, I'd drop a starting buoy and then drive my launch for a while - yeah, that feels like 2000 meters, give or take - and then drop the finish buoy. We won our share, although toward the end of the season I was beginning to wonder if we'd have enough shirts to tide us over. Racing shirts should be sold on big, thick rolls like paper towels. Our best race was back in December, the Christmas Regatta. Only ten of my rowers took part, a much more manageable number. We raced, won, lost, and thoroughly explored the process of winning.

The lightweights finished second at the PCRCs, no doubt improving several notches for having switched to Checks. His reward was to be hired by Ms. Pearson as the new varsity men's coach. Good luck to all.

The X Factor was on my mind in the early months. It stepped aside as the weeks wore on, succumbing to more pressing matters such as battling the fog, rigging the Carrie On, trying to start my outboard. Maybe someday one of my rowers will find himself at a critical crossroads, and he'll answer the challenge in a way that satisfies his soul. Afterward he might think, so that's what Coach Lewis was talking about.

What does one need to do this job well? A good flashlight, preferably waterproof. An electric starter on my outboard would have been nice. Anyone want to buy a Riot Stopper megaphone? We never raised as much money as prescribed in the budget. On the flip side we spent $9,700 less than anticipated. The savings came from not having to make repairs on our outboard engines and assorted vehicles. A hundred dollars in spark plugs goes a long way. With great sadness I finally relinquished the keys to the team van, which by this time everyone called Coach Lewis' van - everyone except Terri, who reminded me on a daily basis that it was supposed to be for official business only. Hell, getting the coach from his apartment to the lake is official business.

Several weeks ago I passed my EMT Final. Now I'm ready if Clement collapses or O.J. shoots himself. The bad news: I'm two pounds heavier than when I started coaching in September. I had my fat whittled down to a decent roar around Valentine's Day. Gradually, as we stopped running and began rowing more, it crept back. The real diet killers were the endless drives to different regattas. I have a feeling that each trip added at least three pounds to my girth. Next book, The Coaching Diet.

Good news. I may have the point to my Peter Matthiessen saga. Months ago I had been hotly anticipating Matthiessen's arrival in Santa Barbara. When he finally showed up, he proved to be somewhat less inspiring than I had hoped. The point: look far and wide for your knowledge. But find your inspiration in the mirror.

I never knew I had such exacting standards until I began coaching. I realize now that I should have had a few strict rules and enforced them without prejudice. I learned to take nothing for granted. Be direct. Set high goals and let the men strive to achieve them. Slackers be damned, rowing is timeless, a worthy challenge for the right student.

From the beginning I had wanted to teach my crew everything-rowing. Did I succeed? Soon after the PCRCs, I had two visitors to my apartment, Michael Kolbe and Tommy Thompson. They had an exceptionally difficult challenge in mind: racing in the straight pair at the IRAs. All they wanted from me was a good luck handshake and to borrow my Empacher pitch meter. These two young men made their travel arrangements, found their way to Syracuse and secured a boat. They prepared, practiced and arrived at the starting line on time. In the actual straight pair competition, they raced well in their heat and advanced to the final. The final? Next year. A teacher's greatest satisfaction comes from seeing his lessons   applied outside the classroom. Knowing that Michael and Tommy had assembled every solitary piece of their IRA endeavor, rigging included, I felt that on a small scale my goal had been reached, a little victory for their coach, 3200 miles away.

Yesterday afternoon, after gathering my tools and speed bag, I took a last, long look - the oar rack, the rolling slings, the whole place clean and neat, the new banner hanging on the rear wall: Pacific Coast Rowing Championship Men's Quadruple Scull Champion. I could imagine years from now a new coach thinking, does such an event really exist?

I slammed shut the boathouse door, climbed into my VW Golf and slipped a cassette into the player, Way of the Dao. Onto Highway 154, one last time, up and over the San Marcos Pass to home.

Once Tozan asked Sozan, "Where are you going?"
Sozan said, "To an unchanging place."
Tozan said, "If it's unchanging, how could there be any going?"
Sozan said, "Going, too, is unchanging."

Rowing, too, is unchanging.